ELISEO ALBERTO
Caracol Beach

Eliseo Alberto, winner of the first International Alfaguara Prize in Fiction (1998), was born in Arroyo Naranjo, Cuba. He is the author of three books of poems, a book for young adults that won the Cuban National Critics Prize, a novel, and a memoir, *Informe contra mí mismo*, for which he was awarded the Gabino Palma Prize in Spain. He has written screenplays for film and television, and has taught at the International Film School in San Antonio de los Baños in Cuba, the Center for Cinematographic Training in Mexico, and the Sundance Institute. He lives in Mexico City.

Edith Grossman is the award-winning translator of major works by many of Latin America's most important writers, including Gabriel García Márquez, Mario Vargas Llosa, and Álvaro Mutis. Ms. Grossman is the author of *The Antipoetry of Nicanor Parra* and of many articles and book reviews. She lives in New York City.

INTERNATIONAL

Caracol Beach

Caracol Beach

ELISEO ALBERTO

Translated from the Spanish by Edith Grossman

VINTAGE INTERNATIONAL
Vintage Books   *A Division of Random House, Inc.*   *New York*

FIRST VINTAGE INTERNATIONAL EDITION, NOVEMBER 2001

Translation copyright © 2000 by Eliseo A. De Diego

This novel won the First Premio Alfaguara de Novela de Alfaguara (Grupo Santillana de Ediciones, S.A., Torrelaguna 60, 28043 Madrid, Spain).

The Library of Congress has cataloged the Knopf edition as follows:
Alberto, Eliseo.
[Caracol Beach, English]
Caracol Beach / by Eliseo Alberto; translated from the Spanish by Edith Grossman.
p. cm.
ISBN 0-375-40540-2
I. Grossman, Edith, [date] II. Title
PQ7390.A375 C3713 2000
863—dc21 99-058954

Vintage ISBN: 0-375-70506-6

Book design by Dorothy Schmiderer Baker

www.vintagebooks.com

Printed in the United States of America
10 9 8 7 6 5 4 3 2 1

Death is that friend who appears in
family photographs, standing discreetly to one side,
the one nobody ever could recognize.

— PAPÁ

The day the world ends will be clean and orderly,
like the notebook of the best student.

— JORGE TEILLER

Preface and Dedication

IN THE SUMMER of 1989, Gabriel García Márquez offered a script-writing workshop to ten students at the International School of Film and Television in San Antonio de los Baños, Cuba. I was his assistant. Among the 1001 stories we told one another was the compelling nightmare of four young Puerto Ricans pursued for an entire night by an assailant, about whom no further details were given. Lacking precise information, the members of the workshop offered our own solutions. One said this character must be a born killer; another thought he was an alcoholic. Better yet, a mute. A drug addict. Or maybe an Armenian. "Wouldn't it be a good idea to include a hunt for a Bengal tiger in one episode?" remarked a student from New Delhi during an animated discussion. Gabriel suggested that he be a psychotic veteran who had the names of his own private dead tattooed on his left arm. I thought he ought to be suicidal. A lost soul. Almost an innocent. The issue of the madman was left unresolved. A year later I heard about a marine from Florida who had kidnapped a Dominican prostitute in Port-au-Prince, and in exchange for the freedom of his hostage his only demand was that they kill him in the rescue attempt. They obliged with six bullets. Then, in Madrid, I was told of a Galician who went on a drinking binge and hung himself with his tie, convinced he was responsible for the death of his two closest friends, who hadn't died—yet. The next morning, in one of those coincidences that happen in this world, the two friends were killed in an absurd traffic accident on their way to the hanged man's funeral.

In 1994, in Mexico, García Márquez asked me to write some of those embryonic fictions from the workshop, and since I had a free hand, the assailant was transformed into a California veteran of the Vietnam war, an Argentine sailor in the Malvinas war, a Sandinista guerrilla fighter in the Nicaragua war, a Palestinian terrorist in the Middle East war, a Soviet artilleryman in the Afghanistan war, an English pilot in the Iraq war, a Croatian militiaman in the Bosnia war, until he finally became a Cuban soldier in the Angola war, 1975–1985. There's no lack of wars. The film was never made. Finally, two years ago, I reread one of Gabriel's stories that begins with this sentence, a narrative jewel all by itself: "Since it is Sunday and has stopped raining, I'm going to take a bouquet of flowers to my grave." Then I sat down to write this novel about fear, madness, innocence, forgiveness, and death.

I dedicate *Caracol Beach* to my dear maestro, Gabriel García Márquez; to the friends who tell me lies and to my students who believe them; and to the guys: María José, Ismael, José Adrián, Laurita, Sergio Efigenio, Cristián, María Fernanda, Andrés Palma, Hari, Sidarta, Jasai, Eli, and Memo. My gang.

Saturday Afternoon

He was awakened by a noise
that he interpreted as a bullet hitting an owl.

— ADOLFO BIOY CASARES

1

CLEMENCY ISN'T a word that is used very often. On the previous night the soldier had dreamed again about the Bengal tiger, and he woke with a start, the taste of rotting meat in his mouth. He spat blood. His nerves had destroyed his gums, and no matter how much he rinsed his mouth with bicarbonate of soda, and even though he drank a thousand cups of coffee and smoked a thousand unfiltered Camels, the acid of the infection kept draining, drop by drop. He dressed under the blanket. Ever since his calvary during the war in Ibondá de Akú, eighteen years earlier, he had taken the precaution of sleeping with his boots on, a habit that eventually devastated his feet with raging fungus infections. He tried to take refuge in a happy memory and escape the trap that way. He failed. Through narrowed eyes he saw the tiger come in. A tiger. The tiger. That one. The yellow one. From Bengal. Its presence took his breath away. It would appear without warning in a derangement of dreams and then give him no peace. Before he caught sight of it under the table, toying with a rat from the garbage dump, he had smelled its rank poppy-cream scent, like a whore's perfume floating in the dawn air, and he woke in anguish. He heard the distant crowing of early morning roosters, the motors of cars driving along the highway, the sound of an ocean he knew was too far away, but only when he saw a ring of seven blowflies resting on the ceiling lightbulb did a snapping twig tell him the devil was near. The flies were startled and stirred the air with the windmill vanes of their wings. Each time he had the nightmare the compass of his mind switched poles and led him down blind alleys. The tiger was slavering. It was thirsty. Or maybe hungry. The rat wasn't enough. It wanted another one. It wanted him.

"Virgin of Regla! In the name of all you hold dear, tell it to go away! Let there be Light and Progress for you," he pleaded. His prayer crashed into the hills. The echo rebounded through the swirling mist.

Since taking the job as night watchman at the auto salvage yard in Caracol Beach, he had lived in a trailer that had once been a circus wagon. The name could still be read in an arc of showy calligraphy that was faded and weathered: FIVE STAR SHOW. TRAVELING RODEO. PERFORMERS AND GYPSY FORTUNE-TELLERS. TRAINED ANIMALS. PRIVATE DRESSING-ROOMS. The sides were painted with images of lions, bearded ladies, and trapeze artists. The interior of the car was equipped with everything needed to make it a habitable prison: the cot attached with hinges to the back wall, a two-burner hot plate to cook on, and a tiny bathroom that barely held one person but had the functional design of a sleeping compartment on a train, with all the fixtures in easy reach—sitting on the toilet you could comfortably turn the tap and take a shower without having to get up. The string of red, blue, and yellow lights that outlined the trailer on all four sides was the one luxury the solitary tenant allowed himself to keep in perfect working order. He liked to turn on the lighting system and see his tin-plate vessel from the highway, shining in the middle of that graveyard for demolished cars.

When he went outside, dazed by the echoes of his dream, the tiger was pacing the roof of the trailer. In the light of dawn he noticed the remarkable fact that the animal had wings harmoniously joined to its body. Wings of a swan or an angel. Two fans of white, silky, well-groomed feathers. It had come from a place where it had been raining because drops of water glistened like pellets of mercury on the edges of its feathers. It was something to see. The tiger sprang with ease from the roof to the clouds, and from cloud to cloud, treading lightly through the field of cumulus, and from there, not moving its wings, dropped in a pronounced curve into the auto salvage yard and was lost from view among the heaps of twisted metal. A beautiful sight. The soldier lit a cigarette and the tobacco tasted like cyanide. "Strike, Strike Two! Where are you, you son of a bitch?" he shouted.

Strike Two appeared at the window of the Oldsmobile. The game of hide-and-seek was repeated with theatrical punctuality. First he showed his pointed ears, then his eyes, his snout, his tongue, his neck, until half his body was visible and he publicly assumed the pose of a great mastiff. He was a puppy. A stray. A troublemaker. He had come to the yard last Christmas and for several days chose to sleep outdoors, under the cars. The soldier did not do much to get close to him, either. They felt a mutual distrust. Sometimes the puppy barked when a customer came in, taking on the sentinel's role that no one had assigned him. He spent his time chasing unreachable butterflies along the alleyways of the graveyard, or biting his own tail in comical whirlwinds. He drank his water from puddles. Neither of them relented. They were stubborn. Very stubborn. But on the night of December 31 the animal came into the trailer and jumped at the soldier's legs just as he was about to slit his veins with a bayonet blade. The dog's incursion prevented his suicide. The soldier gave him a name that reminded him of his days as a baseball player: Strike Two. The soldier was Strike One. On New Year's Day the dog began to sleep in the Oldsmobile, a monstrosity built from parts and pieces of other vehicles, like a mechanical Frankenstein. Every morning the man and his dog repeated the game of hide-and-seek. The man had to pretend he was looking for him in the yard. "Strike, Strike Two! Where are you, you son of a bitch?" After three or four shouts the puppy, with studied complicity, would begin to show his ears, eyes, snout, tongue, and neck. But on that rainy Saturday the soldier greeted him with a kick. Strike crossed the graveyard with his belly to the ground and reached the highway, determined to leave. He stopped on the shoulder. He was panting. He began to look around. Droves of carnivorous trucks, packs of ravening cars, herds of wild buses, stampedes of ferocious vehicles raced along the asphalt track. Strike went back to the graveyard and dropped onto the steps of the trailer. In the human jungle some roads are impassable.

Fear is a straitjacket. The first time he faced the tiger was on the afternoon he lost his mind in Ibondá de Akú. The soldier had been wandering for several days, driven mad by a guilt he would not allow himself to share with anyone, not even the leader of his infantry squad, the only other survivor of the ambush. The officer was an obstinate black who refused to die even though his left lung was torn apart by bone fragments. By some miracle they had broken through the enemy siege and gained a week of hope. The soldier carried the black man on his shoulders. A last shred of sanity obliged the soldier to help him. They liked each other. The maneuver became impossible because they were both delirious: the soldier raving because of his shuddering dementia, the squad leader because of the infection invading his arteries. He didn't stop intoning his own funeral chant: "Yemayá Awoyó. Yemayá Asesú. Yemayá." For three days and four nights the madman carried him on his back, tied to his shoulders with liana vines; at dawn of the fifth day the black stopped chanting; his eyes were open, his jaw hung slack, and a golden insect was in his mouth, but the soldier paid no attention to these clear signs of death, and despite the coldness of his flesh and the rigidity of his limbs and the stink that on the sixth morning made the air unbreathable within a radius of twenty yards, the madman continued to drag him by his feet or his arms, which by then were not limbs but blocks of cement. For a man in his right mind it would have been more logical to bury the body in a clearing in the jungle, but madmen are always in some other place, nobody knows exactly where. He would remember little of those days except for the African leopard that emerged suddenly from the underbrush and began to slash open the black man's torso with the same curiosity shown by a cat clawing at a pillow. No matter how much of a leopard a leopard might be, there are rivals that can overcome him because they do not fear him. So many flesh-eating ants knew about the meal that the big cat gave up his share of intestines after a few superficial bites. When faced with a leopard, the strength of an ant lies precisely in its insignificance. The real animal is the entire ant colony. The leopard can do away with hundreds of ants with a single swipe of his tongue, but the body of the colony will make up for its losses in a matter of seconds. The ants, meanwhile, touch bottom in pools of saliva and diligently bite the leopard's tongue. The madman climbed a tree and searched for salvation but found nothing better than the circle of blowflies clinging to the foliage. An escort of parasitic flies with red heads, like aviator helmets. Memories escaped from his body, leaving it empty. From that distant afternoon until the third Saturday in June, the beast hid in the underbrush of the past, waiting to invade his nightmares. The psychiatrist in charge of his case in a military hospital in Lisbon believed he was recovering: "The medications have begun to have the desired effect. We have not cured his madness but at least we have erased fear from his mind. We can discharge him," the doctor dictated, not knowing that the animal was only waiting for its prey to be left to his fate in a graveyard for cars in order to resume the endless chase. Fear is a straitjacket.

The first lightning bolt of the storm split a palm tree and unleashed a flood. The downpour wiped out the landscape. The earth pounded on kettle drums. A strong odor of burning flesh inundated Caracol Beach, confusing the birds of prey that began to fly over the area, relishing the banquet waiting for them in the slaughterhouse of men. The rains washed the metal of the cars, the springs in the upholstery, radiator pipes, corroded batteries, and rust mixed with the rivers of mud. Vermin splashed in puddles contaminated by that amalgam of muck and corroding scraps of metal. The Camel between the soldier's fingers went out. On that Saturday he would have to get rid of the tiger in the only way his battle with the past was still possible: by exterminating himself. Somebody once told him that fear was a straitjacket. But he couldn't remember who. End of story. The only certainty was the burning palm tree. The exploding bombs of thunder. A dog lying at the door of a circus trailer. The birds of prey. And that second bolt of lightning, a well-aimed blow by God that buried itself in a piece of metal in the graveyard, forging it to a red heat—the same piece of metal on which a boy named Tom Chávez would die some twenty hours later.

"What rotten luck, damn it: I'm fucked, really fucked!" said the soldier. Under his mattress he kept a rope to hang himself with. It would be easier than knotting up a tie. And he began to run, in a hurry to kill himself. Strike Two confused his master's urgency with the start of the game, postponed that day by the images of madness, and he followed him, a warrior and a clown, and sank his fangs into the soldier's socks, bit the bottoms of his overall, tugged at the laces of his boots, demanding a little attention. "Babalú Ayé: don't send any more animals after me!" the soldier said as he entered the trailer, the puppy dragging after him like a plush leg iron with bells.

2

THE LAST RAINDROP of the storm fell on the head of a buzzard flying about 120 feet above Santa Fe, Florida, rolled down the furrow between its eyes and was pulled by gravity from its beak, and dropped at a thirty-degree angle into the courtyard of the Emerson Institute where it hit the bull's-eye between the breasts of the cheerleader Laura Fontanet. That's what Martin Lowell was thinking when he raised his hand and offered his parents' house in Caracol Beach for a boisterous party to celebrate their diplomas. The top student in the graduating class would never have dared to take his classmates to the sanctuary at the beach; or pull out his pecker in public and, with Tom and the Mayer brothers, Bill and Chuck, cross in midair the four soft scimitars of their urine to form the Council of Pissers, a brotherhood based on the heroic sentiment of friendship; much less smoke a joint and he had just had seven long tokes in the school bathroom; and so on that Saturday he wasn't going to deny himself anything. He zipped his fly. Nine months of devotion to his studies and a considerable amount of arrogance had earned him the highest grades, and he believed he deserved the opportunity to fail some of life's courses.

"Some bad isn't bad for you; it does you some good," said Tom as he put the roach away in a match box. His remark made Martin laugh. Tom, simple Tom, had hit the nail on the head. He had to start looking at things in a different way. Some bad isn't bad for you; it does you some good. Could that be true?

"Tom, pass that to me," said Laura.

"With pleasure, babe," said Tom.

"What do you think, Martin? Feels good, right?" said Bill, the older of the Mayer brothers.

"I don't know. It feels funny," said Martin.

"You let me know when the smoke hits your gut. . . ."

"I feel like I'm going to take first communion," said Laura.

"Martin, don't be scared if you see a real buzzard flying over your head, OK?" said Tom.

Martin wiped the glasses he wore for nearsightedness: There's no such thing as a real buzzard, he thought. You're nuts, Tom. Now he saw everything more clearly. Tom was almost never right but almost always on target, which isn't exactly the same thing. He had anticipated that the graduation ceremonies would be duller than a beggar's funeral, and he wasn't wrong. Almost to the letter, the headmaster of Emerson Institute repeated the same speech he had given for the last six years, emphasizing the principal articles of the Constitution; Miss Campbell, who held the chair in mathematics and was dean of faculty, had them recite the pledge in which they vowed to use their knowledge in defense of just causes; moms and dads cried as only the moms and dads of Emerson Institute know how to cry at end-of-the-year festivities; and the ceremony was over in less than one hundred minutes of formal greetings, crocodile tears, and Judas kisses. A chorus of forty voices filled Santa Fe with the school song, accompanied by the freshman band, and Laura said she would turn into Mad

Queen Joan if she spent one more second in that clinic for terminal bores, wearing her good-girl disguise and with the beady eyes
of the Spanish literature teacher following her every move, and so
she proposed to Bill and Chuck Mayer that they go dancing at
Machu Picchu.

"Brilliant!" the Mayer brothers exclaimed in unison.

"Anything's better than putting up with Theo Uzcanga," said
Laura. "This is bullshit."

Tom agreed with her evaluation. Laura added: "Either I get
out of here or I'll kill myself in an explosion of jazz like a Buddhist
monk in Tibet."

"So much studying for nothing," said Bill.

"Why don't we kidnap Miss Campbell and in exchange for
her life we can demand that the president modify the Constitution?" Bill added.

"I know a really nice place where there's no cover charge,"
Tom said.

"What are we waiting for?" said Laura.

"OK."

Martin looked up at the sky and saw the real buzzard a few
minutes before the raindrop slipped between Laura's breasts. A
perfect buzzard gliding in an almost liquid sky. The boy rubbed
his eyes, marveling at the image. His gut was full of marijuana
smoke. He made an inventory of his normal mind and remembered the most recalcitrant logarithms, recited the Mendeleyev
table from top to bottom, thought about the aphorisms of Blaise
Pascal, the formula for exploding the nucleus of an atom, quan-
tum physics, and reached a wise conclusion. He raised his hand
out of sheer academic habit and heard himself say:

"Why don't we go to my house?"

"What?" exclaimed Tom.

"What did you say?" Laura asked.

"I said why don't we go to my house in Caracol Beach?"

The earth stopped and the Tower of Pisa fell in slow motion. Seven stars disappeared from the sky. On a farm in St. Petersburg, Florida, a cow gave birth to ten pigs and a chicken. The Mongols of Ulan Bator heard themselves speaking fluent Hungarian. The pyramids in Teotihuacán melted in the sun and anthropologists from the National Indigenist Institute discovered that the structures were made of butter. It all happened in the wink of an eye. Martin had moved events forward in an act of true audacity. He wanted to go to the bathroom. He tightened his buttocks. He looked down at his shoes. The left one was untied.

"I mean . . . if you want to."

Martin tied his shoe. The group never made the mistake of inviting him along when they went out because they knew beforehand the answer they would get from the future lawyer in the firm of Lowell & Marovic Associates: he had to study for the next exam. He raised his eyes. He felt ridiculous. An absolute jerk.

"A house in Caracol Beach! I could simply fall in love with you this afternoon, Martin Lowell," Laura said with theatrical exaggeration, and kissed him on the cheek.

The sun began to disintegrate in a shower of rockets and fireworks, the planet split in two, and Martin, filled with joy, dropped into the void with his arms outstretched until his feet touched down in the basement of a pagoda in Beijing and he bounced back up the tunnel in the earth in triumphal ascent. "Thanks, Laura," he said on his way back to the courtyard of the Institute, still dizzy from the distance he had traveled.

3

CARACOL BEACH was so conservative a place that milkmen still delivered quarts of the precious liquid door to door, a tradition that has been lost in these frivolous times when the ancient custom of providing service is rejected by some people. The words are don Claudio Fontanet's. What made the small resort really inaccessible was not the twenty miles of highway that separated it from Santa Fe but the sensitive noses of its inhabitants, all of whom, without exception—entrepreneurs, owners of brokerage firms, ladies devoted to the game of canasta—had a sense of smell acute enough to have found a way to live like Robinson Crusoe on the desert island of a chalet. For Laura, that shoreline made remote by chasms of nostalgia was more distant than Sydney, Australia. She had visited Caracol Beach as a child, when it did not appear on any map and was barely a shallow bay protected from Caribbean currents by a barrier of coral reefs. In those days it was not called Caracol Beach but Punta La Galia, and its residents were twenty or so fishermen, the descendants of white Haitians, who sold grilled red snapper and fruit drinks in dried coconut shells as they sang Edith Piaf tunes. Then the place became fashionable. It boasted thirteen residential blocks lined up between the ocean and the shoreline boulevard, three hotels administered by two Swiss managers, and one Japanese, who was married to a Belgian soprano; a French lycée with studios for ballet and oil painting; the Andalusia bowling center with nine lanes; a golf course; a police station; and a couple of black sheep that defaced the landscape: a car cemetery at mile ten on the Santa Fe highway and a bar called the Bastille, the stronghold of the white Haitians. Two catacombs.

"My parents' house in Caracol Beach is available."

"A house in Caracol Beach! I could simply fall in love with you this afternoon, Martin Lowell," said Laura. To tell the truth, she had felt a trembling in her chest and cured it by giving him a kiss. Caracol Beach was linked to the memory of her mother, a Havanean named Maruja Vargas who could not endure the grief of exile and died five years after her marriage to the lawyer don Claudio Fontanet. Her only image of Maruja was fixed in a photograph: mother and daughter are holding hands as they walk along the beach, but since Laura is so small Maruja has to bend forward a few degrees and her face, hidden by a curtain of hair, is not visible. For Laura, going to Caracol Beach meant returning to her mother's womb. Only there, among the coconut palms on the beach, did she recognize her Caribbean inheritance: she allowed herself to be overcome by a sensation difficult to explain by any reason other than blood. Cuba was a piano that someone played behind the horizon.

Don Claudio Fontanet had remarried; his second wife was Emily Auden, a lady from North Carolina who always held high the banner of optimism. Who knows why the lawyer decided to destroy the bridges that might lead back to the island. Perhaps because he was Catalonian. The girl could never get him to talk about her Cuban family. Don Claudio would raise his guard, protect himself with a glass of port, and refuse to share his solitude.

Laura knew that Maruja had been born in a town called El Rincón, and that her life had barely lasted thirty springs: after she gave birth her joints calcified in a slow fusing of her skeleton until she became as rigid as a wooden doll. If not for the photograph, a box with a lock of her hair, and a grave in Santa Fe in the shade of a palm tree, Maruja might never have existed. Laura was left with the consolation of turning her into an imaginary friend who would appear without warning, sometimes at recess, balancing on the seesaw, sometimes on the Ferris wheel or roller coaster at an amusement park. At home the two of them would hide in Laura's room to finish her homework, straighten her toybox, read José Martí's *The Golden Age*. Don Claudio would hear his daughter's laughter through the door, and sit on the stairs and drink port from the bottle.

"Don't worry," Emily would say, "she must be on the phone with a friend."

"I heard Maruja's voice."

"Come on, Catalán, don't be stubborn. It's time to go to sleep."

"Sleep? I want to stay here for a while."

"Then move over and make room for me. I'll keep you company." And they would end up making love on the staircase.

The fact is that the impossible Maruja Vargas displayed great vitality, as if she wanted to break open the padlocks imposed by the armor of her cancer. The other world is closer than it seems. Sometimes she played the piano in her daughter's dreams. Contradances. She played well, considering her deceased condition. It was she who convinced Laura to sign up for gymnastics classes, and even learned the cheerleaders' routines so they could practice the choreography together. On the basketball court at the Emerson Institute, Maruja sold cotton candy. Her visits, frequent in childhood, had grown farther apart as the years passed, and became only sporadic when Laura reached young womanhood.

One night, at the bar in a discotheque, Laura dared confess to Maruja a feeling that had been troubling her for some time: she had begun to love Emily Auden as if she were her mother. Maruja understood that the ghostly cycle of her existence had to end, had to be sacrificed and consumed on the real pyre of life. She did not play the piano again, not even in dreams. On infrequent afternoons they would both be sitting in a movie theater before the lights dimmed, and later Laura would find her in the reflections in shop windows, in the window of a passing car and, on one occasion, in the shadow of her own body. At eighteen Laura felt jealous of her. Mother and daughter were gradually becoming the same age. Maruja Vargas returned to the photograph, not willingly but resigned to dying again in the exile of forgetting. She did not show herself except in Caracol Beach, her natural paradise. When Laura went there she looked for Maruja among the coconut palms on the beach. She knew her favorite places, the prints her swift feet marked on the sand among the tracks made by crabs, the scent of violet water she left behind as she passed. The girl would order something at the restaurant owned by the white Haitians: a fruit drink in a dried coconut shell. Suddenly she would see her mother in the water, balancing on a surfboard. Maruja Vargas didn't even wave. That's how alive some dead women are. Especially Cubans.

4

SOLDIER'S NOTEBOOK. June. 1976. Rain follows us like a curse. On the trip over it rained every afternoon. Just my luck! In the middle of the ocean, the rain can really fool you. Sky and sea are mixed up. Edges are blurred. The ship seems to sink into air made of rough water. Gray. Gray washes over the colors of things, like a black-and-white movie. To make matters worse, since we landed it's been raining in the mornings too. A vengeful downpour, in the words of Silvio Rodríguez. The rain shrivels us into an army of frogs dragging through the mud in the mangrove swamps on our way to the front. What can you do: let a smile be your umbrella! We walked into Ibondá de Akú to the beat of our own special marching song: "Zun zun zun, zun zundambayé! Zun zun zun, zun zundambayé, pretty bird at the break of day!" My mother always sang that song when she was boiling guava preserves; I listened to her from the doorway. The tune floated like smoke. Music goes through walls. Every Cuban knows it: Zun zun zun, zun zundambayé! Leo Rubí, who performed in a folk-dancing group, began to move his body as if a saint had entered him, imitating an owl (the pretty bird!), and Fernandito López really fucked him when he said he looked like a blowfly because then Poundcake gave him a nickname that was too weird: the Fly. When we reached Ibondá de Akú we were dead tired but Lieutenant Lázaro Samá made us inspect the area from top to bottom. "Nothing to it," he said: "nothing to it." The medic Ernesto Aspirin Gómez stepped forward and tried to defend the group with solid medical arguments, physical and mental exhaustion, calories, emotional state, cardiac rhythm: he struck out with bases loaded. End of story. Let a smile be your umbrella. The lieutenant says there are lions and leopards, a shitload of lions, and just one of those animals can eat the whole squad alive. The lieutenant always invents something to make us keep our guard up. He doesn't let us close our eyes for a second. We have to dig a trench. Or go to the river for water. Or have a study circle. After we dig the trench, carry up the canteens, and discuss Fidel's speech, then he tells us stories about the Sierra Maestra and the Struggle Against Hooliganism and the seventy-two hours at Playa Girón. All lies, I bet. Ever since we worked in the port he's been telling me the same damn stories. What balls. Big mouth. Big talker. Shit on his fucking mother. I know he's going to ask for my notebook so he can read it and make sure I'm not writing any military secrets and then he'll find out that today, Wednesday, June 9, 1976, at 09:25 hours, I shit on his fucking cunt of a mother, but I don't give a damn: he shits on ours every five minutes. How can I say anything that matters to the enemy if I hardly know myself what the hell I'm doing here, twenty years old and a million fucking miles from home in a place called Ibondá de Akú. So, here we are, our morale higher than Turquino Peak. Resigned. Fucked. Dragging our asses. And surrounded by African lions and leopards just like the ones in the zoo on 26th. Poundcake said he didn't want to hear about it because he'd dream about the goddamn Bengal tiger. Ruedas the teacher wanted to discuss whether or not we'd be lunch for one of those

animals: "Bengal tigers are from India," he said, full of convic-
tion, and Fernandito said that in dreams, at least in his, all leopards and panthers are tigers, "tigers with yellow stripes, pal, from
Bengal"; Fernandito argued that animals attack when they're
hungry, a pure survival instinct. I agree with Fer. It's true. No lie.
In nightmares all animals are tigers. No shit. Close your eyes and
you'll see. The tiger. A tiger. That one. The yellow one. From
Bengal. In the Nuevo Vedado zoo the tigers are next to the lions,
in the next cage. There must be a reason. God made them and the
devil brings them together. Lieutenant Samá thinks the most
dangerous animals are the ones that have eaten human flesh
because then no other food satisfies them. "They get a taste for
us, especially dark-skinned blacks like me who have clean flesh.
We call those bastards man-eating tigers," he said. I didn't like his
remarks at all. As my comadre Rafaela would say, he missed a
good chance to shut up. [. . .] The captain gives orders not the
sailor. Just my luck! So we went out to reconnoiter the area. It
seemed quiet. Too quiet. I was teamed up with Poundcake, who
kept complaining about his gut. "Talking about tigers fucked up
my stomach," he said, and he went to take a crap behind some
bushes. I waited for him. I smoked a Popular down to the end.
The area around Ibondá de Akú was pretty, like geography magazines. Lieutenant Samá says that the strange place where ele-
phants go to die is around here. Maybe. There was a green green
green valley between the hills, and a really cool falls. A real waterfall. I wish I'd had a camera. And I'm looking at all that, and I'm
gone from this miserable world. Drooling. And not because my
gums are bad. I began to sing, "Zun zun zun, zun zundambayé!
Zun zun zun, zun zundambayé!" And wound up thinking all kinds
of things. The bad thing about wars with no fighting is that you
begin to get ideas and that can be dangerous. In crisis situations
like this you find out what you really know. That's why the officers send us to the river for water even though our canteens are

full. I looked at my hands and they were like mirrors. My life reflected in the palm of my hand. Line by line. Day by day. I'm half crazy. Between my big toe and my thumb cars drove along the shore road in Cienfuegos. At the tip of my middle finger, the cement factory the Russians built. My index finger was a baseball bat. The other hand a pitcher's glove. I found Caterina the Great on the nail of my right ring finger, tossing pebbles into the bay. Strike One. Strike Two. Strike Three. I'm half crazy, just like that loony samurai (me) who goes to war with his teachers in *The Seven Samurai*, the movie they showed us on the ship when we crossed the Atlantic. That's one great movie. That asshole Poundcake still wasn't back so I went to look for him to make sure he hadn't been lunch for the famous tiger even if it isn't from Bengal. No fucking sign of him. The earth swallowed him up. I finally found him. He wasn't where he said he'd be but about ten meters away, in a grove of trees, leaning against a trunk like somebody letting out the string on a kite, not worried, having a good time, in Bethlehem with the shepherds, beating his meat to the beautiful waterfall. What a brain. What a jerkoff. And I thought: if this promising student of electronics at the Technological Institute in Rancho Boyeros doesn't get a letter soon from his bitch of a girlfriend in La Víbora he'll die by his own hand whacking off on the ass of Mother Nature. And I don't have to tell you, some landscapes are real turn-ons. We're not made of wood.

5

MISS CAMPBELL bit into the sandwich and a glop of mustard, carrots, and shredded chicken fell on the collar of her blouse. As she shook off the droppings the roll slipped from her hands. Professor Theo Uzcanga's mind was wandering and without realizing it he kicked the sandwich. Letting his mind wander was a way to evade evil omens. When he woke that Saturday his lungs were sluggish, a prelude to an asthma attack, and since breakfast he had been reading poems to the rain by the Mexican poet Francisco Hernández, his best medicine against respiratory distress. Two lines kept going through his mind. The first said: "I'll sleep standing up to wear myself out. I'm a water spaniel. Your body is a pond." Theo didn't look where he was going. The roll came to a stop beneath the shoes of the equally distracted headmaster of the Emerson Institute, provoking a brilliant piece of ice-skating on mayonnaise that ended in a decisive fall on his ass. Applause. The professor executed a courtly bow to acknowledge his pupils' laughter. Theo thought of the other line by Hernández: "Passing by the cemetery, one often sees the dead rising to beg for alms." Miss Campbell, who felt responsible for the tragedy, wiped the headmaster's buttocks with a paper napkin and smeared the stain over his trousers. In the opinion of Bill and Chuck Mayer, this incident was the only memorable event at the ceremony until Laura suggested going to Machu Picchu to dance and Martin responded with an offer to continue the party at Caracol Beach. A great idea. There they could dance, drink, turn on to their heart's content. The problem was that at the beach, a yellow tiger was playing with a rat from the garbage dump. And nobody told them.

The cheerleader became happy as a clam when she found out they would cross the border into the resort community, and she assured the amiable Agnes MacLarty, the gymnastics instructor, that if she didn't break any bones dancing with Sting that night she would give up her Los Angeles scholarship and bury herself in the cell of some cloistered convent until she died. "I swear I will," she said. And Laura would keep her word. She never talked just to hear herself talk. She had made herself leader of the swarm of cheerleaders, and that talent for authority was enough to assure her control over a hive of friends who followed her to every get-together anyone had in Santa Fe, because a party without Laura's jeans was no party at all: nobody could match her when it was time to dance to a Kiss thunderstorm or a U2 tornado. "You were born a queen, my queen," Tom would say when he saw her presiding over a gathering, surrounded by a court of admirers. "Thanks, champ," Laura would say and throw him a kiss: You're not Sting but almost, she would think. The desire to have fun overflowed her body.

"Believe me. You're a great guy, Martin: the best. You've saved the night for us," said Laura.

"It's nothing, babe," Martin replied and immediately cursed himself. How stupid: how the hell did I say "babe"! Babe! It's nothing, babe. I'm talking just like Tom.

"I swear. I adore you. Shall we go?" Laura said.

"Sure, doll." "Doll" was even worse than "babe."

"What will your parents say?" asked Tom, who had heard something about how short-tempered the Lowells were.

"My folks are terrific. I say, 'Folks, I need the house,' and my folks give me the key. What do you expect? My folks never say no," Martin lied. He hadn't said a word to them, certain they wouldn't give their permission. The indiscriminate use of the word "folks" made him laugh.

"What are you laughing at?" Laura wanted to know.

"I'll tell you later."

"What should we bring? Whiskey?" asked Chuck Mayer.

"Nothing, Chuck."

"Some beer just in case," Tom suggested.

"Absolutely not. There's enough beer to make all the firemen in St. Petersburg drunk," Martin insisted. He wouldn't live long enough to regret that sentence.

"Do you have a car?" Laura asked.

"No."

"You had to have some defect, Martin."

Laura had foreseen that it would be an intense Saturday. She came prepared for any contingency. She went into the gym bathroom and changed out of her nice-girl uniform into the jeans that drove her friends crazy, a Los Angeles Lakers T-shirt (they were Tom's favorite team), and some magic slippers that turned her into a champion dancer. Tom only had to take off his jacket to turn back into the star of the team. He had gone to graduation in sneakers, certain, he told Laura, that feet never show in photographs. Martin Lowell would be dressed up like a penguin, in tails, until his death.

"I'm happy as a clam, teach," Laura told the amiable Agnes while she changed her clothes in the gym bathroom.

"You deserve it. You'll never forget this day. Let's drink to that," said Agnes, and she raised her seventh glass of wine.

"What a drag. The literature teacher won't take his camel eyes off me."

"Me too."

"Why doesn't Theo fall in love with old Miss Campbell instead of with us? That would really be dedicating his knowledge to a just cause!"

"Poor Theo."

"Poor?"

"He's not a bad person. Or maybe I'm wrong."

"I didn't say he was a bad person, teach: he's a bad lover. Lots of talk and not much kissing."

"A toast to your scholarship?"

"A toast," said Laura, and she drank some wine from the teacher's glass. "Are you coming with us to Caracol Beach? Come on, Agnes, don't play hard to get. Come with us."

"I can't," said Agnes. "Harrison Ford is waiting to eat some camel ribs with me at home. Give my best to Sting."

"I will."

Laura kept no secrets from the instructor, and so Agnes MacLarty knew that her favorite student would love to celebrate with Sting the scholarship she had received from a prestigious foundation to study psychology in Los Angeles, Mecca of the mad. Don Claudio had granted her carte blanche to do whatever she wanted that Saturday. She had kept her part of the bargain and achieved an outstanding academic record, and now her father had to keep his and let her fly on her own. The Lowells' house was a gift from heaven. Bill and Chuck Mayer, the marijuana czars at the Emerson Institute, rounded up a group of thirteen of their subjects to take part in the adventure.

"Be careful," said don Claudio at the entrance to the Institute.

"I'm not a child, daddy."

"Oh, aren't you?"

"Of course not."

"There are a lot of crazy people out there."

"Don't worry if I don't come home to sleep."

"What I'm worried about is your driving too fast on the highway."

"Yes, daddy."

"Have fun, honey. Enjoy yourself."

"Bye."

"Bye."

"Don't be that way."

"I'm not being any way."

Tom's Chevrolet pulled out into traffic.

Laura recognized the presence of Maruja Vargas at least twice. The first time was casual: on the other side of the road a dot grew larger until it was clearly defined as it sped by—her mother was riding a racing bike. She didn't even look at Laura as she passed. Indifferent. The girl turned to look out the rear window but Maruja had disappeared: in her place a small whirlwind swirled the dust on the road. The second time was at the guard's booth at the entrance to the resort. Martin was showing the required pass that identified him as a resident of Caracol Beach when the phantom appeared, and this time her behavior was very peculiar: she banged on the car window with her knuckles. Laura did not attribute too much importance to the incident: mothers always think the worst. In fact, she remarked to Bill that she had never seen a prettier sunset. Seagulls circled the masts of the sailboats. Somewhere the Belgian soprano was singing lines by Verdi. They heard her as they drove by, or did they imagine it? It was a nice touch.

"This is the finest afternoon in the world," said Laura, and she remembered a poem by Francisco Hernández that Theo Uzcanga had recited to her on the afternoon he had promised to go over some Spanish lessons with her and they ended up making love in his top-floor studio: "A drop of anise rolls down your thigh with all the indifference of a ship sailing away."

"Nice!" Bill exclaimed, and Chuck memorized the lines so he could repeat them to his girlfriend the next day.

"The sun looks like a mandarin orange," said Laura, after tasting the verses in her mouth. Her metaphors weren't very good.

I ordered it just for you, thought Martin, but he didn't dare say it out loud. He was a little strange.

6

THAT SATURDAY in June, through the good offices of the white wines of California, Agnes MacLarty stopped being a good-looking gymnastics instructor and began to feel like an old woman of thirty-three. Alcohol is a magnifying glass. She knew it. Your pores look enormous. Of course they aren't that big but the lens of intoxication occasionally enlarges things, distorts them, expands them. You think an apple is the moon. The exaggeration of reality contributes to a detailed understanding of reality itself. Pores. Pores! Agnes had the hiccups. She looked in the gym mirror and found a couple of new wrinkles on her neck, a reddish spot on her nose, a nest of brown freckles on her chest, a dust storm of ash under her eyes, and now she didn't even attempt to count the crowsfeet but tried to bring up the eight glasses of cheap wine stored in the barrel of her kidneys. She put her index finger into her mouth. Four fingers slipped in. Room for her whole hand. She almost tore off her uvula. She lost her balance. She needed air. She unhooked her bra. Her nipples burned against her blouse. No. No she couldn't. She couldn't vomit.

"You old . . ." she said into the mirror. A hiccup cut her off but she was about to say "bitch." Oh well.

Oh well: she was alone. For fifty miles around there wasn't a single person who cared about her wrinkles. Oh well. Hours and hours in the gym and when you got home nobody to say how good you're looking, sweetheart. Another glass of wine? Oh well, it occurred to Agnes that Harrison was a professional, busy opening pharoahs' tombs in the desert and she decided to accept her darling Laura's invitation and continue the party in Caracol Beach, but she couldn't find the kids anywhere even though she checked every nook and cranny of the Institute where the Mayer brothers normally sold reefers. Drunk and battered by the attack of hiccups, she resigned herself to finishing that Saturday by doing aerobic exercises until she sweated out her frustrations drop by drop, oh well, and fell exhausted into bed, hoping to dream about being with Harrison on the back of a camel under the Sahara sun. Oh well.

"You haven't seen Laura, have you, don Claudio?"

"She just left with the kids. Not five minutes ago," the lawyer said.

"I missed the boat. Oh well."

Agnes was waiting for a cab at the entrance to the school when none other than Theo Uzcanga invited her for a drink, her ninth, at the Two Blind Cats, where they were paying tribute that night to the Cuban writer Reinaldo Arenas. The worst thing was that Theo Uzcanga asked with so much elegance, restraint, and naturalness that when the gymnastics instructor was about to say no she said, between galloping hiccups, "Yes, all right, I'll go with you, why not?" Oh well, and she was incapable of rectifying the error, something she never would regret, and do you know why? Not because of the stupendous lines by Francisco Hernández that Theo recited in the half-light, or the anecdotes the novelist's friends recounted, or the *guajira* that Albita Rodríguez herself sang a capella on the stage at the Two Blind Cats, no, do you know why she never would regret it? Because when the scythe of sadness slashed her soul barely fifteen hours after that casual encounter, she went back to the literature teacher's top-floor studio and threw her arms around him, dissolving in tears, with her wrinkles, her thousand new crowsfeet, her age spots, and the circles under her eyes, oh well, what the hell, and from that time on Agnes MacLarty and Theo Uzcanga have lived together, shoulder to shoulder, never apart for more than a few days, no, not days, a few hours, dependent upon one another, always calling one another on the phone or paging one another on their beepers, in love or perhaps frightened, some would say neurotic, like Siamese twins, he an asthmatic, and she a fearful woman, trying to have a child, an army of children, for the gratuitous deaths of the boys in the auto salvage yard at almost the same time they were saying goodbye at the door to Agnes's building taught them that the only way to confront with relative success a life besieged by tigers and blowflies is to invent for ourselves a love at any price, do you see? Some kind of solidarity, an imperfect complicity, an alliance, a witch's potion, a charm, whatever, don't think about it too much, nothing can guarantee happiness or justice, nothing can, nobody can, don't forget that, nothing is enough in the face of misfortune, and all you can do is defend that love, kicking and scratching, even if it turns out to be an illusion bigger than the moon. Oh well.

"What did you say about the moon?"

"What?"

"Are you coming?"

"Yes, all right, I'll come, why not. Oh well."

"You look terrific. Really," said Theo.

"Oh, sure!"

Oh, sure? Agnes MacLarty got into the car. That night she had suffered the terror of feeling like an old woman in her thirties, and she needed that kind of compliment because the eight glasses of California wine represented eight successive betrayals: Agnes had been a drunk between the ages of twenty-two and twenty-seven. Through a rigorous program of self-esteem, physical fitness, and group therapy sessions at anonymous associations, she had succeeded in freeing herself from a tenacious dependence on Finnish vodka, her preferred purgative for sorrow, and even though her doctors authorized an occasional drink, she had never dared to empty eight glasses down the transom of her throat: she was not prepared to pay the price of another improbable though possible season in purgatory. Why did she do it? In front of the mirror she had explained it to herself with a devastating phrase: she was sad, but also hornier than a cat in heat.

"People who talk to themselves are remembering all their sins."

"Right."

"If you like I'll take you home."

"I'd rather die first. Kidnap me."

"That's not a bad idea."

"You're a terrific guy," she said to Theo, but she was thinking of Tom, and when he said the word "thanks" she really wanted to make some excuse. Under the neon moon she asked herself what the hell she was doing in Theo's Toyota convertible if what she really wanted was to lie down in bed and dream about Harrison kissing her shoulder and running his fingers through her hair, kneading her scalp, dominating her gently, electrifying her gently, while she, face down, skin tingling, spread her legs in a clear sign of surrender and rubbed her pubis against the folds in the sheet, gently, and bit the corner of the pillow, sucked it to discover that the cotton taste of cloth on her tongue could drive her mad with pleasure. Each dream began with the caresses of Harrison Ford and ended with a clumsy but delicious penetration by Tom but never took place in Professor Uzcanga's Toyota. That's life.

"That's life."

"A drop of anise rolls down your thigh with all the indifference of a ship sailing away," said Theo, quoting Francisco Hernández.

"Don't start," said Agnes.

In the Two Blind Cats it was as cold as an igloo. The first thing Agnes confirmed when she walked in was that no mirrors were hanging on the walls. The second was that the asthmatic literature teacher from the Emerson Institute had a real talent for choosing clubs. The third was that she didn't know anybody. That afternoon, before going to the graduation celebrations, Theo had called to reserve a table for two, near the dance floor, "his table," he had said with pride, and all that planning ahead, all that certainty of success, made the gymnastics instructor feel like part of a suspicious conspiracy. She tried not to attribute too much importance to the matter because its being suspicious did not necessarily mean it would be unpleasant. Whatever happens is fine with me, she thought. She was just sitting down at the table when she displayed a healthy desire for independence: she did not rely on her escort but leaped into the arena to join the crowd of dancers in an act of womanly defiance. Theo enjoyed the scene. The bolero lent itself to having the men least endowed by Terpsichore ask their companions to dance, in this way satisfying one of the basic requirements of an invitation to the cabaret, but the intruder's sudden entrance spoiled their fun. She didn't even pay real attention to the bolero. She twisted and coiled her body, making the unfair competition intolerable. One by one the couples gave up and left the field. The music ended and the athlete continued dancing, away from the lights. Theo took her back to the table—if he hadn't, you know, if he hadn't, Agnes would still be on the dance floor, her back to the wall, dancing by herself. That's life. That's the way it is. Oh well. Pure. . . . The hiccup cut her off but she was about to say "shit."

7

ALL THAT Saturday morning and afternoon he stood in front of the mirror, biting his lips, knotting the tie of his hanging rope with the solemnity of someone dressing for a funeral, in this case his own funeral, while from his sleeve he pulled excuses for not climbing up on the stool, adjusting the noose around his neck, and taking the step he had dreamed about for eighteen years. At the last moment he would find some error in the knots and retie them with a perfectionist's zeal. The resources of his anguish were effective but extremely fragile: either Strike Two barked suddenly and he hid the rope under the mattress, certain that an intruder was approaching along the alleys of the automobile graveyard, or he decided to finish off the blowflies before he wrote a letter to his mother explaining the reasons for his suicide, or it occurred to him that he ought to burn his belongings, wipe away all trace of his passage through this world, and in this way keep other bloodhounds from sticking their noses into the mire. Obsessed by that possibility he stopped twisting the funereal braid, opened the desk drawers looking for the five or six photographs of his family that he had kept, the telegrams and postcards from old friends, the talismans he had accumulated in his long pilgrimage from the city of Cienfuegos to the shores of Caracol Beach. Each object, no matter how insignificant, evoked memories of the island, the jungle, or his exile, and he dedicated himself to the task of deciphering them with no documentation other than the parchments of memory. "Just my luck, Poundcake, just my luck!" It wasn't easy to free himself from the past. One day when he was crazy he had asked the Haitian Zack Duhamel, an expert in tattoos, to record on his left forearm the seven names of his own private dead so they could go everywhere with him. He wore his own cemetery on his skin. Those tombstones prevented him from forgetting his ghosts.

"How'd you kill this SOB, lieutenant?" asked Zack as he inscribed the peculiar name of J. Londoño.

"I'll tell you about it some other time, Zack."

Zack Duhamel was the red-haired Haitian with friendly eyes who worked the night shift at the Bastille. A species facing extinction. All that remained of his ancestors' aristocratic blood was his French last name, a certain elegance in his manner and in some gestures at the bar. As for the rest, many considered him an ass in an apron. The colony of white Haitians was clearly in decline. Its best times had been during Prohibition, and few recalled those years without nostalgic illusions. Smuggling rum and brandy from the Caribbean enriched those who controlled the traffic, though this brief period of prosperity had almost no effect on the economy of Punta La Galia because the most important bosses fled to Marseilles in their yachts, the holds filled with money, leaving behind in America the shells of their ephemeral palaces. Condemned by their historical destiny, and determined to maintain by law the purity of a lineage they considered superior, the decaying community permitted marriages between uncles, nieces, aunts, nephews, and cousins, and soon began to consume itself, poisoning itself genetically. In recent generations a flock of disabled children had been born with an incurable deficiency of red blood cells. Zack Duhamel defended his gallant bachelorhood with all his weapons drawn: in a sense, he really represented the last card in a marked deck.

"Does it hurt? Who was J. Londoño? Is Londoño a first name or a last name?"

"J. is for José. Londoño's the last name. They called him Poundcake."

"Did he put up much resistance?"

"Yes. He fought hard. No. It doesn't hurt."

"Poundcake. What an odd name."

"Poundcake was a brave man."

"I've never met a tiger-killer before. You say it was from Bengal?"

"That's right."

"Aren't the ones from Bengal in Asia?"

"Tigers are tigers, Zack."

And blowflies are blowflies. There they were, the seven insects only a few inches from his head. They made him sick. Saturday dawned overcast with black clouds. The rain started early and didn't stop until the afternoon. The drops machine-gunned the roof of the trailer. Lightning and thunder. For his dying the soldier had chosen the tune about Yolanda as sung by the duet of Silvio and Pablo on a record by the Sound Experiment Group of ICAIC in Cuba. It was his favorite song. Yolanda. Eternally Yolanda. His only sane act in the last ten years had been defending himself against nostalgia, like a cat on its back. At the beginning of his exile in Caracol Beach, his past on the island would appear without warning: a torrential downpour at dawn, for example, or the sudden smell of pencil wood, was enough to ruin the day with the echoes of many questions that had no satisfactory answers because they depended on the possibility of a return that was absolutely forbidden to him. The nights turned kaleidoscopic and the soldier grew dizzy on the carousel of remembrance. Memory left him adrift. It was during this time that he approached the circles of Cuban emigrés in Santa Fe, and on several occasions he participated in the community's traditional fiestas where he even ran into childhood friends and famous baseball players whom he had admired from the bleachers. He met men and women flogged by their recollection of a country they were determined to reinvent street by street, old men in guayaberas who wagered their properties in Havana or Bayamo at the domino table, matrons who exchanged recipes in an effort to keep the proportions from being forgotten, people aged by the bitterness in their mouths who loudly interpreted news from the island as signs that things had begun to change behind the unreachable horizon of sky and sea that they watched as attentively as lighthouse keepers. The soldier, however, did not like to talk about politics, and his apathy regarding what his compatriots called the nation's future eventually excommunicated him from the hive. During a celebration of the Virgin of Charity, patron saint of the island, the soldier dared to publicly criticize one of the expatriate leaders after a speech delivered to a docile crowd of fanatical supporters, and his remarks earned him a permanent cross next to his name on the list of those who could be trusted. Repudiation by his own people was the final straw; as a salve to his pride he told himself he was better off alone. His country was simplifying at the speed of hatred. Hatred for himself. All of Cuba fit into the city of Cienfuegos, Cienfuegos was not welcome in his house, and his house fit into that battered old circus wagon rebuilt lightbulb by lightbulb in the auto salvage yard on the highway. Of all the junk he threw away in Caracol Beach, he saved only one treasure: the record with tunes by Pablo Milanés and Silvio Rodríguez. The colony of white Haitians, in particular Zack Duhamel, had something to do with the solution or absolution for a grief that was wearing him away, twilight after twilight, and thanks to the bartender's advice he found his own way to stay afloat. "Don't chase your own tail, lieutenant. Your country is the bed you sleep in," Zack said as he was tattooing the names on his left arm. The soldier took on the obligation not to love anyone. He sealed himself in impenetrable armor. Except for the tiger, the yellow one, the one from Bengal, that knew how to go through walls like music: "Zun zun zun, zun zundambayé, pretty bird at the break of day!"

"Just my luck, Poundcake, just my luck!" he said, and started to twist the nautical line again.

That Saturday his dead were more alive than ever. He felt besieged by their ghosts. They came back to life in the chassis of cars, they were shadows behind the windows of vans, they glinted in the rearview mirrors of buses and hid in the cabs of trucks and never stopped calling his name, reminding him that it was time to join the army of the dead and let himself be eaten by the tiger. The truth is that minute by minute the afternoon passed with the rain, his hanging rope was set up again and again, a sinister exercise that led nowhere or maybe it led somewhere: to the corral of his cowardice. Desperate, he looked for a new reason to postpone the moment he would climb up on the stool and hang himself from the rope the way hams hang from meathooks, and when he had passed the noose over his head his gums stopped bleeding, Strike Two came in for his bones, and he realized that the weather had cleared.

The soldier tied the rope to a beam in the trailer, fed the dog, and cursed the hour of his birth. He felt as if he were in the middle of an empty baseball stadium. That Saturday would end just like all his earlier nightmares. And he would not have the courage to avoid it. A rat. He would lose his mind again. For the next twenty-four hours he would walk through the jungle and not find his way out of the labyrinth, and he would listen to the voices of his friends hidden under his skin in the graves on his arm. He needed help to kill himself. He went to get it. To war.

"What the fuck: I'm going for what's mine!" As he drove away from the car cemetery in the Oldsmobile, the tiger was running down the highway, following the broken lines that divided the lanes. The ring of seven obedient blowflies crowned the tiger's head. It was growing dark and the figure of the animal was backlit among the speeding cars. The tiger suddenly flapped its swan wings and a furious wind moved the night forward. And brought the moon.

Strike Two stayed at the window, waiting for the soldier, his nose pressing against the glass. He would be on guard there for the next few hours, attentive to the leap of chirping crickets, the croak of frogs in the damp yards of the car cemetery, the light of fireflies celebrating the birth of Sunday, until in the small hours he saw his master return in a different car, holding a girl by the hand, and he left his observation post to give them both a magnificent welcome.

8

CONSTABLE SAM RAMOS had hated toupees ever since he was a boy and had seen a maternal uncle take off a wig as if he were a Mohican removing his own scalp. Uncle and nephew met again in a funeral parlor in Old San Juan, on a night of torrential rains: the boy's mysterious kinsman lay in a coffin, visible to family and friends through a rectangular window, and on that occasion his hairpiece had slipped to the back of his head, revealing one of the many seams left by the autopsy. Sam would not get over that terror until his own hair began to fall out at the military academy. In a few months baldness had made serious inroads on his skull, and someone suggested he use a toupee. Sam shaved his head. From then on he liked to tell his friends that he played Russian roulette four times a week because he shaved his skull with a straight razor and always used a pocket mirror. The edge of the blade and the fragmented image of his head presented a challenge. A real risk, the only danger he faced four times a week now that the days of war had ended for him. On that Saturday in June he gashed the back of his ear. A trickle of warm blood rolled down his neck and spread over his right nipple. His hand wasn't what it used to be. Neither was his patience. One of these mornings he'd end up slitting his throat. Raquel Gould, his wife, told him he ought to learn his lesson: "There's a reason barbers exist." Sam thought about telling her that those early morning shaves were helping him get used to the idea of a fatal accident, but he let her treat the wound and didn't say a word. It would have been the remark of an ingrate.

A soldier with a wealth of experience in logistical operations, his forty years in the service had earned the recognition of his superiors, who considered him an efficient, unquarrelsome subordinate. Captain Paul Sanders would write extravagant praise of him in the letter he presented to the Secretary of Defense when his comrade-in-arms applied for retirement: "I will always remember him at his combat post, with none of the airs of some soldiers who are obliged by their vanity to be brave and instead behave with arrogance, a hateful quality when one is stuck like chewing gum to the wall of a trench. Not many men are his equal: he has an excess of what most men lack." His participation in five armed conflicts, always in the rearguard, had taught Sam Ramos that in a war the most dangerous day is the last, when peace is just around the corner, because nobody likes going home feet first, wrapped in the country's flag like a tamale, and so in the winter of 1993 he asked Sanders to transfer him to Caracol Beach. There he could follow the plan he had devised for his golden years: to rent all the movies he had missed when they first came out because he was taking inventory of canned goods in the warehouses behind the lines. Action movies were his passion. From the moment he had first seen that peaceful curved beach, it had seemed an ideal nest for enjoying an uneventful old age. It reminded him of San Juan. It was a wise decision. Raquel Gould had approved.

"It's for the best," she said.

"Honey, the wars are over."

"Let's eat out tonight to celebrate," said Raquel. "Mandy told me about a restaurant called the Mensheviks, where the food is terrific. Shall I ask him to come with us?"

"You too, Raquel? Don't call him Mandy. It's ridiculous. Nelson. The boy's name is Nelson."

"I'm sorry."

"I don't know where he came up with Mandy."

"It's kid stuff."

"He's not a kid. At his age. . . . Besides, he won't want to go."

"You don't know him at all."

"You should know. He's your son."

Mandy did not want to go with them. Sam Ramos had been running the police station for six months, and he could count on one hand the dangerous situations he'd had to face and still have three fingers left over. The first time he laid his life on the line was the afternoon a rambunctious Siamese cat climbed to the top of an araucaria and he had a hell of a time getting up the tree and preventing a melodramatic ending.

"Here's your cat, Mrs. Dickinson."

"Are you Chicano?"

"Puerto Rican. From San Juan."

"Oh! San Juan."

"Tie your cat to a table."

"God will reward you, constable."

God doesn't reward, he makes you pay, he thought. The second time he found himself in action was on the night during Holy Week when employees at the Andalusia bowling center reported that a Latino immigrant had turned the place into a shooting gallery: he had taken refuge behind the counter in the cafeteria and was firing bowling balls and pins in all directions, along with unrepeatable curses. By the time Ramos got to the bowling alley, the immigrant had escaped.

"The guy's out of his mind, constable," said Manolo the Andalusian, the owner of the bowling center and an old acquaintance of Ramos's. "He was shouting that there was a lion in the room, a lion or a tiger, and he was throwing chairs and bottles to kill it. What lions? What tigers? What that guy needs is a keeper. Can I offer you some tapas to snack on?"

"Tapas aren't bad, but I prefer a Spanish tortilla," said the constable.

"Your son showed up here."

"My son?"

"He came with the bearded Russian."

"Russian or Colombian?"

"Russian. They're all Russian."

"What did he have to say for himself?"

"Nothing. He sat in the cafeteria with his friend. He looked a little queer with his hair bleached blond. Is that natural or a wig?" Manolo didn't say anything else: Ramos's fist slammed into his nose and the Andalusian slid along one of the lanes and knocked over the pins at the far end.

"Shit, Sam!" protested the owner of the Andalusia. "What you have to do is teach your son that men don't wear fake tits on their chests."

Except for the incident of the cat in the araucaria and the episode at the bowling alley, nothing worth mentioning had happened in Caracol Beach. If anything worried Ramos it was that he was putting on a pound a week. In less than a hundred days his belly had grown two sizes. His uniforms were tight. Doing nothing makes you hungry. That Saturday night, Raquel had packed a double hamburger, medium rare, with a bag of fries and a quart of orange juice, but it hadn't been enough. He felt hungry enough to eat a boiled buffalo. He was deciding if he should order in a

Japanese dinner, a few Mexican dishes, or a pizza with sausage and black olives, when the phone rang.

"Caracol Beach police, can I help you?" he said.

"Constable Ramos?" he heard someone ask. At the other end of the line was Mrs. Dickinson. The odious Mrs. Dickinson. The abominable Mrs. Dickinson. The hateful Mrs. Dickinson. The detestable Mrs. Dickinson. Rot in hell! he thought.

"What's the trouble, Mrs. Dickinson?"

Ramos closed his eyes and through will-o'-the-wisps of light he saw the image of a film he had been dreaming for months: a Christmas tree at a window. Wreaths. A smoking chimney. Snow. A light curtain of snow. A snowman with a carrot nose. Carols in the distance. A cat looking for turkey bones in a garbage can. The cat hears a pedestrian. The cat disappears into an opening in the night. The pedestrian is Mrs. Dickinson. The loathsome Mrs. Dickinson. The despicable Mrs. Dickinson, staggering down a dark, lonely alley. She looks drunk but all she's had to drink that night is cod liver oil. Mrs. Dickinson makes a sudden gesture that indicates pain and collapses in slow motion: in the middle of her back one can see an Afghan knife, plunged into her body up to its ruby hilt. The snow slowly covers the body. The snow becomes tinged with red. It's Mrs. Dickinson's blood. A good ending. The cat goes back to the trash and after a moment of hesitation, of justified suspicion, puts its nose into the garbage can. . . .

"What's the trouble, Mrs. Dickinson?"

The constable pictured her ostrich face and for a few seconds imagined her in a nightcap and Peter Pan slippers, scratching her navel. She was alive. And kicking. The crime in the alley was a dream. And so was Christmas, the snow, the cat. All of it a lie. A fake. Ramos felt cheated: how could Mrs. Dickinson be allowed to live? The wicked Mrs. Dickinson. The evil Mrs. Dickinson. His ultimate enemy.

"What did you say?"

"Nothing. I didn't say anything."

"I thought you did."

"You thought wrong."

"Oh!"

Sam Ramos could despise Mrs. Dickinson as fiercely as some wolves hate certain rabbits. If there was one reason he wanted to retire it was to spend the rest of his life forgetting her voice, the voice of a rheumy bird. She called three hundred times a week to report the catastrophes in the resort community: the cat at the top of the araucaria tree, the sound of footsteps in a garden, a couple making love under the streetlight on the corner, some suspicious-looking blacks hanging around her shop. Mrs. Dickinson owned a store that sold fishing gear, barely a hundred yards from her house, and though she had installed a complete security system, she spent the night keeping watch. The first thing he would do after he hung up his constable's uniform would be to take a shit on Mrs. Dickinson's porch. A pound and a half of shit. On this occasion she was calling to report that some depraved kids, probably drug addicts, had broken into the Lowell family's house.

"All right, Mrs. Dickinson. Don't get excited. What are they doing? Are they robbing the house?"

"Worse than that, constable: they're dancing. A girl's taken off her clothes on the table in the garden."

"It isn't your garden, Mrs. Dickinson."

"It's my view."

"I'll come by."

"Hurry, please."

"As soon as I finish shaving my head. . . ."

Mrs. Dickinson concluded her little chat:

"I told Mrs. Lowell. Watch out. You'd better watch out, Liza: there are bad influences out there. Young people are going to the dogs. It was different in my day, constable. God help us. But Mrs. Lowell thinks money can fix the world. She's wrong. She wouldn't listen to me. I'm not in her class. You know? As far as Liza's concerned, I just sell fishing gear. She's never invited me to play canasta with our neighbor, the Belgian soprano who's married to the hotel manager from Tokyo. Not that I'm desperate to play canasta with a singer. I hate opera. And Japanese. But I feel sorry for the boy. I watched him grow up. Martin has a future. . . . It's a shame."

"Who's Martin?"

"What do you mean, who's Martin? The Lowells' son. Come right away. I have a feeling something awful will happen before this night is over."

"Good night, Mrs. Dickinson."

Ramos hung up the phone, convinced he ought to visit an antique shop and buy the Afghan dagger with the ruby handle and commit the crime himself. In the meantime, I'll eat a steamed buffalo and when I've digested it I'll go and take a dump on Mrs. Dickinson's porch even if that buffalo is the last thing I shit, he thought, and his stomach growled as if a set of china had shattered in his gut.

"Were you talking to me, constable?" he heard someone saying from the back of the police station. Ramos had forgotten that tonight he was breaking in an assistant, a young man who answered to the Central American name of Wellington Perales.

"Find me the phone number for the pizzeria," he said.

"What's going on?"

"What's going on is that I'm in urgent need of a pizza with sausage, black olives, and pepperoni. That's what's going on. It's a matter of life and death. Understand? The future of Puerto Rico depends on that pizza. In the right-hand drawer of the desk there's a pink notebook where my wife has written down emergency numbers."

Ramos drank down the quart of orange juice in one swallow. The liquid cooled the chimney in his esophagus and put out the fire in his stomach. A loud sigh of relief set the lightbulb in motion. As it moved, the constable's hairless shadow began to sway on the wall.

9

SOLDIER'S NOTEBOOK. Tell my fortune, fortuneteller. It seems wild animals are no joke. African lions, tigers, jaguars, panthers, leopards, whatever. All big cats are tigers. Ernesto Aspirin was on watch and he came running into camp because he saw one the size of an elephant. He says it stared right into his eyes and its mouth was watering. Lieutenant Samá got really pissed. He read the medic the riot act. Suppose his stupidity means they surprise us with our heads up our asses in our hammocks? Suppose we're ambushed? "Any of you turns tail and runs, I swear I'll hold a summary court martial and put you in front of a firing squad and blow your head off." That's what he said. And he said that cowardice is considered high treason. "You'd be better off shooting yourself." I don't give a fuck. No lions in the Sierra, buddy. But here! Bet your ass. I'm on watch at midnight. And I'll shoot it right between the eyes: I'm not crazy about the idea of traveling this far from home just to be chewed to death by a tiger or leopard. Samá pulled one of his sayings out of his sleeve. He knows a whole lot of those old sayings. I learned it, there's something to it. "Only trees that bear fruit have rocks thrown at them." [. . .]

"Advice?" Samá said. "Not advice, an order: starting today, you sleep with your boots on." Leo Rubí asked, "Because of the wild animals, right, lieutenant?" and the black man answered, "No, you moron, so you all can run when the enemy takes us by surprise." I suggested some recreation: a game of stickball. Four against four. Nobody wanted to. I tried to reeducate them: "What kind of Cubans are you, comrades, if you don't like to play stickball! Antonio Maceo played stickball in the jungle. Columbus played stickball with the Pinzón brothers on the *Santa María*. Rubén Martínez Villena played stickball in the courtyards of the Isla de Pinos Penitentiary. Camilo Cienfuegos played stickball during the invasion of Occidente from Oriente. Stickball is stickball. It's a part of history." They really put me down. "Enough bullshit," Samá told me. "This isn't the time." [. . .] I think I'm missing a few marbles, as Rafaela says. Last night I dreamed I found a dog on the street and brought him home, only it wasn't my house but a strange damn place, though it was clear Caterina and I lived there, I don't know how, because it looked like a junk pile. I've never had a dog. A mangy pup. I take care of him. He turns out to be friendly, playful. My mother doesn't like the idea of another mouth to feed because she says if we don't have enough to eat what the hell are we going to give the dog. In the dream she didn't yell at me. She wasn't even there. I was sure she was someplace around but I didn't see her. The dog went everywhere with me. He protected me. When I came back from the stadium with my bat and glove, the little dog was waiting for me at the window. I told the dream to Aspirin, who says he's something like a shrink. He asked me a couple of questions about my childhood. "What the hell does my childhood have to do with my dog?" I asked. Aspirin said: "I think you need a brother." Maybe. When I get back to Cienfuegos I'm going to get a dog. Maybe what I need is a brother and not a father. [. . .] The good thing about war is that you get to know people better, and yourself too.

Walking the tightrope between life and death, having to keep
your balance, is a learning experience. Danger strips us naked.
You only keep the minimum, the absolute necessities. I'm talking
so fancy. A smooth talker. An acrobat. I didn't know a lot of things
about myself. That's the absolute truth. I had a feeling I was
totally useless and here, in the asshole of the world, I've confirmed all my fears. Even I have to laugh at the weird things about
me. In peacetime it's different. Under fire you discover that a
human being is a worthwhile animal. I amaze myself. Eight men
in the jungle. Eight stones in a shoe. Eight specks in an eye. Eight
men who never would have run into each other on the same road.
And now we're in the same boat. And we're getting by. Each man
is a world. A world. This one talks like a poet; that one turns out
to be a wise man; the other is a great cook. And I write. I write the
first thing that comes into my head. At this rate I'll end up an
artist emeritus of the glorious city of Cienfuegos. The bad thing
is the African leopard. Are there any tigers? Just my luck! I'm
going to light a candle to the Virgin of Regla. The bad thing is
there are no candles. There's not even a place to drop dead here.
The bad thing is that the blowflies are back. What a pain in the
ass they are. The bad thing is you're really far away when you're
here. The bad thing is the bad thing. I wonder which Belarussian
Caterina the Great is sleeping with. Who'll take care of her
chickens? I'm so tired I can't see straight. Wiped out. I curl up in
the hammock. Freezing cold comes in through a hole in the hammock: "Good night," I say. Nobody answers. They put out the
light. Ibondá de Akú is as dark as the inside of a wolf's mouth. Far
away, to hell and back, I hear a dog barking.

10

THAT NIGHT there was a full moon, no doubt a happy coincidence because Laura thought natural phenomena established
channels of communication between what some call cosmic mysteries and others consider natural laws, though the reading of
those portentous signs, at least for her, had its origins in a literary,
even a poetic, sensibility, not necessarily an astral or metaphysical
one as Chuck Mayer, a great defender of zodiacal laws, believed.
"The full moon is auspicious for love," Laura said as they entered
the resort. Martin supposed that such a statement could be interpreted as a coded message, and he decided that if his parents were
going to give him hell anyway over this invasion by his friends,
the best thing would be to accumulate really prodigious misdeeds
so that he would deserve an equally remarkable punishment.
Laura had to be persuaded that he could be a sensational guy, and
he found the courage to throw his hesitations overboard. Surely a
bold strategy for inspiring the love of the prettiest girl on the
planet. Something had moved forward, and Laura had planted a
kiss on his cheek. Martin felt no limits: the marijuana had erased
them.

"Onward," said Martin, and the Mayer brothers could not repress a burst of applause. The Lowells' mansion in Caracol Beach had been built for pleasure, and no luxury had been omitted. A patio with a heart-shaped pool, a bar on the terrace, a music room, excellent sound equipment, a billiard room, five bedrooms, central air-conditioning, and even a wine cellar stocked with single malt whiskeys distilled in Glenlivet, white wines from the Loire Valley, and vintage ports as pale and expensive as mammoth tusks. Martin had learned from his father that each drink ought to correspond to a specific situation, and what suited that gathering of friends was a million beers, except that Martin discovered there were only two cases of Corona in the cellar. He would lament his indecisiveness twelve hundred times in the next few hours. "I had the whiskey in my hands," he would tell Tom. "Think of it! But dude, I didn't have the nerve. Can you believe it? I put it back. How was I to know? How?" Martin locked the cellar with two turns of the key and left his guardian angel inside.

"It's now or never," said Tom as he took off his clothes and did a double forward somersault off the diving board. Bill Mayer was thrilled. Laura, in the meantime, took possession of the place with her authority as the queen in blue jeans. In the moonlight, dancing on the table in the garden, she could be unbearably attractive. She was born to conquer. Beautiful, happy, intelligent, she knew she was a success and did not hide the satisfaction this knowledge gave her. Everybody wanted her that night. She was fantastic, especially when Sting went to have a drink at the bar by the pool and Albita Rodríguez came out of a record to sing one of her *guajiras* among the bougainvillea. Jeans were invented for Laura, Tom thought. Impossible to deny. Jeans had been invented for the nimble thighs of that girl without limits named Laura Fontanet—now she had climbed on a table and was shaking her hips with the grace of her secret Cubanity. The party was all that anyone could ask. Bill and Chuck, bringing up the rear, said they would prepare a memorable Italian pasta and gave themselves over to the task of filling the bellies of their classmates not just with smoke but with spaghetti. Martin, however, had miscalculated their provisions, and the beer ran out at midnight.

"So what? Didn't you say there was enough beer to make the whole St. Petersburg fire department drunk?" said Tom.

I had to have some defect, thought Martin, and it made him laugh. The second joint had produced an unexpected effect: everything made him laugh. The furniture made him laugh. What funny chairs with those ridiculous backs. The four-legged cedar table, a horse without a head, made him laugh. He imagined it galloping through the garden: its heavy wooden legs had acquired a muscular physicality. Mrs. Dickinson made him laugh. And the bougainvillea, what a laugh. And Bill and Chuck Mayer, oh, an even bigger laugh. The heart-shaped pool made him laugh. Who'd want a thing like that? His mother, Liza Lowell, she was so corny. And the shape of Coca-Cola bottles made him laugh. And Laura. Laura's ass squeezed into her blue jeans made him laugh. The Lakers T-shirt made him laugh. Tom made him laugh. Tom, OK, what a laugh. OK, babe. And the clothesline in the backyard. And his penguin's tails. And the glasses. And the foam on the beer. And the tick-tock of his watch. And the photographs of his grandparents in the living room, in their silver frames. What a laugh. And the record by Albita. And Sting. And the sleek refrigerator, what a laugh. And the piano. And the apples in their baskets. And the door handles. And the fake fireplace—a fireplace at the beach! What a laugh. And the toilet bowl. And his farts. What a laugh. And his soft hands. What a laugh. Even the moon, covered with pockmarks, made him laugh. Laugh like crazy. The roquefort cheese of that moon made him laugh. The last full moon of his life.

Tom and Laura were waiting for the moment when they could take off and have their own party somewhere else. They'd had a great time, why deny it, but as it got close to midnight they wanted to be alone: after six semesters of sharing the same classroom, their desks touching, they had finally recognized that they made an ideal couple. Tom was the star of the basketball team and therefore the indisputable stud of the student hive, and queen bee Laura imposed herself by divine right on the school's swarm of cheerleaders with that haughty way she had of denying all importance to the charms of her jeans. The students at the Emerson Institute attributed to Tom a long list of sexual conquests and a bold ability to take any woman who crossed his path to bed, a false rumor he never bothered to deny because it added valuable points to his score on the barometer of fame; the fact is that Tom was terrified of being alone with a woman because the one time he dared to spend the night with Agnes MacLarty his cock was so frightened he could not fulfill to the letter the rituals established for celebrations of intimacy, and in the end he was unceremoniously assaulted in the gymnastics instructor's bedroom. Laura, on the other hand, had a secret that made her even more confident: she had made love to Theo Uzcanga, her poetic and pathetic teacher of Spanish literature, and even though her discovery of sex was not the sublime experience she had imagined in the sexual fevers of adolescence, at least it allowed her to break the membrane of her virginity with comparative good fortune. She kept in her heart the carte blanche authorizing her to be happy on the last night of the academic year, and she swore she would make good use of it. Perhaps things would go better with Tom or Martin. Except that Martin had miscalculated their provisions and the beer ran out around midnight. Tom and Laura decided to leave without saying goodbye to avoid uncomfortable explanations.

"I feel bad about Martin. He's been so nice."

"Forget about Martin."

"And we'll leave just like that? It makes me feel bad. I can't help it."

"It's better this way. We'll make up some story tomorrow. OK?"

Just as they were beginning their escape Martin cut them off with an urgent request: to pick up some beer at the liquor store on the highway. He had smoked a second joint and felt brave enough to crawl up the Himalayas if that would make Laura notice him. For a moment he was tempted to go back to the cellar where the treasure of wines was stored. He controlled himself because there was no drug powerful enough to make him lose all respect for his parents. That hesitation would cost him dearly, but Martin couldn't know that at mile ten on the highway to Caracol Beach the watchman at the auto salvage yard had been dreaming about a Bengal tiger carrying a rat in its mouth.

"I had to have some defect," said Martin. Laura winked at him. So did the moon.

11

THE SOLDIER was thinking that the Havanean Agustín Marquetti, first baseman for the Industriales, could have been a fantastic fourth hitter in the lineup of any team in the majors, when a Ford with Texas license plates beat him to the last spot in the parking lot at the Bastille and he understood the event as a clear warning of tragedy. He left the Oldsmobile in front of a building under construction and started toward the entrance in a foul temper. The driver of the Ford with Texas license plates was a fat cowboy with the face of a Halloween pumpkin who was such a son of a bitch he didn't even thank the soldier for not breaking his neck right there with one of the lead pipes lying in a pile at the construction site, which was what he initially intended to do. The soldier forgave him. For a while.

"I'll let you go this time, you bastard!"

The bar was not very crowded. The Bastille was the most disreputable place in Caracol Beach, a dive frequented by the marked cards of the resort community: true grotesques, an occasional luminous transvestite, and four or five mercenaries who came in on Saturdays to dynamite their livers with the perfumed waters of cheap gin and ambush their hearts as they lay entrenched behind barricades of resentment.

"Hello, Zack," he said to the bartender.

"We've missed you, lieutenant. Since you stopped working with us you hardly come round anymore."

"That's the way it goes, Zack."

When the soldier came to live in Caracol Beach, thanks to the efforts of a veteran's association, Madame Brigitte Duhamel, Zack's mother, offered him a job at the restaurant on the beach. In exchange for waiting on tables they allowed him to eat in the kitchen, where they prepared a stupendous red snapper in garlic, and to sleep in a small low-ceilinged cubicle at the back of the storeroom. After fourteen years he quit his job because he began to develop an allergy to shellfish, but the soldier was always very grateful to the Haitians for having given him a roof over his head, a place to sleep and food to eat, during those difficult moments of his *via crucis*.

"What'll you have, lieutenant?"

"The usual rat poison. How's Brigitte?"

"She getting on, almost a hundred years old."

"That was some rain, Zack!"

The soldier settled in next to the cash register. He never drank more than one beer. During his stay in the lunatic asylum in Lisbon they had prescribed pills to steady his nerves, and he never disobeyed medical orders. He ignored other advice, such as checking himself into a mental hospital every six months for neurological examinations, but he never stopped taking the pills even during the worst crises, when the Bengal tiger came gliding down from the banks of cumulus clouds into the auto salvage yard. He was at ease in the Bastille because in that cattle pen nobody seemed to care about his being a hopeless madman. He adjusted the pistol in his belt. He lit a Camel. The nicotine quieted the itching in his gums. The music's deadly, he thought.

The music was deadly. That Tex-Mex border music drove him crazy and the son of a bitch cowboy with the Halloween pumpkin face insisted on playing records by Los Tigres Temerarios on the jukebox to help him lure, with glasses of gin, a slender transvestite with bleached blond hair who fluttered around the place like a butterfly lost in a crater of the moon. There was a detail in the fragile butterfly's outfit that he found very disconcerting. It wasn't the red boots with slender heels that turned his perfectly depilated legs, or the leather miniskirt that just covered his testicles; certainly not the platinum belt that cinched his waist or the satin blouse cut low in the back or the bracelets at his wrists or the little pads that swelled his breasts or the earrings sparkling at his ears or the false eyelashes that were so exaggerated they could be considered part of his costume. The most outrageous thing about him was an item that was innocent, discordant, almost anachronistic: a wide headband that held back his hair as if he were a young girl at a nun's academy. A headband that was red, white, and blue. A challenge. The soldier thought he could detect in the transvestite a desire to avoid the fat man from the Ford. The butterfly didn't know what to do with his hands. He kept rubbing them together. He kept taking off the headband and putting it back in his hair, an unnecessary action that revealed his growing nervousness. Something about the Texan bothered him. Perhaps it was the obscene way he made kissing sounds or repeatedly touched his fly for no reason. The fact is that the fag with the headband was fed up, and not precisely with gin.

"Pig," said the butterfly as he laid the headband on the back of a chair, "go fuck your grandmother."

"Oh! This girl is playing hard to get," said the man from Texas.

The soldier swallowed hard and considered the possibility of getting his own back somehow: he could turn the cowboy into a murderer. That son of a bitch might be a good candidate. He'd have to provoke an incident. Give him a motive. Declare war. Mobilize him. Tenderize him over a slow flame. Maybe knock down the transvestite. Anything to fuck up his night until the cowboy killed him in self-defense. That way the Texan would soon be free. Not even the worst hack lawyer could lose a case this easy. Zun zun zun, zun zundambayé, pretty bird at the break of day!

"Just my luck: I can't get the song out of my head! Pretty bird my ass!"

The slender, fragile butterfly was doing a sensual dance in the middle of the floor. His snake-like shape seemed to fragment in the sparkles of light flashing from a mirrored ball. His hair floated in the air. The movements of the dance did not correspond to the monotonous beat of Los Tigres Temerarios but to the call of a visceral melody perfectly synchronized with the daybreak bird tune that the madman with the tattoos could not get out of his head. Zun zun zun, zun zundambayé, pretty bird at the break of day! The transvestite gently began to move his arms as the rhythm of his steps accelerated, until he suddenly left the floor, looked for the headband he had left on the back of a chair, and, tossing his mane of hair over one shoulder, approached the bar and asked Zack for a glass of milk.

12

THE MILK had to be low fat and not because of some addiction to dieting but because of habit, a word that has two different meanings, both applicable to the transvestite's request, because habit (a tendency acquired through repeated actions) can be used as a synonym for the noun "custom," and since he was a little boy his mother had taught him to eat healthful, non-fat food; but habit is also the clothing or dress worn to fulfill a vow, and he had proposed to revolutionize Caracol Beach with the image of a diabolically possessed schoolgirl for which he used and abused four surprising strategies: zero makeup on his face, long false eyelashes, a tricolor headband in his hair, and a kiss of milk on his lips. Zack served him reluctantly. It did not matter that the milk was pasteurized and free of pathogenic germs. Bars sell more dairy products than health officials suppose, for patrons do not always come in to get drunk on whiskey or beer; if they did, that would make the business incomplete: in taverns hangovers are also neutralized and livers fermented in alcohol are repaired. The butterfly needed to counteract the half liter of rum he had swallowed that afternoon in his apartment, a purgative that had triggered a childish, impetuous response. His early evening intoxication unleashed a series of aggressions against his Armenian, a tailor with unbearably green eyes. Considering how much they loved each other, why had he displayed so much animosity? He never showed off his black-belt holds or his karate skills or his abilities as a wrestler; still, the Armenian almost ended up in the emergency room. Poor thing, he didn't even try to defend himself. Good as gold. He let himself be massacred. Plain and simple. Though many in the gay community thought his kimono designs were ghastly, the Armenian's heart was in the right place. If there was one thing about him the butterfly liked, it was his perfect sense of justice. In front of other people, in difficult situations, he always leaped to his boy's defense with the valor of a Knight of the Round Table, not caring about defeat and with a violence that represented the best way to prove his love. But in their intimacy as a couple, the Armenian never even raised his hand. Now the transvestite was sorry he had behaved so immaturely. If H.G. Wells's time machine existed, and if he were granted only one chance to travel to any page of history he wished, he would give up the opportunity to visit Golgotha with a video camera or stow away on Noah's Ark, and he would try to turn back the clock to the moment when he proposed adopting a child. Maybe it was a scatterbrained idea, he reflected at the bar, but not as crazy as his man thought. The Armenian explained his reasons. He couldn't see himself as a father. He'd rather have a dog. And the transvestite despised dogs. It ended in a brawl.

Who'd even think of adopting a dog? he thought and asked Zack for a second glass of milk. He felt like a Black Prince at the edge of a quagmire. He couldn't consider the fat man with the Halloween pumpkin face as anything but a hog in a puddle of shit. The one who wasn't bad at all was the guy in the mechanic's overalls sitting next to the cash register. He had noticed the presence of that Lone Ranger at the end of the bar, and if he didn't do anything to attract his attention it was because the pig in shit didn't leave him alone for a second, hounding him with obscene suggestions. Since the Lone Ranger wasn't wearing a mask, the butterfly could see that he had the face of a crocodile hunter. The scar that sliced across his right cheek made him an interesting prospect. Hard. Like a sledgehammer. With a beard he'd be irresistible. For him, only for him, he had improvised his sensual dance under the ball made of tiny pieces of glass. The gyrations in the choreography were an attempt to reproduce the undulating slither of a caiman. He couldn't get past a snake. It wasn't his night. The man didn't even notice him. And the border music didn't lend itself to gallantries. The hunter turned to look at him only once, with "cosmic indifference." The transvestite left the floor, looked for his headband, and, tossing his mane of hair over one shoulder, approached the bar.

"We've missed you, lieutenant. Since you stopped working with us you hardly come round anymore. What'll you have?" he heard the Haitian say.

"My usual rat poison," said the crocodile hunter.

The butterfly controlled his desire to engage the hunter in conversation. That scar looks like a worm wriggling on a hook, he said to himself, and he adjusted his leather skirt. It was too tight. A tailor in the house had turned out to be a misfortune because, having no professional models, he used the butterfly to publicize his stupidities, among them this miniskirt that was like cardboard and pinched his waist. Gigi Col, a prostitute who loved to have fun, promoted the fashion shows that the willful designer organized at the beginning of every season for the enjoyment of his friends and the mortification of his model. His collection could make you cry. The transvestite had accepted the role of Isabella Rossellini, convinced his mother wasn't wrong when she said that every person with an ounce of sense had to be able to make compromises if a loved one's happiness was at stake. And of course the butterfly had made compromises. Especially with his father, a career soldier who had set himself the task of turning his son into a man of action. For his father's sake he had practiced martial arts. Judo. Self-defense. Karate. Wrestling. And placed first in several marksmanship contests. But he still liked men. During his adolescence he agonized over the attraction he felt for the cadets at the military school where he was a student and suffered in secret because of something his artillery instructor tried to explain as a hormonal deficiency, a line of reasoning that caused the boy's expulsion from the academy after his father punched the instructor in the nose and knocked him out. Until one day, years later, the future transvestite read this sentence somewhere: "Not loving anyone is an immoral act," and he resolved to go to bed with anyone who made his heart beat faster. "Get out of the closet," Gigi Col told him. The butterfly remembered her words as he drank the glass of milk. "Don't think about it too much. Be who you are, damn it. You always wanted to be named Mandy. Sounds nice, doesn't it? Mandy. You like it? You're Mandy. Say it out loud: I'm Mandy. Come out of the closet, just do it." Mandy came out. For the past few months he had allowed himself to be dressed and undressed by the kimono designer, and was exactly who he was: a human being.

"Who is that guy, Zack?" asked the crocodile hunter, pointing at the hog. The butterfly was all ears, assuming that butterflies have ears.

"I don't know. I never saw him round here. A stranger. Looks like a Halloween pumpkin."

"You're right. A fat son of a bitch with a Halloween pumpkin face. I hate him. He drinks gin. I hate gin too."

The butterfly returned to the dance floor to make his farewells with a variation à la Selena that would leave those present with the honey of desire in their mouths. He closed his eyes. He moved the levers of his legs in a military cadence, and the pis-

tons of his buttocks marked the rhythm with bewitching seduc-
tiveness. He danced to three records in a row. He was sweating
when he finished. Sweating rum. He imagined himself at the edge
of the swamp. A crocodile. Mouth open. Fangs. Suddenly a man
appeared and risked his life to save her. Right then and there,
without much in the way of formalities, they began to make love.
Hard. Like a sledgehammer. As he was about to penetrate her the
mystery man turned into the Armenian. The days of sexual safari
were over. It was time to settle down. Have a family. Adopt a
child. Or a dog. First he'd go to see his father and tell him. He
missed him. Sometimes he missed him too much. Since he'd
moved in with the Armenian, the transvestite hadn't heard from
him except through his mother, who kept him up to date: "Last
month he rescued a cat that couldn't get down from an araucaria." His father, rescuing cats! Selena again.

The fat son of a bitch with the Halloween pumpkin face bore
down on him like an avalanche of lard and invited him for a drive
in the used Ford he'd just bought. He drooled when he talked
about his car. He touched his balls. His testicles had nothing to
do with the Ford. Absolutely nothing. That gesture was his perdi-
tion. The butterfly lifted him to his shoulders, spun around five
times, and threw him against the bar.

13

SAM RAMOS felt uncomfortable. On Wednesday of that week Captain Paul Sanders had assigned him the task of training the man who would soon replace him as head of the police station in Caracol Beach. A superior's orders are not discussed, they are obeyed. Wellington Perales had just graduated from a military academy in Florida and was eager to see some action as soon as possible in order to demonstrate his abilities. He was a slow-witted but hyperactive boy, an extremely dangerous combination. He believed that a steady hand was all you needed to be a peace officer, and because he had won a couple of spearfishing competitions, he said, he had no doubt he'd be the talk of the resort community. That kind of public recognition was what he needed to marry Sofia Carrasco, his Dominican fiancée, and he was ready to earn it in record time. Life granted his wish. On the third Monday in June all the newspapers mentioned officer Wellington Perales in big headlines, some as a hero and others as a killer.

"This is the happiest day of my life. I've thought a lot about this moment. I'm eager to see some action."

"I'm sorry to tell you that if it weren't for Mrs. Dickinson, you could think of Caracol Beach as a nursery school," said the constable.

"Mrs. Dickinson?"

"When you meet her you'll shit frog hairs and wish you'd been born retarded and start banging your head against a brick wall and be sorry you ever wound up in a place called Caracol Beach. She just called to report some kids dancing on the Low-ells' diving-board next door. Can you believe it?"

"Do you want me to check it out?"

"If I could I'd kill her with an Afghan dagger, the kind that has a ruby handle. I'd sneak up behind her on a dark lonely street and stab her in the back."

"You know what, constable?"

"What?"

"I was born to be a cop. I like it."

"False. Nobody's born to be a cop."

"It's in my blood. I swear."

"There are better things to do with your life. Like holding up banks."

"I love spearfishing."

"Killing sharks is better sport than killing men. One of these days you'll have to invite me along on a fishing trip."

Wellington Perales would tell his story at the request of Captain Sanders, who questioned him regarding the slaughter at the auto salvage yard. Since childhood Perales had been trained to be a soldier, except that his period of apprenticeship was cut short by a stroke of fate on the night his father, a commander in the navy, was shot to death in a tavern in Panama by an unknown gunman. The commander's widow swore that none of her children would be cannon fodder. When he came of age, the temperamental Wellington Perales asked his father's old comrades for letters of recommendation to join the police force, hoping to avenge a death that for him had always been a tragic question mark. And ever since the Tuesday before the events in the auto salvage yard, when Captain Sanders himself informed him that he had been accepted into the police force and his training base would be the resort community of Caracol Beach, Perales had been imagining a long night of pursuits, armed assaults, and battles to the death with gunmen from Panama. But on that Saturday he thought he was off to a bad start, because of all the instructors he could have been assigned to, he got one named Sam Ramos, a fat, bald Puerto Rican who said he hated a woman whose last name was Dickinson and ordered him to hurry up and get him a pizza with sausage, black olives, and pepperoni, which didn't seem a particularly worthy occupation.

"Have you ever killed anyone, constable?" he asked.

"Why do you want to know?"

"I'm curious. How does it feel?"

"No particular way."

"That's impossible."

"Maybe that you're a pig. That's how it feels. More pizza?"

"I was hungry, constable. Thanks. I'm full now."

"I could eat a buffalo," said Ramos as he got to his feet.

"Are we going out?" Perales asked eagerly.

"I'm leaving you in charge of the station."

"Don't worry."

"Of course I'll worry. What did you say your name was?"

"Wellington. Wellington Perales. Captain Paul Sanders was a friend of my father's."

"I heard something. . . ."

"They were in Korea together."

"Any friend of Paul's is a friend of mine."

"My father died six years ago in the Canal Zone. He was

killed. Ambushed. He was after a terrorist or something like that."

"How old are you?"

"Twenty-two."

"Almost the same age as my son Nelson."

"Sanders says the only way they could get my father was in an ambush."

"Right, well, . . ." said Ramos, "take care of the station while I'm gone. And don't kill anybody unless you think they're trying to kill you. That's the only way it's worth being a pig. I have to see the hateful Mrs. Dickinson."

"Oh! Mrs. Dickinson."

"If I don't come back it's because I strangled her and became a fugitive."

"I don't get it."

"Use your imagination."

"I'd rather use my weapon. You became a fugitive, and then what?"

"Then you inform Captain Paul Sanders that I was lost at sea, devoured by sharks, and my wife collects my insurance. Her name is Raquel Gould. Tell her I'll be waiting for her at the beach in Zihuatanejo."

"Zihuatanejo?"

"At Casa El Arrebato. She'll understand."

Wellington Perales walked with the constable to the patrol car. Later he would recall in an amusing way how the shocks in the car groaned with the crushing weight of the driver, "like a circus elephant sitting on a bicycle," he told Captain Sanders. Back in the office he spent his time going through the file drawers, where he found the remains of tuna sandwiches and some candies melted by the summer heat. Bored, he called Sofia Carrasco and told her a few heroic lies. Any conversation between them led to the preparations for their wedding, and tonight was no exception: they were talking at length about their honeymoon on a cruise ship when they were interrupted by the voice of an operator who came on the line to report an emergency call from a bar, the Bastille, where someone named Peter Shapiro, a Texas rancher, wanted to press charges against an ungrateful transvestite who, along with two white Haitian accomplices, had destroyed his brand-new Ford in a public parking lot. Shapiro bellowed his rage, demanding justice. His shouts filtered through the little holes in the receiver like ribbons of sirloin coming through the meat grinder in a butcher shop. To avoid shattering his ear-drum, Wellington placed the receiver on the blotter on the desk and took down the substance of the charge: broken windows, a moronic albino, the name of his insurance company, slashed seats, and a passing reference to an Oldsmobile put together from spare parts "like an automotive Frankenstein monster."

"Thank you," said Wellington.

"What do you mean thank you?" Shapiro protested.

"Excuse me."

"Don't be a moron. Move your ass."

Wellington pressed down the button on the telephone with the delicacy of an expert deactivating a time bomb. Damn, I made another mistake, he thought. He still wasn't familiar with police rhetoric. "Use your imagination," Constable Ramos had said. He made another call to Sofia Carrasco and asked if she had ever heard of a beach called Zihuatanejo.

14

TWO BLIND CATS turned out to be a club intimate enough to allow conversation and crowded enough to keep you from being bored even with a man like Theo who was so given to nostalgia. After dancing the first bolero, Agnes's body was still wound tight. On stage the musicians were taking their places, which promised a good time that night. Agnes doubted her partner's dancing skills, though when the moment came there was always the possibility of being carried away by one of the many Havaneans, male and female, who filled the club, moving their waists at the slightest provocation. Pepe Cortés, the owner, went from table to table, greeting each of his compatriots. A patron of the arts and a born diplomat, Cortés had realized his dream of opening a place in Santa Fe where Cuban immigrants could gather without the burdensome interference of politics, and that cordial effort had won him the blessings of friendship. He lay his hand on Theo's shoulder before saying: "Maestro Uzcanga, with you here the company is complete: welcome to your house," and he continued on his way, leaving a hint of lavender water in his wake. Theo made a modest gesture. He thinks he's Harrison Ford, Agnes

thought, and ordered her first vodka in seven years. Oh well: she
was already drunk. It felt good. She was lucky. Her solitary variation on the bolero brought new invitations. She danced a mozam-
bique with an artist from Bayamo, a tango with a poet from Pinar,
a salsa with an ex-partner of Alicia Alonso, a *danzón* with a good-
looking film actor, two Dominican merengues with a philosopher
from Marianao, a *cumbia* with a seminary student, and even a
guaguancó with a classical ballerina, which received a rousing ovation. Pepe Cortés came on stage and announced the main attraction of the evening: Albita Rodríguez in person. The night was
going beautifully. Theo Uzcanga behaved with style and class,
and didn't bore Agnes with erudite quotations or his "perverse
verse." He didn't recite one sonnet. He didn't recommend a
single book. He didn't say that no one understood him. He gave
her no reason to say no. And besides, he ordered vodka too, even
though he'd been drinking rum and Cokes since the toasts made
at graduation.

"You're a gentleman," said Agnes.

Theo Uzcanga was a gentleman. The moment she had been
anticipating all night, that instant of indiscretion when he would
propose making love in his top-floor studio, a situation that
Agnes intended to resolve with a cutting remark in the style of
Bette Davis, never arrived. On the contrary. He had invited her to
the Two Blind Cats with good intentions and no hidden agendas.
Four vodkas after the first five rum and Cokes, Theo had three
simple reasons for behaving well: first, because he had just completed a study of eroticism in the novels of Reinaldo Arenas; second, he had happened to see Agnes on the street outside school,
swaying next to the traffic light like a long-stemmed rose in flan,
and he had gone over to her to keep her from breaking any bones;
and third, on that night with its full moon, the teacher had been
pierced by the thorn of a fatal presentiment.

"What's the matter, poet?" said Agnes.

"Hmm?"

"Cat got your tongue?"

On the stage at Two Blind Cats, Albita Rodríguez had just performed a *son* that said: "Don't ask me why I'm sad, that's something I won't say; you shared my joy but not my grief, why did you go away?" Five of Arenas's friends, invited by Pepe Cortés, came on stage, and a sweet mix of French perfumes saturated the air with the fragrances of a hair salon. One of them introduced himself as the Mother Superior and presented a sketch of Reinaldo's ghost that touched everyone present: "After he blew his brains out he took up residence in my kitchen, and the stubborn fool insists on rearranging everything, so now I find frying pans in the freezer, salmon filets in the waste baskets, and salt in my silver sugar bowl." The round of memories traced the novelist's life in Havana and ended in a choral piece sung a capella by the flamboyant quintet.

"The night's almost over," said Agnes.

"One more, one less."

"Don't be melodramatic."

"When two are in love, the sadness of one is enough."

The bar closed its doors at 5:50 in the morning. Later they would learn that at precisely the same time, Tom's heart was pierced by an iron rod and Martin carried a spear gun to his encounter with the tattooed soldier.

"Thanks for a fantastic night," said Agnes. "I was feeling miserable."

"Wait," said Theo as he parked the Toyota in front of the apartment building where Agnes lived. Asthmatics develop a sixth sense: they have hunches.

"Smell that."

There wasn't enough air in his impaired lungs to say more than that minimal command.

"What is it?"

"Smell that."

Agnes sniffed. There was nothing unusual. Or was there? The constellations were in place in the firmament. And the moon. The city smelled like a village, the business street like a tilled garden, the air like water, the water like earth, the asphalt like cedar, Sunday like Thursday, the ocean like the countryside, the old like the new. She inhaled morning air. Dew. Beginnings. Even foolish butterflies were fluttering around streetlights, convinced they were wild tulips, and color-blind dogs crossed from one corner to the other each time the traffic lights changed. It had been raining, and the flashing neon lights were reflected in glassy pavements, creating a very convincing theatrical effect of telegraphed mirrors. A bell tolled six slow strokes that slipped around the contours of houses and other things. A woman in a flowered apron, one of Agnes's neighbors, hung a birdcage on her terrace. A train sounded in the distance, behind the baseball stadium. The whistle of the locomotive that was arriving, or perhaps departing, mixed with the trills of the canaries, and the trills of the canaries mixed with the bells of an invisible church calling the faithful to six o'clock Mass. Silence. Finally Agnes could throw up. The mouth of a sewer swallowed the dregs of the wine. Theo pressed her stomach firmly. He offered a handkerchief. She liked lavender water.

"What's going on? Why so much perfection?"

"Who knows? Not even God can understand this life," said Theo. Asthma closed up his thorax.

At that moment, in the auto salvage yard at mile ten on the road to Caracol Beach, a Bengal tiger spread its wings and a sudden wind saturated the air with drops of saltpeter. Beads of Oyá hung from the animal's feathers, along with other protective amulets: branches of *cundiamor*, stalks of bitter carpet grass, little copper medals in the shape of crutches, lockets, scapularies. When its wings closed the wind stopped. And the moon went out.

15

TO KEEP the door from slamming in its face, the tiger entered the Bastille close on the heels of a customer and walked among the tables, measuring each step as astutely as a sapper in a minefield. The soldier saw its image reflected in his glass of beer. A fleeting spark. A clear sign. He had been waiting for it. He knew the tiger would find him even if he hid at the center of the earth. It never admitted defeat. It kept fucking with him. Coming after him. The tiger. The yellow one. From Bengal. Seconds before he saw it in the bar, waiting for his reactions, the soldier had the taste of shit in his mouth again, and his gums, bitten by the ants of infection, were itching. With the same caution as his rival, he followed the tiger's maneuvers in his glass, like someone observing in a mirror what's going on behind him. He saw it lick the plastic of the jukebox. The image was distorted in the curve of his glass. Its head looked enormous compared to the ridiculously contorted body. He saw it stretch out on a distant table and flick its tail over its back. He saw it scratch at the seat of an empty chair, sharpening its claws. He saw it playing with the lightbulb hanging in the corridor where the bathrooms were located. Until the music stopped for a moment, and the animal passed through the back wall and simply vanished. A scent of withered poppies hung in the air. The blowflies were outside, crashing into the window, attracted by the light from the Bastille. Tack tack tack, you could hear them from the bar. Attacking blindly, violently. Tack tack tack. The glass was streaked with a viscous liquid. The tiger walked up the street. It moved its wings without taking flight. The blowflies stopped their assault on the glass and flew after their king in perfect formation.

The soldier drank the rest of his beer from the bottle. And his mind divided in two. The carousel of madness had begun to turn. In memory, as impossible to drive away as the blowflies, the medic Aspirin Gómez was reading aloud the letter from his girl-friend, again provoking the rage of the machinist Fernandito López, in the next hammock. Lieutenant Samá intervened in time and stopped them from hitting one another. The Brain Ruedas and Leo the Fly Rubí were playing checkers in the light of a kerosene lamp: they had received no letters from home. Fernandito kept spitting and spitting through the window. On the far shore of the soldier's dementia, Zack was mixing a drink in the blender. The soldier lit a Camel. Border music was deadly. The butterfly lost in the crater of the moon adjusted his tricolor head-band. He was drinking a glass of milk. The soldier belched up beer. Zack applauded.

"What are you thinking about, lieutenant?" the Haitian asked and pulled him out of his reveries.

"I was far away. Very far away. Who is that guy, Zack?" he said, pointing at the fat man.

"I don't know. I never saw him round here. He's a stranger. Looks like a Halloween pumpkin."

"You're right. A fat son of a bitch with a Halloween pumpkin face. He comes from Texas. At least, his Ford has Texas plates. I hate him. He drinks gin."

"You bet he does, lieutenant. Should I poison his drink?"

"I can't stand him, Zack. He took my spot in the parking lot. I had to leave the Oldsmobile in front of the next building."

"It's not right."

"You bet it's not right."

"If you want, I'll grab him from behind and you can beat the shit out of him. Then I'll tattoo his name on your arm: 'Here lies a fat Texan with a pumpkin face.' Too long, right?"

"He took my spot, can you believe it? I had to park in trash, Zack, all because of a cowboy pervert who comes chasing butterflies in our bar. Our bar, Zack. He deserves to die."

"He does," said Zack. "Like the tiger. Tell me again how you hunted it down. It's incredible."

"Another time, Zack."

"I told Gregory Papa Gory, the albino. I told him I knew a guy who fought one of those wild animals with his bare hands to save a friend. When I told him about it, Papa Gory made the sign of the cross. He's very Catholic. He baptized the whole flock of Mongoloid kids in the community. A real Samaritan. You don't know Gregory, do you?"

"Gregory?"

"Gregory Papa Gory. He just got back from Port-au-Prince after a few months in the French Caribbean. Maybe I'll hire him on as cook. He has a way with shellfish. And lots of experience. His wife died a couple of years ago. I hear he's coming over today. He's all alone, like a dog in a doghouse."

"I don't think I know him."

"He's godfather to all the idiot children in Punta La Galia. Know something? Papa Gory wrote me a letter and said in black and white that nobody can beat up a Bengal tiger with his bare hands."

"Yes you can. . . . He should have seen how its eyes were shining in the middle of that jungle, Zack."

"You bet they were shining, lieutenant."

"It tore off my friend's leg."

"That's what I said. And you made him a tourniquet."

"He was bleeding to death. His belly was full of ants."

"He owes you his life, lieutenant."

"I strangled it. Just my luck!"

"Papa Gory says no human being can strangle a tiger. I really want to see Gregory. We always talk on the phone."

"Look, Zack, look: the queer with the bleached hair is ready to explode."

"You're right. Fat pumpkin-face doesn't know who he's messing with: that queen's a real tiger on ice."

"That's a good one: a tiger on ice."

"Another beer, lieutenant?"

"How much do I owe you, Zack?"

"Nothing. I'm the one who owes you. I like talking to you. You know a lot. Don't be a stranger. If you decide to leave the salvage yard, you can always have your place behind the storeroom. How are your allergies?"

"Bad, Zack. Everything's bad."

"You're right about that. Everything's bad. Aren't you waiting for Papa Gory?"

"My fifteen minutes are up."

"What's that mean?"

"It doesn't matter, Zack."

"Good luck, lieutenant."

As the soldier was leaving the Bastille, he looked around for the fat cowboy son of a bitch pumpkin face who drank gin by the bucketful, and he caught sight of him just as the slender butterfly applied a judo hold, lifted him to his shoulders, and threw him against the bar like a stick of margarine. Zack applauded the fight with childish enthusiasm, not caring about the damage. When he reached the street, the soldier saw that the right rear tire of his Oldsmobile was flat, punctured by a mason's spike.

"God damn it to fucking hell," he said.

The soldier felt like finding a steel bar in the debris around the construction site and smashing the Ford's windows to smithereens. Not satisfied with breaking glass, he thought, he'd begin by kicking in the fenders and slashing the seat covers with the bayonet blade he carried at mid-thigh, and he'd pull apart the fuel lines so the fucking Ford would burn to a cinder. He swore by all his dead that he'd do it, and he was true to his word, but first he had to get rid of the tiger. When he started the engine of the Oldsmobile, the headlights illuminated the figure of the animal as it raced away with folded wings and was lost from view at the distant intersection, without taking flight.

"God almighty: Jesus, just my luck."

The black albino, Gregory Papa Gory, was approaching the bar with all the serenity in the world. He had shuffled his feet when he walked ever since an attack of gout weakened the muscles in his lower extremities, which was why he always looked as if he were splashing through puddles. He was in no hurry: "Better late than never" was his favorite saying. His maxims were effective because he said them in the solemn tone used for reading the Psalms. After the boys were buried, Ramos would go to the Bastille to put away two liters of Puerto Rican rum, and Papa Gory would tell him that the night before, on Saturday night, the night of the killings, he had seen the famous madman of Caracol Beach get into the Oldsmobile and heard him shout some obscenities. "I'll never forget his face. One second is long enough to recognize a man on the road to hell. I swear. When he passed me our eyes met, and his were wild, they looked like balls of fire to me. A bad sign. If I had known, I would have tried to stop him. Don't ask me how," he said. A pensive Gregory Papa Gory walked into the bar. Zack welcomed him like a hero brought back from the dead by the legions of the Evil One.

16

SOLDIER'S NOTEBOOK. I see him and say to myself: "What hat did they pull this black out of?" I swear. This Lieutenant Lázaro Samá is a real pisser. A tough customer. He's a *ñáñigo* or *abakuá*, I don't know much about that stuff. He doesn't hide it. Doesn't brag about it, either. That's why they wouldn't give him a Party card, though with his record he should be on the Central Committee. When he tells his war stories he never mentions battles or ambushes or anything like that: he likes to talk about funny things, crazy stories about a bunch of characters who belong in the circus. A comedian. Ever since I first met him hauling sacks of cement in the port of Havana, not acting tough or showing off, just nice and calm, piling up the bags, I've liked that dark-skinned black. I can still taste the *malta* I drank with him. Even though Samá's from Santiago. I swear I can't stand Santiagans. I don't know what it is about them. Like a kick in the stomach. Even though I wasn't born in Havana. I'm from Cienfuegos, a city full of half-French whites. (Now it's full of Russians, Bolshies.) It's not that. Maybe it is. What's the difference. What happens, happens. It must be the heat, right? People from Santiago de Cuba

can't keep their mouths shut. Five minutes after you meet one
he's telling you in gory detail about the guy who's sleeping with
his wife, how they're hung (him and the other guy), how many
times he fucked his girlfriend during Carnival. I swear. Lázaro's
different. I'll have to rip this page out of the notebook so he can't
read it when he asks for my diary. I don't want him to think that
the son of Caterina the Great is a shiteater, an asskisser, a
bootlicker, a brown-noser, a lousy yes-man. Yesterday or the day
before, when the letters came from Headquarters, he started
telling stories about Juana Bacallao. Too much. I know who Juana
is. What Cuban doesn't know about that five-hundred-year-old
black woman who walks down the middle of the street like she
was a car. And what tail fins she has on her. "I've never seen anything like it," Samá told me. "When this war is over and we're
back in Cuba the Beautiful with a whole lot of medals on our
chests, I'll take you to the Palermo so you can see what a wild
woman that *rumbera* is. You know the Palermo? A real dive. It's in
Old Havana. Behind San Rafael Boulevard. A real shithole: the
worst, but a little drink of mint makes it all OK. You even forget
about the stink of piss." The truth is the lieutenant didn't stop
talking. Fernandito López was supposed to relieve Benemelis on
guard duty but he kept him there, running off at the mouth, all
because Fernandito didn't get a letter from Cuba (he made the
mistake of getting married before he left). Samá is a lot of Samá. I
like the stars. Samá knows that. So he keeps coming over and asking me about the constellations, the moon, Saturn and Venus—
blacks love the planet Venus. Come to think of it, what day is
today? I think it's Saturday June 10th or Sunday the 11th. I have
to ask. Here comes Poundcake. He says he swears by his sweet
sainted mother that it's true, gentlemen, he saw movement of
enemy troops in the distance and. . . . [The page in the notebook
is cut off at this line.] Everybody's making plans for the future.
Maestro Ruedas dreams about a teaching job at the Pedagogical

Institute in Matanzas. Aspirin says that with his record as an internationalist fighter he can matriculate to study medicine at the University of Pinar del Río. It's true. All Benemelis thinks about is having ice cream at the Coppelia in Camagüey. Good idea. Fernandito's out of it. Like the beggar they call the Gentleman of Paris. I think. I don't like him much. Or dislike him either. Lukewarm. Maybe I haven't talked to him enough. He's weird. He keeps spitting. He spits the whole damn day. He spits on his hands. He spits on his boots. He spits on his canteen. He spits and spits. He even spits in his food like a toothless old man. Lázaro says not to mess with him. He'll get over his craziness. Leo is a mystery, who knows what the Fly is up to. He keeps his mouth shut. A worm, like all the ones who run away and betray Cuba. Somebody (I won't say who) says he's a faggot because he talks like one. I don't think so because he's always getting letters from his girlfriend. That's what he says. That his sweetie writes every blessed week, a darling ten-page letter with dear little baby kisses drawn all around the edges. The army won't ever catch me again. Ball's what I love but that's a square peg in a round hole. My fifteen minutes are over. My elbow's fucked up. Not my lucky day when I got on that bike. I have to stop writing. Samá's worried. Serious. Poker-faced. He's lost contact with the rear. Communications are a holy mess. Sometimes I operate the radio and all you can hear is a bunch of damn noise. Lots of times you pick up enemy frequencies but can't understand shit. The air's full of static. Must be the blowflies. A hell of a lot of blowflies. Maestro Ruedas, our glorious squad translator, doesn't know enough English to get a Coca-Cola. Looks like Ibondá de Akú is only a stone's throw away. Today I feel like listening to Chucho Herrera's Nocturno program, lying in the hammock, the transistor glued to my ear. Something by Los Brincos. Caterina loves Los Brincos. And chickens. Today I caught forty winks in the afternoon. I had a dream. No, not the one about the dog, OK? This time I dreamed I was falling down a well, wrapped up in a sheet. The chickens were following me. I wasn't scared. The chickens were fluttering all around me like angels. And cackling. What a dream. I'm dead tired. God almighty. Damn. I don't even know what I'm writing anymore.

17

"MY AUNT JESSICA'S dying," Tom said and grinned from ear to ear. He was a bad liar. And he wasn't very good at telling jokes, either. He lacked imagination. Not only because he was an uncomplicated boy, but because Tom was simply Tom. "There's no difference between him and a good-looking stud," said the other cheerleaders at the Institute. Laura would come to his defense: "For God's sake: don't expect pears from an elm. Tom is Tom, and in this school nobody's better than he is at being Tom. He had to have some defect." The apple of Tom's eye was the Chevrolet he had won in a sweepstakes sponsored by a soft-drink company. He equipped it with every sophisticated device on the market, not to mention gadgets as useless as air-fresheners that smelled like the snow-covered forests of Canada, Lakers decals, and a spray to inflate the tires in an emergency. When Tom found himself obliged to throw up the smoke screen of a lie, he never expected anyone to believe him. He would say the lie, and that was it. Plain and simple. With no dramatic elaboration or any liar's techniques. His talents were more muscular. Sports were his passion.

He spent a fortune on specialized magazines that focused on football, basketball, and ice hockey. He read them with the fervor a monk brings to scripture. If anyone has ever wondered who buys the sports publications that fill the racks in drugstores, an answer close to the truth would be Tom. The Emerson Institute inherited his periodical collection. For him, the body represented the temple of a new religion. He passed his courses with grades just high enough to keep his parents paying for athletic coaching. He was always the hopeless loser in difficult situations he could not resolve with his fists, though he always tried to feint first with a lie.

"What about my aunt? If you ran out of beer it's not our fault. Drink vinegar," Tom said.

"Give me a hand, Tom. It'll only take us a couple of minutes in your Chevrolet. Is that too much to ask?"

That night it would have been criminal to deny Martin anything. To the surprise of his classmates, the peaceable and punctilious scion of the Lowells, always so correct, had devised a memorable party for them without giving a thought to the punishment that awaited him when his parents learned from Mrs. Dickinson that their son had unleashed a real hurricane in the resort community of Caracol Beach.

"Count me out. And my Chevy too. I'm sorry," said Tom. "I have to go to the hospital. My Aunt Jessica's dying."

"We'll go and come right back," said Martin. "It won't take a minute."

"Isn't there any wine?"

"That wine is sacred, Tom."

"Call your folks."

"They'll skin me alive if I open a bottle of Glenlivet, or port."

"Nothing ventured nothing gained. You don't lose a thing by

trying. Bell invented the phone so children could communicate with their parents."

"Get in," said Laura, and she opened the door.

"What about Jessica?"

"Jessica can wait, Tom. Tomorrow I'll go with you to the cemetery so you can bring your aunt some flowers," said Laura.

"OK. You're a sweetheart," Tom replied without enthusiasm. "Seeing is believing."

Martin could not bear the idea that Laura would leave the party without giving him the opportunity to summon the courage he needed to say how much he had wanted her ever since the afternoon he first saw her at the Emerson Institute cheering for the basketball team.

"Thanks. You two are real friends. I mean it. I swear I'll never forget what you've done," Martin said melodramatically. The drinks had gone to his head. Tom started the engine in the Chevrolet and Laura began to hum one of Sting's songs. On the way, Martin discovered a detail that could complicate their plans: his bank card showed insufficient funds at the ATM. He had used up his money on his penguin suit.

"I'll pay," said Tom.

"No way. You're my guests," said Martin.

It was Laura who had the idea for the final escapade of the evening. She planned the job with great precision. While she distracted the clerk in the liquor store, Tom would stay at the wheel with everything set for a fast getaway, and Martin would steal some cases of beer.

"What do you think of my idea, Martin?"

"It's fabulous."

The top student in the graduating class backed the adventure because he loved the leading role Laura had assigned to him. In only a few hours he had developed a new image as a decisive person even more daring than the basketball star.

"You take care of the clerk, Tom stays at the wheel with every-thing set for a fast getaway, and I steal some cases."

"We can't miss."

"That's a fact," said Martin.

Tom was not happy about the possibility of complicating the night with dangerous adventures, and he counted the minutes, like the beads of a rosary, until he could get rid of Martin and be alone with Laura in some dark corner of Caracol Beach.

"Count me out," said Tom.

"It was a joke. You have no sense of humor," said Laura. "I'm happy as a clam."

Tom was so annoyed at behaving like an idiot that he lost his concentration at the wheel and almost collided with a red-painted Oldsmobile that was crossing the highway on a perpendicular road without its headlights on.

"Watch it!" said Martin. Tom avoided the crash with an Indy 500 maneuver.

"Drop dead, asshole!" he shouted.

The soldier thought it wouldn't be a bad idea. That's what it was all about: getting himself killed. He put the car in reverse and decided to follow the Chevrolet that was swerving down the highway. The scene was pretty funny. Like the movies. First this way. Turn the wheel. Then that way. Turn the wheel. The car looked drunk, as if its tank were filled with rum, not gasoline. The soldier imitated the actions of his prey, and the Oldsmobile began to zigzag back and forth about twenty yards behind them. Drop dead, asshole. Turn the wheel. You were born, ass-hole. Drop dead, asshole. You were born, asshole. Turn the wheel. Drop dead, asshole, the madman repeated to himself, his eyes not fixed on anything. He put the pistol between his legs. The barrel was pointing at his testicles. Maybe it would go off by itself even if it didn't have a firing pin because he had bought it at an amusement park. It was a Browning, useless but convincing. A catalogue piece. Maybe it would go off by itself. Bang bang. The devil can perform miracles too. Drop dead, asshole. Turn the wheel. You were born, asshole. Drop dead. The air in the Oldsmobile's right tire was low, and it squealed on the asphalt, just like a rat in the mouth of a Bengal tiger.

18

THE PIZZA with sausage, black olives, and pepperoni was still dissolving in his stomach's gastric juices when Sam Ramos arrived at the Lowells' house with a search warrant signed by himself, only to find Albita Rodríguez singing in the garden, a trail of empty bottles, and Bill and Chuck Mayer asleep on a rubber float in the peaceful waters of the pool. On the mirror over the bar someone had written a message in crayon: "Where'd you go? God won't forgive you. Ciao." Three caricatures illustrated the text. Ramos found them amusing. The first drawing showed a skinny boy who wore a tie and had enormous bulging eyes behind the thick glasses of the nearsighted; in his hand he held a scale. Albert Einstein, Ramos thought. The second drawing exaggerated a competitor in the Mr. Universe contest, with a mouth like a slice of watermelon, protruding ears, a Greek profile, and a touch of stupidity in his expression. "Tarzan of the Jungle," he said. In the third sketch, a voluptuous Amazon posed without clothes and covered her breasts with two banana peels, while in a comic-strip balloon she tried to justify her nakedness with these words: "Oh no! What dirty minds! I only wanted to dance at

Machu Picchu." The drawings were so well executed that when the constable found the original models in the auto salvage yard, Tarzan run through by an old piece of metal and Einstein riddled by bullets, he could identify them by the caricatures.

Sam Ramos was thinking up a good insult to describe the nefarious Mrs. Dickinson when he heard Albita Rodríguez through the speakers in the bougainvillea. The ceiling of the night fell in on him, star by star, and he thought about Old San Juan, parties with his friends from the neighborhood, his dreams of glory, his son. He felt a sharp pain in his chest. Nelson was his best failure. His worst achievement. The last teacher he had talked to about the boy's future had told him he was on the verge of flunking out. "Maybe some judo classes would be a good idea. He has his hormonal problem, you know, and masculine role models are not always appropriate for a sensibility like his," said the artillery instructor in the main office of the academy, and Ramos knocked him out with one punch. The following year Mandy would complete his education and go out on graduation night with his pals to celebrate the heroism of being hairdressers. Stylists. It was time he became more involved with Nelson, and the first thing he had to do was learn to call him Mandy without feeling ashamed. The boy caused him pain. Father and son had not dared to talk about homosexuality because Ramos was—and he did nothing to hide it—an old-fashioned homophobe. When did the mistrust first appear that eventually opened an impassable chasm between them? At what point did they begin to fear each other? Where did the fault lie? Ramos had trained hundreds of boys, and in most cases he had succeeded in turning them into hard, strong men, but he had been careless on the weakest front: his home behind the lines. I have to go and see Nelson, he thought as he tried to turn off the sound equipment in the Lowells' living room. Tomorrow I'll invite him for a drink. Better yet, a meal. White rice and beans, green plantains. The reason for the change in plan was his ravenous hunger despite the pizza with sausage. "I'm an idiot," he said, and he decided to have supper with Nelson to see if he could make up for lost time in the human heart he loved most in this world. Why not? It's never too late to tell your son you love him. One of them had to give in, and he would be the one: a fat bald pig named Sam Ramos. He loved Nelson. Wars don't always end in victories or defeats. Someone had to propose a truce, hoist the white flag, say enough is enough. The fat bald pig named Sam Ramos would let Nelson bring his new boyfriend so he could try the red beans. A Siberian bear. Was the bear Russian? No, Lithuanian. Maybe Uzbek?

"Russian. They're all Russian."

Albita Rodríguez laughed among the bougainvillea. Ramos rescued the shipwrecked sailors with the garden rake, and before he pulled them onto dry land he dunked them in the water of the pool to extinguish the last embers of their inebriation.

"Let's go, sailor boys, the party's over: go sleep it off some-place else. Don't make me arrest you," he said.

"Thank you, officer," said Bill.

"Move it."

"If Martin or Laura or Tom comes back, tell them we got tired of waiting and left."

"Martin or Laura or Tom?"

"They went out for beer."

"I'll tell them."

"What time is it?" Chuck wanted to know.

"Time to go."

Ramos let them leave only when he was sure one of them could drive a car with some degree of safety. Then he used the radio in the patrol car to communicate with the shark-hunter Wellington Perales.

"What's happening?"

"All quiet at the front."

"Then I'm going to stop by my son Nelson's house. If you see a tidal wave coming, you can find me there."

"Yes, sir, constable."

Ramos couldn't help it: he looked toward the house next door and saw Mrs. Dickinson as he had imagined her at the police station, a nightcap pulled down to her eyebrows, peering through the curtains. Ramos spat on the grass. His tolerance and capacity for forgiveness had a limit: the abominable Mrs. Dickinson. The horrible Mrs. Dickinson. His hatred was stronger than his courtesy. He would gladly shit on her porch tonight. By way of greeting he made a very Sicilian gesture with his arm. Then he got into the patrol car and drove away. Albita Rodríguez was still singing among the bougainvillea.

"Yes, I am a pig," he said when he couldn't keep his belly from pressing against the steering wheel. Four blocks up the street a strong smell of white rice and red beans hit him in the face. He stopped the car at an intersection. Who'd cook up a pan of white rice and a pot of red beans at this time of night? The windows of the nearby buildings were shut tight, like niches in a strange kind of mausoleum. Then he realized that everything, absolutely everything, was cooking inside his chest, steaming in regrets. He never let himself be overcome by longing for San Juan, a city he barely remembered except for the smells and tastes of a distant youth. Ramos had fled the island (he always used the verb "to flee") at the age of twenty and swore he would never set foot in his house again unless he could do it with glory. And a chest full of medals. After his flight he gradually moved farther and farther away from his family until he was lost from view in the distant corners of the planet, but as time passed he began to return, inch by inch, to the Caribbean. What unconscious mechanism was allowing nostalgia to bring him to his knees? In the small hours of that morning, at an intersection, hidden away in Caracol Beach, he found the reason and learned that you need your homeland twice in your life: at the beginning of the story, when you're a child, otherwise you end up an orphan with no sky or roots, and when your back begins to bend under the burden of years, for an old man weighs less if he's led to the grave by the hand of the innocent he once was. And suddenly that aroma of beans, that dreamed-of rice steaming on the fire. White rice. Hulled rice. With cloves of garlic fried in olive oil. Some parsley. The beans thick and creamy. A piece of squash. The woody odor of cumin. So much lost. Childhood shit. Ramos leaned against the wheel. He was uncomfortable. The place where he cut himself shaving was stinging. His panic was Mandy. The boy lived in one of those apartments. Raquel had told him where, but he had forgotten. The building on the right? Or was it the one on the left? No, on the right. Fourth floor. One, two, three, four. Sure. There, in that cage with a balcony facing the street where a ridiculous little Puerto Rican flag was hanging. "Do I go up or not?" he wondered. A second before he fled—he was always fleeing—Ramos caught a glimpse of his eyes in the rearview mirror, and though he tried to avoid it, he felt a sickening whiplash of pity.

19

LAURA SAID that the expression "happy as a clam" was outstandingly stupid because nobody, absolutely nobody, could know how clams feel, and therefore the comparison was of doubtful poetic value. Martin gave an erudite discourse on the miserable life of both pelecypoda and annelida, in particular intestinal worms ("good only for letting girls lose weight without having to go on a strict diet"). Still, he granted to earthworms the value of bringing to the earth's crust fertilizer to make humus, but in any case feeding on shit like a worm or burrowing in mud like a clam did not seem a good reason for feeling happy. Bored with the conversation, and annoyed with himself, Tom lost control of the wheel and almost crashed into the soldier's car. "Drop dead, asshole!" he shouted.

The air on the highway made the alcohol fumes go to their heads. There were no customers in the liquor store. Martin would remember seeing the red-painted Oldsmobile that Tom almost ran into at the crossroads, but at that moment he thought nothing of it. Laura chose to stay in the backseat of the Chevrolet and doze: "Don't be long," she said and pillowed her head just under the window.

"It'll only take a couple of minutes," said Martin.

Tom saw a man come into the store and noticed that he had a poorly sewn scar on his cheek. As they passed in the aisle he felt a bad vibe: the man smelled of cod liver oil. Tom didn't say anything to Martin. The stranger dropped a chocolate bar into his pocket and began to walk backward like those comedians in silent movies who retrace their steps when the film is rewound.

"What are you thinking?" asked Martin.

"I'm thinking this world is full of crazies. Seeing is believing."

Before he paid, Martin once more became the correct Lowell he had always been. Near the shelves that held the beer he felt obliged to play fair and confess to Tom that for love of Laura he was prepared to meet him on any field of battle. Tom marshaled his patience and listened without saying a word until Martin traced the history of his passion all the way back to the distant days when he had first seen her on the basketball court. They were playing for the district championship against a rival school. Agnes MacLarty was directing the cheerleaders from the stands. Martin's family had just moved to Santa Fe, lured by the possibility of finding a nice house in Caracol Beach, and the boy had not yet selected the school where he would finish his studies. That afternoon he visited the Emerson Institute and did not find it very appealing. He thought it was too liberal. He was about to leave when the roar of the fans drew him to the basketball court. Laura was dancing in the middle of the court, baton in hand. The girl's nimble thighs would soon become an obsession. Tom was blossoming into a hero. He scored thirty points and carried them to victory. Martin was hoarse for a week.

"I was hoarse for a week."

"OK. Very debatable. From start to finish," said Tom. "I scored thirty points."

"I've loved her ever since."

"OK. You've loved her ever since. So?"

"So I can't stop thinking about Laura. I know you love her too, Tom. I know. You don't have to tell me. I knew it that afternoon. You scored thirty points to officially inform all the students and faculty at the Emerson Institute that the great Tom loved Laura Fontanet like a blind man loves his cane. OK? Tell me the truth."

"OK. What else?" Tom thought that Martin's interpretation was not entirely correct. He hadn't been flirting with Laura but with Agnes, and to a point he succeeded because he got her into the frying pan and warmed her in the butter of his kisses. That night he took her to bed, and despite his dubious erection, the conquest could be considered a triumph.

"You wanted us all to know that Laura would be yours."

"Agnes said something similar to me that day."

"I don't understand, but that's your charm, your style: you don't let anybody understand. Every time you made a basket, you turned around to look and Laura smiled back at you. Don't deny it."

"I'm not denying it."

"I was in the stands. I didn't know either of you. I was new. An outsider. Rara avis. An ordinary spectator."

"I don't remember you."

"Nobody remembers me. I always go unnoticed. I'm a zero to the left. A solitary earthworm. That's my principal attribute."

"What were you doing there?"

"Don't tell me it's not so: you were hunting the queen."

"That's one way of putting it."

"What do you expect? I love her, Tom. I swear. I'm ready for anything. Kill me if you want to. You must think I'm out of my mind. OK. Whatever. I'm out of my mind."

"OK. You're crazy."

"Shit: you always say OK."

The scene could have gone on indefinitely. Tom decided to cut off the dialogue with a gentlemanly suggestion:

"Let her decide," he said, absolutely convinced of the advantage he held over his rival.

It seemed an acceptable arrangement to Martin, and with renewed optimism he walked to the register to pay and get back to the Chevrolet as fast as he could. On the ramp down to the parking lot he was telling himself that he would invite Laura to his room. With a bottle of white wine under his belt he would tell her how planet Earth had split in two when she kissed him on the cheek just a while ago. Or was it a century? Tom took a few more seconds, looking for some chewing gum in the candy rack. At that precise instant, though they didn't know it, the two friends had begun to die near mile ten on the highway between Santa Fe and Caracol Beach.

20

SOLDIER'S NOTEBOOK. Here's the problem life poses: it has thorns and it has roses. That's what the song says. Tomorrow it'll be [words crossed out] that we've been in Ibondá de Akú and it feels like a century. What's happening is that nothing's happening. During training, back in Cuba, they showed us movies about the Great Patriotic War, and naturally the defense of Stalingrad that lasted months and months was condensed into two hours, in color, with music in the background, and so the battles were exciting, but in real life you learn that wars are full of dead time, routine, the worst boredom, you dig trenches and fill them in, climb a tree, get water from the river, and you don't see shooting anywhere, or you hear it like thunder in a rainstorm falling in hell, until I guess the day comes when it's your turn to get wet in the shower of lead and others see our lightning in the distance while they're digging and filling in their trenches. Poundcake says we really are the seven samurai (I'm the crazy one), because just for a roof over our head and a few sardines we've come to defend the future of a people we never even heard of. All I know is that I don't know what I'm doing here. As for us killing the enemy or the enemy killing us, what we have to kill is time. [page missing] Fernandito spends all his time spitting. Leo told me the other day that Fernandito told him he's thinking about deserting. He wants to go home. [page missing] Lieutenant Samá was sleeping with his mouth open, under the tree where we sometimes sit to eat, and Poundcake went to find a tube of toothpaste so he could squeeze some into his big blubber mouth. And he did. Lázaro jumped up like a bee had stung him on the ass and pulled out the pistol he always carries in his belt. "What happened?" he shouted, spitting out toothpaste, drooling all over himself: "What happened here? What happened?" "What happened was that your mouth was open, lieutenant," said Poundcake. Lázaro put away his weapon and answered with that damn self-confidence of his: "That's because I opened it. Applaud, OK?" [Written in the margin in red ink, in a different hand: "You'll pay for this, you little shit!"]. We died laughing. Wow! If it wasn't for moments like that. After a while, Lázaro told a joke. A dud. Nobody thought it was funny. He tells the worst jokes. Aspirin read his girlfriend's letter out loud, and that made Fernandito really mad. Poor guy. He's shitting with fear. And that's exactly why he's in such a lousy mood, so damn touchy, ready to start a fight with anybody for no reason at all. You never know how a coward will react. It comes full circle. Acute fearitis, said our medic, who has a clinical eye. The Brain and the Fly haven't gotten any letters from the island. I was outside, writing. Not much to say. Lázaro sat down beside me. "Juana Bacallao is a phenomenon, my friend. What a woman! I've never seen anything like it. When this war is over and we're back home in Cuba the Beautiful with a whole lot of medals on our chests, I'll take you to the Palermo so you can see what a wild woman that *rumbera* is. You know the Palermo? A dive. It's behind San Rafael Boulevard. A real shithole: the worst, but with a little drink of mint you have a good time." [. . .] On Sunday, I think it was Sunday—or was it Monday?—Lieutenant Samá gave a rousing speech to raise the fighting spirit of the troops, he said, which had begun to weaken after a few cans of sardines turned out to be rancid and we started shitting little fish in the bushes. Well, he began by talking about Carlos Manuel de Céspedes and the Baraguá Protest, moved on to the blowing up of the *Maine* and the annexation of the republic, and ended by quoting the words of Enrique Arredondo, TV's Cheo Malanga. As a finishing touch, before he repeated the slogan "Fatherland or Death," he said from the platform of the chair: "Compañeros and compañeras" ("compañera" was for Leo Rubí, I guess), "comrade soldiers," the lieutenant shouted the conclusion to his patriotic speech: "Let us be better today than tomorrow!" And a second before the applause, Leo himself came right back with: "Yes, Lazarito, sure, a teeny bit worse every day." I swear. It was really funny. Wow! The lieutenant's speech reminded me of something that happened a long time ago. It must have been five or six years back. Comadre Rafaela was in the house, scraping the pot for a little burned rice for the pigeons. I was reading the paper *Revolutionary Youth*. And you, Caterina, were eating a guava that somebody had just given you. And then the bottom half fell on the floor, remember? You got down to pick it up and there you were on all fours, your hands on the floor and your ass up in the air like a rose on the keel of a cement barge. "Watch out," I said, "that's just how they blew up the *Maine*," and you answered, sighing, with the guava in your mouth: "Oh, honey! Some boats have all the luck." Rafaela—Felita—almost died laughing that day. Applaud, OK?

21

"TOO MUCH excitement for one night," Laura said to herself as she unbuttoned the top of her jeans. She felt liberated. She sighed. The end of school, the confirmation of her Los Angeles scholarship, the discovery of a new, daring Martin, and the unexpected attraction to Tom, had been a lot of surprises for a full moon. Knowing she was desired by the young men in her generation who, each in his own way, were the most promising, swelled her vanity. She would play with them like a cat with two mice, and at the moment of triumph she wouldn't take either one, at least not tonight, because tonight all she wanted was a bed where she could sleep for at least two hundred years. How many glasses of brandy had she drunk? Twenty? Thirty? And five thousand beers. I don't know anymore, Mom: I lost count, she thought. Laura didn't know when she could take off the jeans that were cutting off her circulation. On Friday afternoon, before a jury composed of don Claudio Fontanet and Emily Auden, she had modeled a dozen outrageous outfits adorned with her stepmother's jewelry, but at the last minute she ignored the suggestions of the family tribunal, which had voted for a beautifully made rose-colored

Mexican dress, and chose the old blue jeans that had seen a thousand battles and had brought her so much luck in her cheerleader's career, though she knew she would hate them in the end: dancing would make her perspire so much that the cloth would stick to her skin like a siren's tail. "I don't know where I am/ because I don't know where you are," she said. They were lines by Francisco Hernández. And she closed her eyes. She saw Sting. Perhaps because she was in Sting's arms she never knew what nightmare that madman jumped out of when he put her in a choke hold and held the barrel of a pistol to her temple.

"Applaud, OK?" the man said.

"What are you doing?"

"Will you ask me in?"

"Don't hurt me."

"Shhh. Be quiet. Shut your pretty mouth. I was watching you. Watching. And I said to myself, They left her standing at the plate. And I came. Did you see my pistol? Why would I hurt you? Do you know who I am? Do you? You don't know anything! Don't do anything stupid. Look, if you behave nothing's going to happen to you."

"Please."

"Your friends don't know that the tiger's on the way."

"Who are you?"

"Tell my fortune, fortuneteller."

No. He wasn't Sting but a man about forty with the muscles of a bull, a Latino to judge by his lousy English, wearing mechanic's overalls with the sleeves cut off to reveal a list of names tattooed on his left arm. Fear sharpened her instincts, and the infinite power of desperation allowed Laura to fix the image of her attacker in her mind until she saw details that would have gone unnoticed under normal circumstances: the scum of solid grease that covered the nail of his trigger finger, the military tag hanging around his neck, the bayonet blade he carried at mid-thigh in a leather cartridge belt, and the badly sewn scar that twisted along his right cheek like an earthworm wriggling on a hook.

"Haven't you seen the tiger?"

"I don't know what you're talking about."

"The tiger."

"The tiger?"

"A yellow tiger. From Bengal. The devil is walking the earth," said the soldier. "I know. I know a lot. People are born to die. I'm going to tell you a little secret, but don't tell anybody else or I'll kill you. Listen, pay attention. Pay attention to me, damn it! What happened is that the fat man took my spot in the parking lot. Why'd he do that? You tell me why. Just my luck!"

Laura wanted to put herself in God's hands but couldn't remember the words to any propitiatory prayer. The man had to be crazy since he did not have to use so much force to make her do what he wanted, and precisely because of the way he spat the most vulgar insults at her, the fire in his wild-looking eyes, the tension in his jaws, his hot dusty smell, she knew that this maniac who was putting his fingers on his nose now and scratching his head compulsively could also kill her in the backseat of the Chevrolet. For a moment she thought the scene would fade and she'd find herself at home, lying in bed, ready for another dream about Sting. The illusion that she was imagining a man with the muscles of a bull lasted only a few fragile seconds, and then he returned her to reality with a saliva-ridden laugh.

"Pay attention to me, damn it!"

"I haven't done anything."

"Ask Zack. He saw the fat man. A fat creep. Don't you know Zack?"

"I haven't done anything. Who's Zack?"

"We're going to die. We're all going to die."

"I don't know any Zack."

"It'll be easy. The tiger's on the way. It's hungry."

"A tiger?"

"Do you think a rat can fill a tiger's belly? Come on, girl! It's hardly a mouthful. That tiger's a lot of tiger. Haven't you been to the Bastille? What world are you living in? Ask Zack. You be still. Nice and quiet. Don't upset me. Don't make me nervous. Don't fuck with me. Nice and easy. You're coming with me."

"Where?"

"Where do you think, girl? To hell!"

Five hours later, when she recalled the montage of events, there was one detail Laura could not clarify or understand no matter how often she ran the sequence on the screen of her memory. Until dawn of the following day she kept asking herself if she really had heard the buzz of blowflies that seemed to surround the madman. She would swear that she had. And that Tom's Chevrolet was filled with the kind of mechanical, confused noises insects make. Only a moment before the sun came up on the third Sunday in June, Laura was certain she had heard the blowflies—the furious beating of their tiny wings—because that was the sound death made as it came toward her in the auto salvage yard.

Martin looked in the car window. The soldier pressed the Browning between the boy's eyes. Martin began to tremble like a bird in a downpour. There was Laura, crying without tears, held down by the brute strength of a man who was the image of madness, and there he was, peaceable Martin who had never harmed anyone, more insignificant than ever, his belly twisting in panic, obeying the absurd orders that the shouting lunatic was spitting at him. The bags of beer slipped from his hands. Tom, who came toward them chewing his gum, immediately recognized the man with the scar on his cheek who smelled of cod liver oil. He attempted a counterattack, trusting to the advantage of surprise, but all he accomplished was that the soldier squeezed Laura's neck as if he were tightening a garrote and violently jammed the pistol against her forehead.

"Don't cross the line, assholes, don't cross it," said the soldier. "I'm from Cuba the Beautiful, the Liberated Territory of America. Don't say I didn't warn you: you can't fuck around with Cubans. Get in. Sit down. Sit down, damn it! Take the wheel. Take the fucking wheel. Move, damn it! Compadre, you sit up front!"

In the blink of an eye, Martin, Tom, and Laura had been caught in the net of a deranged hunter who thanked them for having wished him dead at a crossroads; a psychopath who talked endlessly about Bengal tigers, African leopards, blowflies in the air, and military ambushes in Ibondá de Akú—a Cuban who giggled and showed off the many dead weighing on his conscience without a drop of guilt.

"Ask Zack, the white Haitian."

"We'll give you everything we have. Everything," said Martin. "My wallet, my watch—it's a Rolex."

"What do I want a Rolex for?"

"We'll do whatever you say but don't hurt Laura. Don't hurt her," said Tom.

"Your name is Laura?"

"Laura. I'm eighteen."

"I didn't ask how old you were. What are you trying to do? Impress me? Me? You're nuts, girl. God almighty. Nobody impresses me. I'm Lieutenant Samá, see? Lieutenant Lázaro Samá, a real pisser. A funeral, a testimonial, it's all the same to me. I've taken the vow. From now on, for your information and discussion, from now on you follow my orders, damn it, if not I kill the bitch or the tiger kills us all. I don't know which. I kill her."

Tom was going to say "OK" but he felt as if his vocal cords had twisted shut, crusted over with fear. Shit. He couldn't get the key into the ignition. Martin huddled against the window, over-come by a physical terror that shook him down to his bones, and he cursed himself for not having bought enough beer to last through the party. When Tom put the car in reverse and pulled away from the liquor store, he thought he saw the same Oldsmo-bile he had almost hit at the crossroads.

"Sing, damn it!" the soldier suddenly commanded. "Zun zun zun, zun zundambayé. . . . Zun zun zun, zun zundambayé, pretty bird at the break of day. . . ."

"Who are you?"

"Sing, I said! What language do I have to say it in, cunt? You're a cunt. A little cunt, that's all. Now. Repeat after me: Zun zun zun, zun zundambayé. . . ."

"Who are you?" Laura screamed.

"God almighty, who else would I be, shit, I already told you: Lázaro Samá, a tiger on ice!" And he brandished the pistol in the air as if it were a samurai sword. "And don't yell at me, I don't like it when people yell at me."

Midnight

An instant later the stone, tearing off all the
flamboyán leaves in its path, hums over the precise spot
where the little bird had been sitting.

— JOSÉ LUIS GONZÁLEZ

22

THE ARMENIAN opened the door. He was wearing a raspberry-colored kimono with a dragon embroidered in gold thread, and in his hand he carried a glass of fine Baccarat crystal where a scoop of vanilla ice cream was floating in coffee liqueur. He wasn't more than twenty-five though he looked as if he were in his thirties, surely because of the heavy beard that covered his face like a bala-clava, and the thick round glasses that distorted his unbearably green eyes. The Siberian bear, thought the constable. The plunging neckline of the kimono revealed a forest of hair divided by a cross of Lorraine hanging from a silver chain. Ramos had never felt so ridiculous. The Armenian, accustomed to making people uncomfortable, invited him in with a friendly gesture.

"Don't be afraid. My house is yours," he said.

"That's very kind of you, young man."

"The famous Constable Ramos, if I'm not mistaken?"

The famous Constable Ramos nodded with a resigned expression.

"Excuse me for coming so late."

"Is it late?"

The Armenian looked at his wristwatch.

"It's early. Around here we sleep during the day. What can I get you?"

"Something that'll shock me, Russky," said the visitor without thinking. "That's it, something that'll shock me."

The Armenian laughed, put his glass of ice cream on a shelf of the bookcase, spat on the knuckles of his left fist, and without giving or demanding explanations hit Ramos square on the chin with so much precision that he was knocked off his feet and into a leather armchair. When his head cleared, the teeth in his lower jaw ached.

"So, you're a southpaw," said Ramos. He found a more comfortable position in the chair.

"A southpaw, a designer, a cook, and an Armenian," he heard him reply.

"Armenian? I would have sworn you were Russian."

"Armenian."

"Manolo the Andalusian said you were Russian."

The living room was in disarray, as if a pitched battle had been staged there. Chairs overturned, chessmen scattered throughout the room, the table upended, pictures hanging crooked on the wall. Half a dozen roses in a puddle of water next to a broken vase. The constable's guard went up. He cocked his pistol. It was pure instinct. He wouldn't use it. Then he became aware of a strong odor filling the room: Mandy's husband was brewing coffee somewhere.

The Armenian appeared at the door to the kitchen and said:

"Manolo the Andalusian can say whatever he wants but I'm Armenian. With or without sugar?"

"With cognac," said Ramos. "So you're a cook too. . . ."

"Co-owner of the Mensheviks. We serve everything but chicken."

"Come to think of it, I heard about the restaurant."

"Can I call you father-in-law?"

"No."

The Armenian served the cups of coffee, knotted the sash around his robe, and began to straighten the furniture. The constable got to his feet and helped him. He picked up the roses and the chessmen. He put the pieces of shattered vase into the trash can. The kitchen was as neat as a pin. After a while, Tigran said that Mandy shouldn't be much longer.

"What's your name?"

"Tigran Androsian. Tigran, like Petrosian, the world champion, Boris Spassky's rival."

"Do you play chess?"

"I enjoy it. Once I played Larry Evans to a draw in a simultaneous match. I don't play anymore."

"What happened here?"

"An earthquake."

"Seriously."

"Seriously. Before supper, your son and I had an argument. You know. Mandy is very violent."

"I know."

"From what I can see, he had a good teacher."

"I taught him self-defense. Judo, some karate."

"Things well taught are never forgotten. That's what my stepfather used to say. You and he would really get along. You'd like each other, I can tell."

"And my son?"

"Your son almost killed me. You got here just in time. I had decided to eat a ton of vanilla ice cream. Did I hurt you?"

"You loosened one of my teeth."

"I'm sorry, father-in-law."

"I told you not to call me father-in-law. I'm not your father-in-law."

"I won't call you father-in-law, but you are my father-in-law. I love your son with my balls, if you don't mind the phrase. It's a macho thing. It's Puerto Rican."

"I'd like to kill you."

"You wouldn't be the first. You've killed a lot of men, haven't you? Mandy's told me all about you. Your wars. Is San Juan nice?"

"You almost wrecked the place. Why were you fighting?"

"Mandy wants to adopt a child."

"Oh, shit!"

"That's just what I said: Oh, shit! What a stupid idea. I can't bear the idea of fatherhood. A queer with a maternal vocation is pathetic. Do you want to know how this movie began? Mandy wouldn't let me talk. He knocked me down when I got sad."

"He hits hard."

"The bitch wants to be a mother. Have a family. I wouldn't be surprised if he starts going to Sunday Mass. He says the boy's name will be Alberto. What he doesn't understand is that I hate my stepfather."

"Oh, shit!" Ramos exclaimed. His teeth hurt. "Do you have any aspirin?"

"When I was thirteen and we lived in Erivan, my stepfather used to come into the bathroom to see me naked in the shower. It made him hot. And he'd jerk off. Me too. No. We don't have aspirin."

"Why are you telling me that, you bastard?"

"So you'll understand and talk to Mandy. I'm afraid I'll end up doing the same thing with my son."

"You're a pig."

"That may be, but a responsible pig. I'd rather take in a stray dog. Don't you like dogs? They're like kids but with tails. Dogs fascinate me. I dream about being an old queer who sits by the fire and knits little wool coats for his pets."

"Do you know where he went?"

"I'd bet my balls he's at Zack's bar, because he put on the miniskirt I sewed for him and his red, white, and blue headband. I hate your son when he puts that band in his hair. False innocence is a real fraud. Mandy knows I can't stand him hanging out with the Haitians. They rub me the wrong way. Their children are imbeciles."

"Zack's bar. . . ."

"Zack's a sicko. Have you seen the people who go there? Real grotesques who want to dynamite their livers with gin. I don't like it. I don't like any of it. I'd like to go to that bar and carry your son out over my shoulder like a sack of shit."

"Do it."

"I don't know. Sometimes the bitch scares me."

"Fear is a straitjacket."

"Don't fuck around. Fear is a lot more than clever words. You know that. Don't fuck around."

"I'll go with you."

"Finish your coffee."

"If he gets violent I'll arrest him. A night in the lockup wouldn't do him any harm. Did you say he wants to call the kid Alberto?"

"Yes. Alberto. Do you know anyone named Alberto?"

"Me? Maybe. In the army you meet a lot of people."

"You didn't answer my question, constable. Or did you? My memory's awful."

"What? My tooth!"

"Can I call you father-in-law?"

"No."

"I knew it."

"Let's go find him."

"And some aspirin for your tooth. I'll change. I don't want my kimono to get torn. I'll be right back," Tigran said, and left the room.

"Can I pour myself a drink?" Ramos called.

"Make yourself at home. I don't have any cognac, just vodka and some Bacardi. Oh, and milk. Your son's taken to drinking milk. Three quarts of milk a day. I think there's some caviar left in the fridge. At least that's Russian. I told you, father-in-law, my house is yours," the Armenian answered from the bedroom.

Ramos stayed in the living room. As he was replacing books on the shelves, something caught his eye: in a niche in the book-case was an altar of photographs, a real altar in the shape of a pyramid, with candles on either side. Along the base of the tri-angle the story of his son's childhood was told in a line of nine or ten photographs: Nelson in a cradle. Nelson dressed for his first day of school. Nelson and his parents looking at a cake and nine candles. Sheriff Nelson Ramos aiming a water pistol at the cam-era. A portrait of Sam Ramos wearing a marine dress uniform and a heavy beard drawn in with crayon. A photograph of Raquel in a bathing suit. Nelson in a judo stance. Nelson on a karate mat. Nelson the boxer. In the center of the triangle a newspaper head-line announcing the death of John Lennon. From this point on, Nelson disappeared and Mandy emerged. With long hair in a ponytail, embracing the Colombian with a face like a quail. Mandy with his friends at a fashion show. Mandy at a bar sur-rounded by men. Mandy with the tricolor headband. Mandy naked, about to jump off a diving board: in the background the Armenian Tigran drinking beer from a bottle. Crowning the altar was a photograph that twisted his gut. He barely looked at it because he heard Tigran's voice behind him:

"Mandy adores you, constable. You're his idol. His model. You did the right thing coming here."

"I was looking at the pictures. He drew a beard on me with crayon. You know, I once grew a beard during maneuvers. When I shaved it off he didn't talk to me for a week."

"When he gets crazy I want to kill him. If he doesn't beat me up, he treats me with a contempt he calls 'cosmic indifference.' I don't know which is worse."

"He never forgave me."

"That's how he is. He loves men with beards."

"What the hell are you suggesting, you pervert?"

"That he made me grow a beard. That's what I'm saying. Now he calls me Tigran the Terrible."

"You're a perfect pig from the Black Sea," said Ramos.

"Don't say another word or I'll end up falling in love with you."

Before they left, Ramos took another look at the altar with its candles. He suffered an attack of gastritis: in the top photograph of the pyramid his son Mandy, dressed as a woman in a polyethylene skirt and wearing a headband in hair bleached sunflower yellow, looked like a butterfly lost in a crater of the moon.

"No. We'd better not," said the Terrible as he climbed into the patrol car. "They bark, they bother the neighbors, and you have to take them out to shit. A stuffed dog, maybe, or one you wind up, or blow up. . . . Don't you think so?"

The constable stepped on the gas. At an intersection a prostitute was fishing for sharks to spend the night with. Her breasts, the size of footballs, were good bait. Tigran waved to her as they passed. The streetwalker didn't see him, or pretended not to see him: she wasn't looking for poor Armenians.

"That's Gigi Col, the Mexican with the rabbits," he said.

"I know who she is," said Ramos. "She was in school with my son. Whiskey rotted her from the inside out. Gigi has rabbits?"

"A cage with six rabbits. A good-hearted whore, that Gigi. A real honey."

"I'll rip out your Armenian tongue!"

"You'd leave me without my love weapon."

"One of these days you'll wake up with your mouth full of ants."

"One of these days."

"Rot in hell," said Ramos.

Gigi Col swears it had been a decent enough Saturday, a little long maybe because her workday began at noon when an old-guard client, addicted to his perversions, called her to arrange for a house call. In the evening she found a new romance in a hotel on the beach. This client turned out to be an Italian businessman who obliged her to dress as a vampire so he could feel in his own flesh the whiplash of pleasure that made a torture of love. The businessman paid generously and in cash. Midnight found her on the street. She liked to walk through the resort community and put her thoughts in order, and at that moment she wasn't fishing for sharks, as Ramos supposed, but had fallen under the spell of a soprano who, from a balcony somewhere, was singing a melody by the Italian Giuseppe Verdi, though Gigi never did find out who the composer was. It wasn't a piece of information that would make her lose any sleep, "what with all the shit that was going down," she would tell Sam.

23

THE TIGER was pacing the roof of the bar very close to the neon signs, and as it walked past there were sparks and electrical shorts. The soldier went back to the Bastille to keep his word. Death, that is, dying, is a quick way to cure madness. The Ford with the Texas plates was still in the parking lot, which made it easy to suppose that the fat man with the pumpkin face was still inside, fucking around with the lunar butterfly. Zack Duhamel would be sick of serving gin to a hippopotamus. From the street you could hear the beat of another border band. The soldier felt euphoric: the sense of danger reminded him of earlier situations, in particular the days of basic training in the fields of the provincial militia school, when he thought he might become a lion at the vanguard of the troops and because of his daring comeback with rows of medals on his chest. Caterina the Great would have magnificent reasons to be proud of her son, but life is much more complicated than death because death is final, categorical, and life is a mined road. An endless series of traps. And so on that Saturday he would have to be able to die, this time he'd do it, he'd have to forget that when death approached him the first time he felt an icy fear, a panic that could not be repeated now. That night he would fall in combat, and defeat would be his victory, because then the seven blowflies would stop swarming around him and the Bengal tiger could spread its swan wings and return to its cage of hate in the hell of the jungle. All he had to do was let himself be killed in the ambush.

"Destroy the Ford," he ordered.

The boys smashed the Ford with steel bars.

An hour later, Tom admitted to Martin that he had felt an unexpected pleasure, as if Satan in person had told him what to do. Laura watched from the backseat of the car and would never forget the figures of her friends silhouetted against the cardboard of the night, because something told her she should do everything in her power to superimpose that moment on all the other moments of that interminable Saturday, to fix the image in her memory in the event those fears and tensions drove her to reproach them one day for cowardice. And that is how she kept them in her heart: haughty and raging, doing battle with a steel Ford, a caiman asleep in the parking lot, until they beat it into submission. Tom led the attack, as one might expect, but Martin did not lag behind. His tactics complemented Tom's. Tom struck the first blows without precision, while Martin seemed to study the target in order to deliver a master stroke. Tom was a battering machine, Martin a stylist. If one needed eight swings to break the taillights (four of them shattered the bumper), the other required only a single stroke to destroy the windshield. Laura looked at the soldier and it troubled her that the madman, busy trying to light his cigarette with a defective lighter, was not even paying attention to the scene.

"Applaud, OK?" said the soldier. A flower of flame was reflected in his eyes. "Hey, you, you guys. . . . Get over here. Don't overdo it," he shouted at the boys. Tom and Martin came back to the car. Laura heard them panting, choking on adrenaline. Martin let out a counterproductive whoop of jubilation.

The tiger was waiting on the sidewalk, asleep under a tree that from a distance had the shape of a woman. The soldier saw it as soon as they reached the corner of the shore road. The tiger. From Bengal. With swan wings. The nightmare had never lasted this long or been so vivid. So real. The tiger wasn't a dream. Just a tiger. That's it. A tiger sleeping on the sidewalk. It never gave up.

"The dog. . . . Kill that dog or the girl pays!" he ordered.

Tom and Martin were certain he would keep his word. Laura would not be his first victim. After they had smashed the Ford, during that aimless ride through the streets of Caracol Beach, the soldier had proudly counted the rosary beads of supposed rivals whom he had killed for the sheer pleasure of killing. On his left arm, from his shoulder down to his wrist, he had tattooed the names of his own private dead, and nothing seemed to give him greater satisfaction than caressing those epitaphs engraved in his flesh while he recalled the circumstances of each execution.

"The dog or the girl," he threatened.

Laura's teeth were chattering, iron against glass.

"I can't," said Martin.

"Let's go, damn it," the soldier said, and he burst into laughter. "It's no big thing. Let's go, let's go. . . . Lázaro Samá will teach you to fuck with him."

"For God's sake, Tom, do what he says: just kill the dog," Laura pleaded.

The pharmacist Langston Fischer would tell Captain Paul Sanders that Bingo was his only companion. "Every night I took him for a walk around the block. It was an excursion, almost a religious ritual. Bingo looked forward to it with so much excitement. That Saturday we made our nightly rounds three hours later than usual. I had a headache. I couldn't sleep. I suffer from migraine." As proof of his love, as you will see at the end of the novel, Langston had the dog cremated at the Santa Fe cemetery. But that came later. After the finale. When those two boys blocked his way and almost with regret said they were very sorry but they were going to kill his dog, Langston Fischer replied that Bingo was vaccinated against rabies. It didn't make much sense but that's what he said. The soldier looked out the car window and with an unmistakable gesture reminded them of their orders.

"We're sorry, sir," said Martin.

"You're crazy."

"We have to kill the dog."

"You're going to kill me," said Langston.

Tom saw Laura's silhouette moving in the darkness of the car: he set his conscience free and begin to kick the dog.

"My head's splitting!"

Martin neutralized the old man from behind, apologizing all the while, until Tom picked up Bingo and, to make it a fast death, smashed him against the wall. The dog died instantly.

"He's had it," said Tom.

As they drove away, Laura saw the old man through the rear window: he had sat down on the curb under a streetlight, holding Bingo on his lap.

The third trial the madman subjected them to was stealing a prostitute's purse. He hated prostitutes. The memory of Caterina the Great had tormented him since childhood. The arrival of a Russian meant he couldn't sleep in the house that night. He would stay awake till morning, drinking mint liqueur and crying as he looked out at the city, hoping to see the stars from the courtyard. Whenever he could he tried to do harm to whores. The scar that twisted along his cheek like a worm wriggling on a hook had been cut by a cheap Havana whore, like the one walking along the dark street now in Caracol Beach, one night when he wanted to be with a woman who smelled like Caterina the Great: like marmalade.

"You're crazy."

"Of course I'm crazy."

"What do you want now?" said Tom.

"What do I want. What do I want now. Nothing to it. I want you to beat the shit out of that whore and take everything she has," ordered the soldier. "That's what I want. Make her suffer so I'll enjoy. . . ."

"Why?" Laura exclaimed. The soldier's answer nailed her to the seat:

"Because my mother's a whore."

Gigi Col saw the boys coming and thought she'd end the day with a flourish. "Look, officer," she would tell Captain Sanders, "President Lincoln said it: every man is responsible for his face. Those two johns looked all right. Listen, one was dressed up like a penguin, in tails. The other looked like a TV star, an actor in the soaps. I gave them my sexiest smile. Tigran the Terrible says I have a million-ruble smile. What never occurred to me was that they'd turn out to be a couple of shits." What Gigi never imagined was that her clients would respond to her smile with so much violence. Tom greeted her with a punch in the pit of her stomach. As she fell Martin made a grab for her handbag.

"Motherfuckers! Sons of bitches!"

Gigi Col couldn't catch her breath as she lay on the sidewalk. "It was like being on a roller coaster, captain. Nothing like that ever happened to me. A lot of things went through my mind, none of them good, I swear," she said in the police station. Tom and Martin returned to the car with her handbag.

"That's it, isn't it?" said Martin.

The madman looked at them in disgust:

"Trash."

"I can't stand any more."

"Now Lieutenant Lázaro Samá is going to show you how things are done. It'll be a real blast!"

And from somewhere he pulled out a pair of handcuffs and chained his left wrist to Laura's right wrist.

"We're going back to that liquor store," he ordered, and he dropped the key to the handcuffs. "Now you'll stay with me. Till death do us part!" The key fell between the seats. It stayed there until the following Wednesday, when Tom's older brother found it after he picked up the car at the police lot.

The tires squealed on the asphalt as the Chevrolet made a 180-degree turn and disappeared into the night.

Gigi Col shouted at them from the sidewalk:

"'Faggots!' That's what I shouted at them. It came from the heart, captain."

Paul Sanders says that Gigi confided something strange to him. Is it worth repeating? When she picked up the bag that the boys had thrown on the sidewalk, a chill ran down her spine that made her skin crawl. She was scared. Very scared. So scared she decided to go to the police station in the resort community and report the attack. She didn't want her friend Sam Ramos to take any action, she just wanted to talk to somebody, be questioned, sleep in a cell near another human being. She wanted to forget her solitude. Solitude is shit. The veins in her body had turned into a nest of snakes. All slithering around. She considered herself a realistic woman, skeptical and not easily shaken. She called a spade a spade. She didn't believe in ghosts or spirits. Or angels. Until that night. Until that shudder.

In Gigi's words, it felt as if the tail of an enormous cat had brushed against her calves in a light, delicate caress. Then she clearly felt the invisible feline rubbing its back along her leather skirt, at the height of her hips. It nudged her. It pushed her against the wall of a nearby house. She could smell it. And it smelled of rat. Garbage-dump rat. Captain Sanders asked if an animal that size was comparable to an African leopard or perhaps a Bengal tiger, and she answered, Yes, sure, especially because of how big its tongue was—it was disgusting, that porous, slavering, warm tongue, more a slab of boneless meat than a tongue, licking her back for she didn't know how many unbearable minutes. Gigi swears that "the shadow" flew away, but the only proof she has is this: in the middle of the night a few white feathers were floating in the air, blown back and forth by the wind.

24

SOLDIER'S NOTEBOOK. To Caterina the Great, in Cienfuegos, Cuba. First Liberated Territory in America. Beacon to the Continent. June something, 1976. I'm starting this letter to you though I don't think I'll send it because I suppose you're very busy with your Russians from the cement factory and won't have time to think about your son Me-Without-A-Father's-Name, so far from Cienfuegos by the grace of God, but I don't have anything to do at this post, sitting in a tree reconnoitering, and so to hell with you, Caterina, because I'm thinking about home and even if you don't believe me, because you've never believed me, I miss you, I miss you a lot, I miss you, yes I do, in spite of your whoring, and you know, I think I've been unfair to you, very unfair, I think I couldn't understand you before but I do now, I'll prove it, here in the devil's own house: finally I understand that you don't have to understand this life but just live it, and everybody's free to do whatever they want to do or can do, not only what they should do, and I'm not the one to judge you or anybody else, and so, Caterina the Great, I beg you to forgive me if I said anything stupid to you, or mean, or insulting, if I threw your dirty linen in your face or washed it in public, or even worse, if I was embarrassed because I didn't know who my father was, even if he was some fucking pimp from the neighborhood, a one-night-stand, but with a last name to give me, I don't know why I'm telling you all this, it must be that death is a real, concrete possibility, a fight to the finish with no gloves on, and I don't want to leave this world carrying the grief of not having told you I love you, at least in a letter I'll never send, I believe, I think, I suppose, but maybe they'll find it in the notebook I keep in my pack and tell you that I told you, my old lady, that you did right when you did half of Cienfuegos, the fun you've had nobody can take away from you, not even Mazantín the Bullfighter, let a smile be your umbrella, and even some of those big-bellied Russians who slobbered all over you morning noon and night for ten cans of potted meat were nice to me afterwards when I saw them on the Prado or in the ice cream store and they even bought me a combination, the most expensive dish of ice cream at Coppelia, so you see, they weren't cheap with your son, I never told you because it made me a little sad to know I gave in on account of hunger, accepted their charity of a dish of ice cream, even when it was a combination with five flavors and you could choose the ones you wanted though I always ordered five scoops of chocolate mint, that was the one I liked because it reminded me of the bottle of liqueur you hid behind the altar to the Virgin of Regla, remember? the same bottle of mint I would sneak drinks from, especially on those long nights when you were fucking your Bolshies and your son, mama, your son could only look at the specks in the sky, the constellations, the Soviet satellites traveling among the distant stars, and I drank the whole liter sip by sip so the city of Cienfuegos across the bay would look nice with its wreath of colors and the lights of the cars heading for the Hotel Jagua, the one with the cabaret, the cabaret where you took me one night to celebrate the great feat of my having struck out Agustín Marquetti when the count was three balls and two strikes. What a night! Strike one. You were so proud. Igor Sergeyevich, the Bolshie engineer, got the table. It was cool. I thought he was a nice guy for you. He was a buddy of Yuri Gagarin's. Strike two. I got drunk. And slept in your bed. Your bed! I'll stop now. Happily ever after. Strike three. I have to get out of this tree. I'll write more tomorrow. I won't tell you about Ibondá de Akú because this letter isn't for talking about the war but about the two of us even if you never read it because that's the way life is. I'll just say that I've had a great time. Some pretty scenery. You'll get to know my friends. The ones in the squad. Poundcake, the Fly, Aspirin, a guy they call Camagüey. The Brain is teaching us English. The Brain is a graduate of the Pedagogical Institute. He says I have a facility for English. The best of them is named Lázaro Samá. I told you about him. A hell of a guy. You won't go to bed with Lázaro, I'm warning you, because he's black and you don't like dark meat. Just blondes. He's been like a father to me. And comadre Rafaela? Send her my regards. I think about her. What a good person. What a pretty pigeon coop. I may be whatever I am, mama, but nobody can call me ungrateful. As Enrique Arredondo, the great Cheo Malanga, used to say: to think there are people who get up at five in the morning to bake bread for the breakfast of a miserable swine like me. Caterina the Great, nothing to it, if I pardon you will you pardon me? I still love you. Your bed! Your bed forever.

25

TIGRAN SMELLED of bath talc. Ramos felt like a jackass driving the patrol car along the streets of the resort community. The odor of talc was driving him crazy. Not to mention the brilliantine in Tigran's hair and his jeweled rings, and the Terrible had applied so much gel that the lights sparkled in the mirror of his hair, cut in the style of Nureyev, and he touched it constantly with his ringed fingers as if he were adjusting an ill-fitting toupee. The constable had attempted to make conversation about any subject that would keep them from exploring bedroom intimacies, but his "son-in-law" side-stepped his traps with the feints of a boxer. The bone of Mandy was stuck in his throat.

"The bone of your son is stuck in my throat," he said and spat out the window. The Terrible recounted how he had met Mandy in Manolo's bowling alley. The Colombian with the face of a quail had just returned from his own country with bad news: the HIV virus was swimming in his veins like a dolphin, and Mandy was certain his days were numbered. "He wanted to kill himself. He thought about slashing his wrists," he said. "Before that he tried to set himself on fire, but he's so vain he wasn't happy with

the image of himself as a crisp pork rind in a refrigerated coffin."
The Armenian convinced his lover to face the situation and have
the necessary tests. As a gesture of loyalty he went with him to the
office of a doctor who was a friend of theirs. The results were
negative. A second round of analyses confirmed the good news,
and they decided to live together.

"He never told me. He talks about those things to his
mother."

Tigran leaned his head out the window in a way the constable
thought more appropriate to a dog than a man. Stiff as plastic
because of the gel, his hair did not move in the wind that blew in
from the street. Could it be a toupee?

"Raise the window. You'll break your head open on a pole."

"Now he wants a son."

"Rot in hell," said Ramos.

"What do you think about a dog? It might be a good idea,"
said Tigran. The constable kept to himself what he thought about
his possible lineage. He couldn't see himself as a grandfather taking the dog out for a shit or the baby for a walk. Especially if the
kid's name was Alberto.

Ramos and Tigran reached Zack's bar just as the fat man with
the pumpkin face discovered that a gorilla had destroyed his Ford
in the parking lot. Zack and Gregory Papa Gory were acting as
United Nations mediators. Mandy was urinating with cosmic
indifference against a lamp post.

"Son of a bitch!" said the fat man and pointed at the transvestite. Zack held him back with powerful arms.

"Take it easy, pumpkin face."

"I'll kill him. I swear I'll kill him."

"Never spit into the wind," advised Papa Gory.

Ramos approached the group. Out of the corner of his eye he
saw the scene he had feared: Nelson and Tigran were kissing on
the mouth. And yes: the Armenian was wearing a toupee. The

constable did what he had to do. He checked the Ford. He found that the windows had been pulverized and the seats slashed open from top to bottom, like the belly of a cow in a slaughterhouse. There were a number of loose ends. No attempt had been made to steal anything from the vehicle, it had only been vandalized with no explanation other than the pleasure someone took in violence. He reached a conclusion that seemed to fall right off the tree and into his lap:

"It must have been a gorilla."

"A gorilla or that damn blonde, officer: the one with the bleached hair, right over there," said the fat man as he pointed at Mandy, who was still kissing the Terrible.

"What did you say?" asked Mandy.

"My car! You son of a bitch!" shouted the fat man.

"No insults, cowboy," said Gregory Papa Gory in an undertone. "No need to insult anybody."

Mandy moved away from the Terrible, removed his red, white, and blue headband, and bore down on the fat man.

"I've had enough, asshole."

"Enough what? Bleaching your hair?"

"You're a pain in my balls."

The constable watched the scene in silence. That night he learned what a varied menu of improprieties his son had at his disposal, a vocabulary enriched by Colombian, Russian, and Armenian insults. In several of them Ramos recognized his Puerto Rican influence: "With my apologies to hogs, you're nothing but a ton of lard." "When you're born to live in a sty, shit falls on you from the sky." Ramos, too, enjoyed comparing pigs to certain human specimens. Like father like son. Like boar like piglet.

Zack let the fat man go.

"He's all yours, butterfly," said Zack, putting his money on the transvestite. Papa Gory sat down on the sidewalk.

"It was you, you fucking son of a bitch."

"No accusations without evidence," said Zack. "The law's here. Let the constable decide."

"Your name?" asked Ramos.

"Peter Shapiro."

"Occupation?"

"I'm a rancher, from Texas."

"What brought you to Caracol Beach?"

"Does that matter?"

"No. It doesn't matter."

"I closed a deal and I bought a car."

"What happened here?"

"That blonde hit me. Threw me against the bar. The bartender's a witness. . . ."

"I didn't witness anything. Right, Gregory?" Zack countered. The black albino didn't take the hint.

"Why would I destroy your car if I already smashed your face in? Asshole!" said Mandy.

"The kid's right," Ramos said calmly.

"Do you believe him?"

"It's your word against his."

"The bartender saw everything, constable."

"I'm blind," said Zack.

"I hate faggots," said the man from Texas.

"What's the good of saying things like that?" Gregory Papa Gory observed.

"That's why this country's in the shape it's in, constable. Bastards!"

Now it was Tigran the Terrible who stepped forward and threw a hook into the fat man's belly. He must have been a boxer. Probably won a couple of championships in Armenia. The fat man, the wind knocked out of him, hit the canvas in the parking lot: Zack the referee could count all the way to a thousand. Ramos pulled his pistol from the holster and pointed it at Mandy.

"Hands behind your head. Don't give me any trouble, boy."

"He was touching my ass, dad," said Mandy.

"Dad?" said the fat man from the ground.

Mandy stared at him.

"Yes, my daddy. . . ."

"You can tell me all about it at the station," Ramos interrupted. "You're under arrest until this is cleared up."

"Under arrest!"

"That's what I said."

"You go to hell," said Mandy, but he put his hands behind his head. The Armenian slipped his arm around his waist.

"Come with me."

"You go to hell," Mandy repeated.

"I'm already in hell," Ramos muttered under his breath.

Mandy did not hear him. The fat man began to move. He was down on all fours. Gregory Papa Gory gave him his hand to help raise the enormous bulk of his body.

"On your feet, boy," said the albino. "Welcome to the fourth or fifth circle of hell."

"Where am I?"

"Madison Square Garden, Mr. Shapiro," said Zack.

Ramos led Nelson and the Armenian to the patrol car.

"Don't fuck around, damn it," he said, and slammed the door.

Tigran pressed his mouth to the window and Ramos read his lips: "Thanks, father-in-law." The bones in the constable's back cracked. He cocked the pistol and aimed it at the Armenian through the glass. His hand was shaking. Ramos raised the barrel of the pistol. His finger tensed on the trigger. He knew he could do it. It would be easy. Very easy. He had killed before. He was prepared to repeat the experience. An exile from behind the Iron

Curtain couldn't be very important. Captain Paul Sanders would fix it. They had been together in trenches, bunkers, bombing raids. He fired into the air. The bullet struck its target on the moon: the pole of the flag that the astronaut Neil Armstrong had planted in the sand back in July of 1969.

"Rot in hell!" said Ramos.

The gunshot set the finale in motion. The fat man with the Halloween pumpkin face had the really bad idea of smoking a Marlboro, but when he lit the wooden match, made in Tijuana, the shot rang out and he was so frightened he dropped the match into a rivulet of gasoline that started at the carburetor and ended at his feet. The flame ran upstream to the headwaters of the fuel. There was no explosion though it did burn in a slow, vigorous, uncontrollable blaze. Zack put his arm around Gregory's shoulders. Neither one was interested in seeing what was going on behind them: what for? The bartender preferred to talk about the visit of the lieutenant who had killed a Bengal tiger.

"Nobody can kill a tiger with his bare hands," said Gregory Papa Gory as they walked into the bar. "Unless, of course, Lucifer is helping him."

Peter Shapiro remained in the parking lot. The cigarette dangled from his lower lip, held there by saliva. His shoulders sagged, his arms hung limp beside his body, and his right leg was placed a half-step in front of his left. In this posture he began to melt in the heat of his Ford until he disappeared from this novel without a trace.

26

WELLINGTON PERALES checked every page of the notebook with pink covers where Raquel had written emergency numbers, and he couldn't find the number under the letter S for Sam or R for Ramos or N for Nelson; he should have looked under M, but how was he to know that the constable's son called himself Mandy, a pseudonym de guerre for confronting his profession as a transvestite with a more tender sobriquet. That simple setback put his nerves on edge. The night was getting complicated. First, a Peter Shapiro who reported that some bastards had just set fire to his brand-new Ford; then an old man who came in to report that two thugs had smashed a dog named Bingo into a wall. The only thing missing was Mata Hari.

"Those two boys are animals."

"Did he bite anybody?" Perales interrupted.

"The dog? What an idea!"

"Just asking."

"You don't know Bingo. He couldn't."

The old man made a chaotic statement. He said that Bingo was an affectionate pet with all his shots who brought him the paper every morning and had been with him for three years, a great help and an ideal companion because his children had moved away from Caracol Beach, bored with life in a resort community where nothing ever happened.

"Let's see, from the beginning. What do you remember, granddad?"

"They apologized."

"What do you mean apologized?"

"They apologized. I don't know. Officer, do you have any idea what's going on?"

"What kind of work do you do?"

"I'm a pharmacist. Langston Fischer. Pleased to meet you."

"Langston. Pharmacist. Fischer. What else?"

"I already told you. Bingo. Three years together. And now there's Bingo, wrapped in my jacket. And he's dead. Understand? He'll never bring me the morning paper again. Never. Those hoodlums killed him. What should I do? Tell me. Should I bury him? Have him cremated? I have a half-witted godson who works at the crematory in the cemetery. Those kids!"

"What did they look like?"

"How should I know? Your age. Do something."

"Constable Ramos will be here any minute."

At that moment a prostitute, her jasmine scent noticeable from twenty feet away, came into the station. It was Mata Hari. She crossed the room in three strides in spite of a miniskirt that restricted her movements. Wellington observed the whore's breasts galloping in the saddle of her bra. She had enough momentum to win the New York City marathon. She was mad as hell. She came up to Perales's desk and, not taking her eyes off his, slammed it so hard with her handbag she made the paperweight jump.

"Where the fuck is that no-good Ramos? Tell him Gigi Col the Mexican is here."

It was Langston who replied: "The constable's on his way."

"I'm officer Wellington Perales and I'm in charge of the station. Well, young lady, what can I do for you?"

"You can give me a whiskey," said Gigi Col.

"Make that two," said the pharmacist.

"I know Constable Ramos," said the future winner of the New York City marathon. "I trust him. He's never thrown me in the slammer. I'm a good friend of Mandy's."

"Mandy?"

"Mandy. Sam's son."

"Isn't his name Nelson?"

"Nelson, but he changed it to Mandy. Just a whim. Ask him about Gigi Col. Everybody calls me Gigi the Mexican. Anybody looking for trouble can find it up my ass. I'm here to make a complaint."

"A complaint . . . right."

"There are two punks running wild in Caracol Beach and I hope they break their necks. I almost lost a whole day's wages. Easier said than done."

"The boys who attacked the young lady are the same ones who killed Bingo. I'm certain. They're the ones. Two lunatics."

"I don't know if my boys are the same ones who killed Bingo. Who's Bingo?"

"Bingo is Bingo, my dog."

"Your dog?"

"Well, he was Bingo."

"I want justice. I never cared much about justice, I don't believe in any of that shit, but they have to pay. Pay for what they put me through. That's all. It would be fucking great if you threw them in the can for a while. Do you believe in ghosts? That cat's tail was so damn cold!"

"Take my statement right now," said Langston, and he placed the dog, wrapped in his wool blazer, on the counter.

"All right. What happened?"

"Bingo has his shots. I mean, he had."

"I thought I'd finish up the night with a hand full of aces. I don't like dead things. Least of all dead cats."

"He brings me the paper every morning. He's been with me since my children moved away from Caracol Beach."

"You don't let anybody talk, mister," Gigi said to Langston.

"Show a little respect, my girl."

"Don't piss your pants, grandpa."

"Don't what?"

"What about my whiskey?" said Gigi.

Wellington felt lost. What should he do? If only the phone would ring. Miracles do happen. The phone rang. Now he knew what to do: pick up the receiver. And answer. The earpiece was colder than a witch's tit. It wasn't St. Peter, but the call came from heaven.

"Caracol Beach constable," he said.

"When were you promoted, soldier? What's going on?"

"I think we're at war," he said, distraught, and he outlined what had happened: the little dog Bingo, the pharmacist Langston Fischer, the streetwalker Gigi Col and her vocabulary worthy of an Aztec princess.

"I know two out of three."

"Believe me, this place is like a loony bin. I don't even know my own name anymore."

"You're drowning in a glass of water, my fisherman friend. I'll be there as soon as I can," said Ramos.

"What do I do in the meantime? They don't stop talking. Gigi says she's a friend of your son Mandy."

"Nelson. His name is Nelson. Give some coffee to Fischer

and a J&B to Gigi. A double, with ice and mineral water. The bottle of whiskey is in the desk, on the right. I appoint you constable. Now you can say it."

"The old man wants some too."

"What does Dr. Fischer want?"

"Whiskey."

"Make a decision about something, damn it," said Ramos, and then he cut him off.

"Yes, sir."

He had just hung up when the phone rang again. This time the call came from the very center of a volcano. A young cashier wanted to report the robbery of a liquor store. The thieves emptied the cash register but then threw the money away in the parking lot. They broke everything and took nothing. Not even a pack of gum.

"They're crazy, if you ask me," said the cashier.

"Crazy. You say they're crazy."

"Well, sure, crazy. Come right away."

"Don't worry."

"Are you sure this is the police?" said the young man, and he hung up.

Wellington Perales remembered the constable's order.

"It's time for action. Let's go."

"Where?" said the pharmacist.

"Where do you think? To war."

"Ah, shit!" Gigi exclaimed, and not because of the reference to war but because she had just noticed that the young policeman's hands were trembling, as she told Captain Paul Sanders when she gave her version of events: "They looked limp, like empty gloves. He was hiding the same fear a lot of big machos feel when the time comes to take off their trousers in front of a whore, especially if she's sexy, because the ugly ones, well, shit, they're more relaxed with them. Those are the times, captain, when you have to count to ten, nice and slow, and think about Pancho Villa's mustache, and be as patient as a saint. I counted to twenty, I remembered that I had to buy some carrots for the rabbits, and I got into the goddamn patrol car. That dumb fuck pulled away in second."

27

THE SOLDIER swept the Jamaican rums off the shelf with one hand, and with just a nudge of his shoulders he knocked over the display of kitchen utensils, the momentum dragging the handcuffed Laura behind him. He was euphoric, drunk on the lust for violence. And he was singing: "Zun zun zun, zun zundambayé! Zun zun zun, zun zundambayé, pretty bird at the break of day!" When the young man at the liquor store came to the defense of the establishment, the soldier grabbed him by the lapel and pushed him against the refrigerated cases where the fish were displayed. Then he went toward the exit door, knocking down shelves left and right, with Laura in tow, and in the blink of an eye he emptied the cash register. When the soldier was outside he tossed the bills and coins in the air like confetti to show that money was nothing but trash and the act of committing a crime for the sheer pleasure of the crime itself was the only authentic pleasure worth anything in this life. The Cuban had reached the plenitude of his madness. Handcuffed to Laura, and holding up the torch of the pistol in his right hand, the individual who said he was Lieutenant Lázaro Samá began to walk from one end of the parking lot to the other. Martin used the time to clean his glasses. Suddenly the soldier was marching like a cadet, following the ceremonial norms of a battalion on parade; just as suddenly he halted, came to attention, did an about-face, and came back moving his shoulders to the beat of an imaginary rumba until at last he stopped in front of the boys, wielding a fiery glance like a weapon. Tom took Laura's free hand in a gesture that somehow meant to say "I'm with you." Martin had the impression of being observed through an inverted telescope that distorts distance and shrinks the object to its smallest possible size. The madman was going to subject them to a final trial. He would. They perceived the danger in the early morning breeze that began to blow from the east. The soldier raised the pistol to his mouth and licked at the cold candy of the barrel. He laughed between his teeth.

"What happens now?" said Tom.

"Who's the boss? You'll see. . . ."

"I don't understand," said Martin.

"All right, who's in charge? This is serious. Very serious. Don't make me mad. All right. Don't say I didn't warn you. You'll be sorry. You'll see. I'm Lieutenant Samá. I give the orders here. Period. Period, end of story. Enough said."

"That's just it," said Martin. "What do we have to do?"

"Lieutenant . . . you call me lieutenant or I'll bust your damn head open."

"What do we have to do, lieutenant?"

"I'll tell you. I'll explain it step by step so you don't screw up. Nothing to it. Piece of cake," said the soldier. According to his own words, which he pronounced with difficulty since he did not take the pistol out of his mouth, the definitive proof of manhood was a matter of life or death: every man had to be able to kill another. He was prepared to offer them the opportunity. He did not say that for eighteen years he had tried to commit suicide, and he did not mention his plan in Zack's bar to get the fat man from

Texas to cut off his head like a chicken, and he did not even speak of the hanging rope he had set up that Saturday in the trailer in the auto salvage yard. He only said, with the authority of a judge passing sentence, that Tom and Martin would have to kill a man before sunrise. They would have to kill him.

"You have to kill me. God almighty. You have till dawn. We'll meet in the car cemetery, mile ten on the highway. Fantastic. That's the ticket. You kill me and we're done. You can go home. Two against one. And no tricks. All right? No cops. I can smell them. I'm a dog." And he walked toward the Chevrolet hopping and jumping like the character of the madman that Toshiro Mifune interpreted so masterfully in Akira Kurosawa's *The Seven Samurai*.

"You drive," he said to Laura.

Tom and Martin remained in the parking lot. A bat flew very close to them. A car horn reproduced into infinity the chords of a popular song. The ordering of reality was no consolation to Martin because before he lost his mind he lost his glasses. At this point in the story the top student at the Emerson Institute was gone from this world: dementia is a form of losing one's way.

"Where are my glasses?" he exclaimed.

"Fucking son of a bitch," said Tom, and he walked toward the soldier's Oldsmobile.

"What should we do?" said Martin.

"This old bucket has to run," said Tom.

And it did run, with pistons clanking and oil leaking from the gaskets, with barely two gallons of gas in the tank and a flat tire, but it started to move. The old bucket was moving. Tom spun around in reverse at such high speed that the right door suddenly opened through the pull of centrifugal force. Martin was almost thrown from the car. It would have been his salvation, but he managed to hold on to the window, lean the other way, and keep his seat, while Tom pushed the gas pedal to the floor and the

Oldsmobile lurched forward like a bumper car in an amusement park, in the same direction taken by the soldier with the tattoos.

"My glasses!" exclaimed Martin. The tires on the right side of the car had run over them. In any case, the boys kept moving. Do dead men wear spectacles? Tom and Martin did not dare to talk about what had happened: that's how frightened they were. Then Martin suggested going to the police. Tom wasn't sure. Lieutenant Lázaro Samá had said no tricks, and if he felt cornered he wouldn't hesitate for a second to take it out on his defenseless captive. He was a lunatic. A killer.

"We shouldn't face him alone," said Martin. "It would be suicide. We have to think of something."

"What does he have that we don't have?" Tom retorted.

"He's crazy. That's what he has: he's crazy. Don't even try it."

"Of course I will. For Laura's sake. Haven't you thought about Laura? Think. Imagine what that nut will do. He'll rape her. Abuse her. And us? We'll be sitting with our arms folded! What time is it?"

"Believe me, Tom. I haven't stopped thinking about Laura. I swear. That man will squash us like two cockroaches."

"You're scared, right? You're shitting yourself you're so scared. What time is it, cockroach?"

"Of course I'm shitting myself, Tom. We have to tell the police. We have to get help. We can't do it ourselves."

"Why not? Why?"

"What do you mean why, Tom? Because we're only eighteen years old!"

28

SOLDIER'S NOTEBOOK. It rained all last night. I like it to rain at night. In Cuba, when the sky has to take a leak, it starts raining in the middle of the night. It pours. It sounds nice. The smells of things come alive. Wood smells like countryside. Countryside like wall. Wall like sheet. Sheet like mama. And mama like milk. Like cow! Then the roosters stop crowing. The sun sits on his ass. Rises late if he rises at all. In the middle of the morning, in the middle of the sky. He's not worried. Here I am, he says, finally got here. And the whole day is turned around. Lázaro was talking about the *orishas*. The African gods are really something. I didn't know much about all that. When Olofi the all-powerful decided to make the world, he turned smoke from the fire into clouds and water came down from those clouds and put out the flames. The ocean is the fountain of life: Yemayá. I learned a lot about Yemayá. She's terrific. She wears a necklace made of seven glass beads and a robe decorated with symbols of the sea. [...] This was the worst day of the war. Know why? Because it lasted a century. It never ended. A dead fucking calm and we were really depressed. God almighty. The hours were three thousand min-

utes long. The sun didn't move, it stayed in the same place in the
sky, between the branches of a tree, like a fiery grapefruit. How
great to do something, kill some time . . . but no. If only Lieutenant Samá had sent us to the river for water. Poundcake said he
was going to fill the canteens and Samá went crazy. Like a wild
fucking animal. He ordered us not to leave camp. To nail ourselves to the ground. To go into the tents and jerk off together. To
get out of his sight. We cursed the day we were born. The lieutenant was in worse shape than anybody and that's not like him.
Not like him at all. I never saw him so damn angry, so silent, so
lost in his own thoughts. In Bethlehem with the shepherds. I
went over to try to have a conversation with him and he told me
to beat it and cursed and insulted me. I left, I didn't feel like taking crap from anybody. If I didn't take it from you why would I
take it from him? I've been thrown out of better places. In the
afternoon, with the sun still between the branches of the tree, he
came over to see me. He leaned against the rope of my hammock
and I didn't ask a thing but he told me what was wrong with him,
the whole story. It made me sad. He showed me a tattoo he has up
near his shoulder: a bow with three arrows. I hadn't noticed it
before. I hate tattoos. A *majá* snake is curled around the bow. On
one of the arrows there's a bird. For Ochosi, the Christian St.
Peter, the patron saint of people in trouble with the law. The children of Ochosi are always full of plans. They go to the front without thinking too much about it. They love change, they're clever
hunters, and they love their families, though sometimes what
they do makes their people suffer. I didn't know Lázaro had a son.
His name was Felipe. An irresponsible kid. I say "was" because
Felipe died in '67, at the age of eighteen, when he tried to cross
over into American territory at Guantánamo, near the river, and a
mine exploded on this side of the line and he was blown, you
know, to bits. God almighty. They scooped him up with a shovel.
A friend who went with him and lost a leg told Lázaro the explo-

sion blew his son ten yards into the air and the body came down missing its head and one hand. They found the head on the other side of the river. The hand never turned up. End of story. They made him into mush. Lázaro says it was his fault. He blames himself for not spending enough time with him, for always being too busy with union and militia business, with Santería. He's never forgiven himself for Felipe's death. And never been able to explain it. For better or worse, he loved him. Why did he go over to Yankeelandia? Why was he leaving his people? That's the question Lázaro asks himself over and over again. Who knows? He was a child of Ochosi. They lived pretty well. He wasn't interested in politics, only in parties. A worm, the kind who runs away from Cuba, a real worm, he didn't seem to be one of them. He wasn't doing too well in school, but being a rotten student is no reason to risk your skin in a stunt as dangerous as that. You'd have to be crazy. Even comadre Rafaela knows the Yankee base at Guantánamo is mined on all four sides. Lázaro can't accept it. The anniversary of Felipe's death is right about now, and that's when the lieutenant gets depressed and can't shake it off even with a purification. That's what he told me and then he left. I kept thinking about it. I dreamed the scene except that yours truly was the one flying through the air like Matías Pérez. I woke up scared. My gums were bleeding. I decided to walk for a while. Then I saw him. Lázaro. Standing under the trees, talking to the saints. He was singing: "Awadé Omó Lenikí. Awadé Omó O Ma Fe Wa" (We search for the hunter, powerful child we greet thee. We search for the hunter, child we always longed to be), "Awadé Omá Omá Ochosi Omó Obatalá" (Ochosi knows, he knows. Ochosi, child of the king of white cloth), "Awadé Omó Lenikí. Awadé Omó Ya Ku Ará Kayakú Ará" (We search for the hunter, child we know thee dead. His kin had the pleasure, they were friends of the dead). His saints come from around here. You never know what you have until you lose it. The black man misses his son. I miss my father, though I don't know his face. What he looked like. What he looks like. What he will look like. Bald. Big mustache. Tall. A midget. Nice. A fisherman. A bastard. A grocer. Snub-nosed. Fat. Elegant. A *santero*. A stevedore. A sailor. A hick. Intelligent. A *machista*. A bureaucrat. Irresponsible. A hustler. A manager. A bugger. An athlete. An ambassador? If we could join our misfortunes—there's a word for you—Lázaro and I would kill two birds with one stone: he'd have a new son and your son, Caterina, would have a replacement father on the pitcher's mound. It's complicated: love isn't so easy to arrange. Awadé Omá Omá Ochosi Omó Obatalá. Men are divided into two groups: those who are near and those who are far away. I like that. Fantastic. That's it.

29

IF A MAN'S WHISTLING, he can't be dangerous, at least for as long as he's whistling, thought Laura. She began to detect a change in the soldier's attitude starting from the moment they left the parking lot. The person who said he was Lieutenant Lázaro Samá suddenly became calm. "Miraculously" would be a better word. He started to whistle a tune. No doubt about it: he was passing through the eye of the hurricane. The residents of Santa Fe faced an average of seven major storms a year and knew perfectly well that a candle doesn't even flicker in the epicenter of the whirlwind. There's calm after the storm, asserts an old but not very wise adage, because what it doesn't say is that after the calm the storm usually attacks again with devastating effects. The soldier stopped whistling, stared at her, and held the pistol two inches from her nose; with the skill of a professional he began to load and unload the magazine.

"One, two, three. . . . Eeny meeny miney moe, catch a tiger by the toe. . . . Ready, aim, fire."

"If you're going to kill me just do it, damn it. Shit. Fuck. Asshole. Cunt. Motherfucker. I know how to curse too!" Laura screamed, and she slammed on the brakes, opened the door, and tried to get out. This could be viewed as a suicidal act, though it must be acknowledged that it had a certain possibility for success based on the strategic principle of surprise.

"God almighty!" shouted the madman and pulled on the chain that connected him to his prisoner's right hand. Laura slammed into the wheel.

"Shit. Fuck. Asshole. Cunt. Motherfucker!" the soldier repeated in a musical way. And aimed the pistol at her again, this time at her forehead, and holding it at eye level he took out the magazine and triumphantly showed her a Nestlé bar, the ephemeral loot he had kept from his assault on the store.

"It can't be," Laura moaned.

"It's for you, girl: a chocolate bar! Let's keep moving," the soldier said. Laura forgot to turn on the headlights. Fifty yards farther on they passed Wellington Perales driving in the opposite direction in the patrol car, where Gigi Col couldn't understand why the fuck Langston Fischer kept slamming the crown of his hat into his thigh if it was only a damn animal—four legs, a head, a body, a tail, but only a dog after all—and it wouldn't be hard to get another one like it, even better than shitty little Bingo complete with pedigree and certificates of ferocity. Look on the bright side: if the dog's dead at least he doesn't have rabies, and first thing Monday morning all he had to do was go to the pet store in Santa Fe and buy a killer Doberman, a German shepherd, a Rottweiler, because nowadays not even nuns and whores could feel safe.

"Caracol Beach is getting dangerous. I'm moving to the Vatican," said the Mexican with the gift of gab.

"And what should I do?" said the pharmacist.

"Shut up," answered Wellington. Coming toward him, on the other side of the highway, he saw a Chevrolet whose headlights were not turned on and the officer automatically felt tempted to give the driver a ticket but since he was in a hurry to get to the liquor store he let the car go on, not without first flashing his headlights in warning and commiting the license number to his elephant's memory so he could report the infraction. "I didn't know what to do," he would admit to Captain Paul Sanders during the investigation. "Today things seem much simpler but at the time I thought a robbery in the business district was more pressing. I tied up loose threads. Tell me, was I wrong? And it's not so serious if somebody forgets to turn on his lights, or is it? Shit, I make a lousy cop."

Langston Fischer still had not decided what to do with Bingo: whether to bury him at the beach or cremate him in the Santa Fe cemetery, where his godson worked. That indecision, which might seem like a tempest in a teapot, was becoming a persistent anguish.

"You're drowning in a puddle, grandpa," said Gigi. "Throw it in a ditch and buy a new one tomorrow."

"He's a dog, not a hat."

"That's just what I'm saying, pal."

"It's all so simple for you, young lady. If Bingo could have talked he would have been human."

"Look, grandpa, don't piss your pants. I'm a whore and a masseuse who makes house calls and I feel entitled to talk about my clients," said Gigi. "Those gentlemen in shirts and ties you see on television, those political leaders, those spokesmen for humanity, are more like dogs than a lot of dogs who can't talk. Some men bark. Fuck it. Let that relative of yours burn him. At least that's what I'd like them to do with my bones. I can't imagine the worms having me for a banquet. So much exercise, so much effort, so much body without an ounce of fat, just for some lousy worms. No way."

"Do you think they'll take him at the cemetery?"

"Well, your godson works there, doesn't he, not too bright and a lush, right? Well, you've got it made. You give him something for his trouble. Money opens any door, here or in Hong Kong, and I don't think they put locks on that crematorium. Ashes are ashes, dust, powder. Whether they're a dog's or a man's."

Tom and Martin saw the patrol car in the distance and decided to ask for help. They had no choice. They had discussed it, and any other solution would be suicide. Tom stopped the car. Martin got out on the road and signalled to the police car over the top of the highway divider. He put a smile on his face, the most foolish one he could, to arouse sympathy. He felt ridiculous and had the terrible impression he was naked in the middle of the desert, faking an innocence no jury would believe. He couldn't stop thinking about the dog smashing into the wall, and the sound its bones made when they broke came back as precisely as a scene from a movie that you can't get out of your mind. Tom was the one who shouted the alarm: the old man with the dog and the prostitute they had just roughed up in the middle of the street were riding in the patrol car.

"Fucking sons of bitches," screamed Gigi Col.

"God help us," said Langston Fischer.

"Murderers!"

Wellington Perales got out of the patrol car, pistol in hand. "I was scared, really scared," he would confess to Captain Paul Sanders. "It was a bad idea to take along the Mexican and the old man. But what could I do? Leave them at the station? And besides, I was afraid. I admit it. Gigi babbled like a parrot and the pharmacist never stopped moaning. Like they had killed his kid. It was all so stupid. Horrible and stupid. I felt obliged to act. At that moment those boys were a couple of criminals. How was I to know what was happening in Caracol Beach? It was my first night on duty, captain. You remember. The constable left me in charge of the station. Martin, I think it was Martin, came running toward us. Waving his arms like he was swimming in air. The other one, Tom, was walking, sure of himself. I saw, or thought I saw, his hand at his waist, where you keep weapons. I assumed they were high on drugs. I don't know. I shouted at them to freeze but my finger slipped and I squeezed the trigger."

"Freeze!" said Wellington and three shots fired into the air. Tom and Martin started running. They got into the Oldsmobile. The highway divider saved them. There was no other choice. Now they were fugitives from justice.

30

SAM RAMOS had called the station from a phone booth at the entrance to one of those brightly lit cafeterias that are proud to keep their doors open twenty-four hours a day, and since the waiter had not yet brought his two double burgers, fries, and Coke, he decided he wasn't going to sweat the small stuff, so he forgot about Wellington's reports and went back to the table in the smoking section where Tigran the Terrible was trying to convince Mandy that adopting a child was a foolish idea and proposing three alternatives to strengthen their relationship: traveling as soon as they could to Armenia so Mandy could meet his stepfather (who was consuming himself with rage in an old-age home), renting an apartment in Old San Juan (where they could live like tourists), or buying a dog in some pet shop (and amusing themselves with something more wholesome than chasing men in the Haitians' bar). Mandy threw his arms around Tigran's neck. Nothing more serious happened because the waiter brought their order. They didn't speak of the matter again. Ramos asked them to please accompany him to the station, where Gigi Col was threatening to drink up the reserve of whiskey he kept hidden away for difficult moments. Like this one.

"You're in charge, father-in-law: we're your prisoners of war," said Tigran the Terrible. "It's my treat."

Ramos let the "father-in-law" pass; he was prepared to let a camel pass through the eye of a needle just so he could stay with his son. He even displayed infinite patience by keeping quiet during this dialogue: "When we lived in Los Angeles, dad used to take me with him on his night patrols until he stopped asking me because I started to flirt with the thieves, right, dad?"

"Some criminals are divine," said Tigran.

"Divine. That's the right word."

"In London I met an arms smuggler who was a honey."

"I don't like it when you tell me about your lovers."

"I didn't love him. . . . It was just physical. Do you like honey, father-in-law?"

"Yes," Ramos growled.

One hundred yards before they reached the station, Ramos knew something was wrong in his precinct: parked in a row with their motors running, four patrol cars colored the night with red and blue flashing lights.

"The party isn't over," said Tigran.

Wellington Perales explained to the constable that he had decided to ask Santa Fe for help because Caracol Beach was an active volcano. In a few words he brought him up to date on what had happened: the assault on the liquor store and the skirmish on the highway.

"I couldn't catch them. They were heading toward the east end of town. They're driving an Oldsmobile from the time of Roosevelt."

"Any injuries at the liquor store?"

"Just damage to the store, because it turns out they didn't even steal anything: they threw away the money in the parking lot."

Mandy and Tigran, meanwhile, were consoling Gigi Col, who didn't need moral support but another whiskey on the rocks; she had already accepted the incident with comparative good humor and told her friends about it with great enthusiasm. The twelve police reinforcements, meanwhile, went back and forth like wasps angered by the smoke of a fire. Captain Paul Sanders himself had taken charge in Ramos's absence and, installed behind the barricade of the desk, was asking Operations Center in Santa Fe for information that could help solve the case. Ramos did not attribute too much importance to the fact that a comrade-in-arms had usurped his place: he had a pound of ground meat in his stomach to digest; he would soon reach the age of sixty-two, safe and sound; and the station clock indicated it was not the best time for arguing about a dead dog, least of all with a man like Paul. Besides, Paul was his boss.

"Hi, Paul."

"Hi, Sam."

"I'm glad you're paying us a visit."

"Wellington called me."

"How are the girls?"

"Fine: loading me up with sons-in-law."

Through the good offices of Captain Paul Sanders, Ramos had gotten a job in that peaceful resort community where nothing ever happened until Mrs. Dickinson called to complain about some wayward kids dancing to rock music in the Lowells' garden. He had to convince Captain Sanders to let him shit on her porch that very night. If not, I'll show you a spider, Paul, Ramos thought.

"Did they give you your whiskey?" he asked Gigi.

"Thanks, Sam: that drink saved my life. You cut yourself behind the ear."

"Yes. When I was shaving. What did they do to you?"

"Not much, that's the worst part. To tell you the truth, they hardly touched me. A punch in the belly," said Gigi, and she gave a very feminine description of her attackers, not forgetting to mention that one was nearsighted and the other had the shoulders of an athlete. For a moment Ramos thought of the caricatures he had seen in the Lowells' house. "I had about three hundred dollars and a radio, and those little punks didn't even take my condoms. I wanted to talk to you, Sam. I'm scared. Has a dead cat ever licked your back?"

Captain Paul Sanders walked over to Gigi and asked her to go with him to make a formal complaint.

"Know what? I better not. I called for a taxi. Look, officer, President Lincoln said that every man is responsible for his face. Those two johns looked fine. One was wearing tails, dressed up like a penguin. The other was like a television star, an actor in the soaps. It never occurred to me that they were a couple of ingrates."

"Ingrates?" said Captain Saunders.

"Let's just leave things be, OK? Tomorrow's another day. Don't mess me up with a trial."

"I didn't say anything about a trial."

"But you thought it. I'll be honest with you. I'm illegal in this country. But I pay my taxes. And I get regular checkups. I pay my dues to the sex-workers union. What else do you want? I'm not perfect. The constable knows where to find me."

With a gesture Ramos asked the captain to accept her excuse. Paul Sanders let the pigeon fly the coop.

"You've got a half-ton belly," said the captain.

"Peace makes you fat, Paul."

Mandy and Tigran walked Gigi to the door, and when she got into the cab they stood arguing on the sidewalk. They were so close their noses crossed like swords. Ramos looked his son over from head to toe. Until that moment he had gone out of his way not to notice the details. Now he saw the boots with slender heels that turned his perfectly depilated legs; the leather miniskirt; the satin blouse; his padded breasts; and, like an ignoble crown, the red, white, and blue headband extending from ear to ear. To get his son back he had to accept him just as he was. Easier said than done. Could he do it? His loose tooth hurt and his intestines were growling. The hamburgers were only half-digested. "I'm a thousand pounds overweight, but I don't give a shit about tarantulas, Paul," he said to himself.

Langston Fischer was coming out of the bathroom with his baby Bingo wrapped up in his blazer. The constable chose not to approach him. It was enough to hear him repeating his mournful litany: "Why did they apologize before they killed you? Why? Why?" Ramos went into the bathroom to urinate. His bladder was heavy, his urethra full of orange juice and Coca-Cola. The cubicle smelled like a veterinarian's office. Like dog hair. The water in the toilet bowl was stained red. A clot of blood had stuck to the porcelain. Bingo's blood. A jet of urine spattered on his trousers. Now he'd have to wait for it to dry. He felt nauseated. His tongue tasted like a rag. He ran to the sink, turned on the tap, and splashed water on his neck, his forehead, his eyes. It was a way to deceive himself, to think he wasn't crying—and he was crying. For Mandy. Or for himself. He sat down on the toilet. His buttocks overflowed the plastic seat. He rested his head in his hands and dozed for a few minutes. Again he smelled the steaming white rice. Hulled. With cloves of garlic fried in olive oil. Some parsley. Old San Juan. Puerto Rico. So much fighting and all for nothing. A voice woke him: "Dad, dad, are you OK?" With some difficulty, Ramos pulled the chain while still sitting, got to his feet, opened the door, and walked past Mandy without looking him in the face.

31

TO BE FIFTY-SEVEN years old and as lonely as a hyena in the zoo are two insufferable calamities when one has not been able to sow a single seed in the furrows of this world. Albita Rodríguez was still singing through the speakers in the bougainvillea and Mrs. Dickinson still could not sleep no matter how much cotton she packed into her kangaroo ears. The hours Mrs. Dickinson feared most were just before dawn. Every night she prepared a cocktail of sleeping potions to defeat insomnia, though she did not always succeed. She got up, invented a few curses, and decided to call the Lowells' house in Santa Fe. She'd tell them a thing or two. There's a limit to everything and she had reached hers: another round of songs and she'd set fire to her neighbors' mansion. She looked up the number. She dialed with decision. One ring. Two rings. Wake them up. They're going to listen to me. Three rings. Four rings. And Albita Rodríguez in the bougainvillea. At the fifth ring, she heard Mr. Lowell's voice on the answering machine: "This message is for you, son: it's fine with us if you celebrate with your friends at the beach. This is a great day. But be careful. Don't do anything crazy. There's wine and liquor in the cellar, and some beer. We're proud of you. Talk to you later. Your mother says she'll fix a leg of lamb tomorrow. Love you. If you care to leave a message, wait for the tone. Thank you." Mrs. Dickinson had a diabolical inspiration. Changing her frigid cockatoo's voice into that of a menopausal fox, she whispered this horrendous joke: "Your son is dead." And hung up. The petty vengeance of a lie eased her irritation. That Sunday, two police detectives knocked at the door of Mrs. Dickinson's house with an arrest warrant signed by Captain Paul Sanders: she had to answer several questions regarding the tragic end of Martin Lowell, whom she had killed off three hours before police officer Wellington Perales annihilated him with six bullets.

"Let that be a lesson to you," said Mrs. Dickinson and she slept soundly for too short a time because she was awakened by the siren of the burglar alarm and knew someone was breaking into her fishing-gear store. Albita Rodríguez was still singing in the bougainvillea: "Oh, hope, if one day I find you I'll never let you go, hope of good fortune, my hope."

That's what Albita Rodríguez was singing when Tom and Martin came into the house and found only the message their friends had written in red on the mirror over the bar. The simplicity of the caricatures, the comic reproaches for their lateness, the reference to the rock concert at Machu Picchu, calmed Martin down: he began to believe it was a dream, and that when he woke up the party would go on till sunrise. Time was running out. Safe in the summer refuge of the Lowells, Tom looked for the joint he had hidden in the matchbox. He had been thinking about that talisman all night. The knowledge that he was carrying it in his right pants pocket had been a consolation. Now he could enjoy it. He wouldn't let the opportunity pass. He was in a house. A welcoming house with family photos on the walls and a heart-shaped swimming pool. He lit it. The smoke kicked like a mule in his throat. He absorbed the blow. That was the only tranquil moment misfortune had granted them since the soldier cut them off in the parking lot, and the star of the basketball team intended to savor it. Martin didn't want any. He felt ridiculous, insignificant, opening and closing the cabinet drawers where the kitchen knives were kept. He called his parents in Santa Fe. He got the answering machine: "This message is for you, son: it's fine with us if you celebrate with your friends at the beach. This is a great day. But be careful. Don't do anything crazy. There's wine and liquor in the cellar, and some beer. We're proud of you. Talk to you later. Your mother says she'll fix a leg of lamb tomorrow." He dialed again. The line was busy. He tried a third time: "This message is for you, son: it's fine with us if you celebrate with your friends at the beach. This is a great day." He hung up, not leaving a message. What for? When they heard it, the horror would have ended, who knows how.

"Damn," he said and imitated his father's voice: "This is a great day. There's wine and liquor in the cellar, and some beer. But be careful. Now he tells me!"

"What's the difference?" said Tom as he stretched.

"I had a case of whiskey in my hands. I can't believe it. But I didn't have the courage, buddy. Just think. I put it back. How was I to know? How? I locked the cellar with two turns of the key."

"What's done is done."

"That idiot almost killed us," said Martin.

"It was a miracle we got away."

"That moron."

"You should have gone out for the track team: I was in front and you flew right past me, your heels kicking away at your ass. You ought to call yourself Martin the Roadrunner!"

"I felt the bullet whiz past my ear. I swear. I never heard a gunshot before."

"There were three or four."

"It sounds awful."

"Did you see the whore?"

"And the old man. He's the pharmacist. Lucky he didn't recognize me, or he'd tell my mother. The dog was a Chihuahua?"

"Or a Pekingese. I really gave it to him. Zingo!"

"Zingo . . . Bingo."

"Shit, it's a small world."

"It's a small Caracol Beach, you mean."

"The cops! They're a big help!"

"Maybe we should turn ourselves in."

"You're nuts!"

"What a long day."

"The longest."

"The longest, right. Bingo."

Tom talked about graduation and even quoted the words of
the headmaster and Miss Campbell; the concepts of civility
and good conduct the students had ridiculed that afternoon suddenly reclaimed a significance that Tom intended not to forget if
he walked away from his battle with the soldier, just like those
terrible morals at the end of fairy tales that you never think about
when you're young, perhaps because they're so obvious, but as
you grow older they turn into a fountain of sage advice.

"I can't see anything. Without my glasses I'm helpless. From
here you look like a cow," said Martin.

"Moooo!" said Tom and exhaled smoke. "Can I tell you
something, Martin? When we were smashing up the Ford I
enjoyed it in a way I can't explain."

"So did I," said Martin. "As if the devil himself was telling us
what to do."

"Exactly."

"The soldier didn't order us to rip up the seat covers, but
that's what you did."

"We did."

"Well, yes, we did."

"And in case that wasn't enough, we broke all the lights!"

"Every one of them, Tom."

"This tastes great. Want some?"

"We're like two soldiers talking in a foxhole and waiting for the fighting to start again."

"Two soldiers in a foxhole. I like that. Can you imagine when we tell Bill and Chuck what happened? They won't believe we killed the madman to save Laura."

"I can't even see my hands in front of me. I want to kill him, Tom. I hate him. I hate him. I hope to God I'm the one who does it."

"Watch out," said Tom. "Be careful what you wish for."

In a burst of intimacy, Tom admitted to Martin that panic was not a new experience for him because he'd had a similar feeling the evening he went to bed with Agnes MacLarty. He didn't hold anything back. Pursued by death, he felt an urgent need to share his sorrows with a friend. His being afraid when he stood naked in front of a woman like Agnes MacLarty was easy to understand (the gymnastics instructor at the Emerson Institute had served as the masturbatory inspiration for several classes of students); in Martin's opinion it should not be considered a stigma. For an athlete like Tom, spoiled by success and applause, that ordeal, which had earned him so much undeserved fame among his classmates, had meant the most resounding failure of his life. He recounted the scene in detail—the icy vodka from Finland, the music in the background, the astute Agnes's plan of conquest—and did not deny his weak showing in the confrontation of bodies, in particular his indecisive behavior when it was time to go in for the kill with his novice bullfighter's sword. Word by word, as he laid out the truth of his lies on the confessional table, Tom began to see things from an unexpected angle and he felt light, unburdened, free of guilt. Martin was intelligent and he was also right: they were only eighteen. He put out the joint. He exhaled: three smoke rings linked in the air.

"I wanted to run out of there, Martin," he said.

"Does she have big tits?"

"Oh, brother, what tits!"

"Tell me. Tell me about it, Tom. But remember, from this moment on anything you say may be used against you by the distinguished members of the Council of Pissers."

"Understood, Your Honor. OK. That afternoon I had just scored thirty points in the final game of the championship. Suddenly she says to me: 'Come to my place for coffee.' You know what women mean when they ask you over for coffee. . . ."

"Especially cappuccino!"

"Guess what? It was cappuccino!"

Doubled over with laughter, Tom finished telling how the horsewoman Agnes MacLarty had ridden him bareback in the rodeo of her bed. That night's horrifying events had cleared his recollection of that other afternoon of adolescent love, which now seemed like a page out of a novel. His laughter infected Martin. It was desperate laughter but it helped: for ten minutes they forgot about the soldier.

"And you haven't gone to bed with her again?"

"I think she wanted to this afternoon," said Tom.

"Really?"

"I swear."

"You're dreaming."

"She kept looking at me. That woman's so hot."

"Do you like her?"

"Who doesn't?" said Tom.

"You're right."

"And I could feel my cock getting as big as a pickle."

"A pickle!" Martin repeated, choking with laughter. "A pickle!"

"Until Laura suggested going to Machu Picchu to dance. I loved that phrase."

"Laura's wonderful! She kissed me. You saw how she kissed me."

"She kissed you?"

"Don't be a jerk."

"I didn't see."

"She kissed me. I felt as if the sun was beginning to disintegrate in a shower of fireworks and the earth was splitting in two, and then I fell into the void with my arms outstretched, Tom, I swear, I fell until I touched down in the basement of a pagoda in Beijing and then I bounced back up like an arrow. . . ."

The reference to Laura broke the momentary spell.

Tom stood up and said: "What time is it, damn it? We have to do something. . . ."

He reminded Martin that barely two hours earlier he had sworn that for love of Laura he was prepared to do battle on any field of combat. Martin defended himself with the shield of his intelligence: given the circumstances, the only thing they would get if they accepted the madman's challenge was Laura's corpse, for the truth was that the possibility of emerging victorious from so unequal a contest was minimal. Their first attempt at informing the police had failed, but trying again had the indisputable advantage of turning the matter over to competent people.

"The cops! They're a big help."

"Tom, I'm scared."

"He's crazy."

"Let's call the police station. . . ."

"Do you know the number?"

"No."

"So?"

So Martin gave in. He remembered that his father kept a revolver loaded with six bullets in his night table, and on the shelves in the garage Tom found a cleaver that might help if things got desperate. They gathered everything that might help them in a fight: a baseball bat, clothesline, hooks from the fake fireplace. They would soon find another resource once they were under way. But for now they loaded their weapons into the Oldsmobile and started for the auto salvage yard at mile ten on the highway to Santa Fe. Albita Rodríguez was still singing in the bougainvillea.

"This car stinks of codfish."

Tom was ready to go on the offensive when Martin mentioned Mrs. Dickinson's fishing-gear store. If a harpoon was an effective weapon for killing sharks, why wouldn't it work just as well ripping open Lázaro Samá's chest? The store was the only business on the block and he was sure it didn't have any special security system.

"That's good to know," said Tom, and he floored the gas pedal, changed the Oldsmobile's direction with a rapid turn of the wheel, and rammed straight into the store window.

"Shit!" shouted Martin.

The windshield shattered in a shower of glass. The alarms went off, and so did the sprinklers in the fire alarm system; the closed-circuit video cameras began to roll. On the console at the police station a bulb went on and gave intermittent shrieks of red light. Now Tom and Martin had harpoons for hunting down the soldier. And in this novel, they had barely a hundred minutes left to attempt it.

32

SOLDIER'S NOTEBOOK. Ah, shit! Things are getting serious. Clear signs of enemy troop movements. I'm saying the prayer Lázaro taught me, the one about the seven roads: "Yemayá Awoyó, you who are far away, in the sea, mistress of the water, you who devour the innocent lamb, Mother with hair of silvery metal who gives birth to the lagoon, Mother our protector, woman perfect and unique who widens the sea, Mother who thinks, save us from death, help us." Samá says that whenever I'm in danger, just a step or two away from death, Yemayá will mount me. I have to endure it. Let myself be carried away. You feel a shudder on your skin. You get gooseflesh. The saint invades your body. Disarms you. It's like the hand that goes inside the puppet and makes the doll live [...] Ruedas the Brain spent the whole afternoon trying to communicate with headquarters, but he couldn't get through. Something's going on. They don't answer. The radio's fucked up, said the Brain, and Fernandito spit on the equipment. The lieutenant's in a lousy mood. Today we're going out to reconnoiter. I hardly have time to write these notes. The guys look nervous. You have to be crazy to fight in a war. I'm serious. Being crazy is the best strategy. If you think about it too much you run away and go looking for your mama. I don't know why I'm looking for mama. I left Cienfuegos to get away from the Great. I must be looking for something else and got mixed up. [. . .] Nobody knows what to expect. Leo, Ernesto, Fernandito, Elías Benemelis, names that don't mean anything to our enemies, and God only knows what *their* names are. Samá talked to me in private. He looked into my eyes and said that he and I would take point. It's my baptism by fire. So much waiting for this moment and now that it's just around the corner. . . . I told him I was scared. "Me too," he answered, but as hard as a stallion's prick. This black man doesn't know fear. He says he's the child of Babalú Ayé and I'm the child of Yemayá. A fearless, righteous goddess, mistress of the waters and representation of the sea, the fountain of life. She scares me: Lázaro says her punishments are harsh and her wrath is terrible. She likes to dance with a *majá* snake coiled in her arms. On one of her many roads she is the wife of the god of war and weapons. We children of Yemayá like to test our friends, we resent offenses and never forget them even when we forgive them. It's true. "Aren't there any virgins who play ball?" I said and he laughed. "Let Yemayá mount you," he told me. It's time. And I'm thinking about my house. The neighborhood. The port. Ice cream. And what would have happened if I hadn't climbed on that bike and broken my elbow. Where would I be now? Which baseball team? But I did climb on the bike. I wanted to get away from the house. Caterina the Great was making love with my best friend. Paco. Paquito. Paquito wasn't Russian. Paco played right field on the team. Sixth in the batting lineup. I was ashamed. I stole Paco's bike. I needed an ice cream. I didn't see the pothole. Big enough for a whole pig. Shit. I flew into the air. I landed in the hospital. That was when the war started. My war. I haven't dreamed about the dog again. I really like dogs.

33

IF DOGS END UP resembling their owners, the soldier with the tattoos must have been a good man because Strike Two gave the hostage a magnificent welcome with acrobatic leaps, demonstrations of great joy, all the tricks of a well-trained animal. A happy pet doing somersaults is something to see. Under the circumstances, those displays of affection seemed somewhat gratuitous, even offensive, undeserved in any case, but in a way they helped to calm Laura. They don't have visitors very often, she said to herself as she unwrapped the Nestlé bar.

"Strike, stop bothering the girl!" the soldier shouted as he unsheathed the bayonet blade he wore on his thigh and threw it some distance. "The young lady is my guest. Go get it!"

The dog responded instantly, rewound his enthusiasm, and took off like a shot after his prey in comical leaps and bounds; his claws skidded across the floor and he dived under the table at the spot where the tiger with swan wings had sat that morning to eat a rat from the garbage dump.

"You're wrong, soldier," said Laura. "I'm not your guest. I'm your prisoner." Her teeth bit into the candy bar. She had seen a slight muscular contraction in the soldier's face, a tense, almost imperceptible grimace, as if a tiny spring had popped in his cheek.

"The only prisoner here is me," he said.

Laura swallowed the piece of chocolate without chewing it. Strike Two came back, growling. He was pretending to be a wild animal. A bloodhound. A fox in a henhouse. Could the soldier be doing the same thing? His master took the knife out of his mouth and threw it to the far end of the trailer. The routine was repeated five or six times.

"I really love animals!" said the soldier.

Laura used the pauses in the game to observe the inside of the trailer. It was a strange place. Certainly something about it was wrong, anachronistic, though at first glance she couldn't tell what it was. She felt as if she had entered a young boy's bedroom. Military trophies hung on the walls, weapons of every type and caliber—from sophisticated machine guns and hunting rifles to hand grenades, axes for chopping wood, rifles with telescopic sights, shotguns, automatic pistols, machetes, bows and arrows—and yet, surprisingly, the collection did not terrify but produced the opposite effect: an atmosphere of tranquillity, almost of peace. Perhaps it was the arrangement of the pieces in elementary geometric shapes (circles of grenades, triangles of rifles, hexagons of daggers), or the eclectic, haphazard nature of the display: next to modern infrared search equipment hung a semiautomatic water pistol with see-through chambers, a slingshot, and a toy bow with plastic arrows. Laura felt relief, though the word may be somewhat inexact. It could have been worse. This was the gallery of a lunatic, the museum of a very special madman. In addition to weapons, enough to equip a company of cadets, there were banners of athletic teams mixed with marine insignias, contact mines alongside catcher's masks, religious images among photographs of naked women, and on the back wall, over the cot, a small map of Cuba tacked to a cork board. The madman had drawn in pencil a flag that looked like a flying carpet. Laura believed she could detect the incongruity in the arsenal: it was tenderness. Until she saw the bench and the noose tied to the ceiling beam in the trailer. The rope was swinging as if someone had just broken open a piñata.

"Go get it, Strike: under the bed! Bring the knife. Find it, Strike, don't let it get away!"

"I don't understand why you want them to kill you. Much less what good it does you to kill me."

"You haven't seen the tiger."

"The tiger?"

"A Bengal tiger. Nobody believes me."

Strike Two wanted to go on playing. The soldier kicked him. The puppy bit at the bottoms of his trousers. When he tried to shoo him away with his hand, the chain on the handcuffs tightened and Laura fell to the floor, pulled down by the movement.

"I'm sorry," said the soldier, and he offered his hand to help her up. "Are you hurt?"

Laura saw the knife three inches from her free hand. She didn't have to think twice. She brandished it in her own defense: "Take these handcuffs off me," she shouted menacingly.

The soldier did not try to disarm the girl. When she sliced the air with two swipes of the blade, the soldier broke into raucous laughter: "God almighty, girl, think it over."

"I'm going to die anyway, aren't I?" said Laura. "One solution is to take you with me."

"What?"

"I'll pay your fare. First I'd have to bury this knife in your heart. Take the cuffs off me or I'll kill you."

"You'd have a hard time: it's a rubber knife," said the soldier, still laughing, and he fell onto a chair. The tiger, going down the highway back to the kingdom of Ibondá de Akú, suddenly heard the man's laughter multiplied by rebounding echoes, sniffed the air to find the scent of its prey among the natural smells of the countryside, and headed for the auto salvage yard, unhurried, calculating, stepping so gently on the twisted roofs that not even Strike Two sensed the hunter's approach.

In spite of so much destructive power, the Cuban could find no adequate response to the counteroffensive that Laura decided to undertake without delay: she would overcome him with a woman's weapon. When her initial fear had passed, the girl understood that the best possible defense was an attack, and to save time she took a shortcut, certain that in her case time would be her principal ally. She knew she was beautiful and she made use of this advantage. She waited for the right moment. Alone, in that lunatic trailer, Laura began to cook her prey over a slow fire. For his part, the soldier recounted with incredible brashness the origin of each piece in his museum, where he got the Thompson, the person he took the automatic pistol away from, which rifle he'd use to blow away his friends at school. War was a recurring theme. Whether or not it was pertinent, the trauma of that experience appeared over and over again in the madman's rambling monologue, and that was where she saw the opening for what she had to say. But first she said she really, really had to pee.

"I'll wet my pants," she said. Laura clutched at the only thing that would save her life: the illusion of being alive.

"What?"

"I said I'll wet my pants."

"What the hell!"

The soldier was not prepared for so embarrassing a situation: she had to urinate and he had thrown away the key to the handcuffs. They both tried to squeeze into the trailer's tiny bathroom, but the maneuver was not only ridiculous, it was impossible. They went outside and in the midst of so much old metal they looked for a place where she could take care of her needs in relative privacy. When Laura squatted down, her pants halfway down her legs, she knew she was not lost because the tattoed soldier looked away with discreet delicacy and began to whistle one of Silvio Rodríguez's tunes between his teeth. The madman's gesture revealed an unexpected quality of gentlemanliness. With the moon for a witness, Laura began a conversation about the coolness of the night, and its smells, and he allowed himself to be led tamely by the cadence of that amiable talk. To the girl's surprise, he had a profound knowledge of the stars. He had become interested in the subject as a boy, when he had sat for hours and hours on the kitchen stool and waited for Caterina the Great to finish her transaction of love. He had spent entire nights in the awful solitude of the auto salvage yard, and many others beneath the stars of war, and in time he had come to know the cosmos better than the palm of his hand. The reference to the military adventure in Ibondá de Akú aroused the furies of his madness, but Laura contrived a way to make the memory less oppressive.

"Really, wouldn't it be a good idea to unlock the cuffs?"

"Maybe, but I lost the key."

"That means. . . ."

"That means we'll be together till death do us part. What did you say your name was?"

"Laura Fontanet y Vargas. My mother was Cuban."

"Cuban! No kidding. It's a small world! What part of Cuba are you from?"

"Well, where my mother's from, because I was born in exile. Mom came from El Rincón."

"I'll be damned!"

"Do you know El Rincón?"

"Honey, what Cuban doesn't?"

"Shall we go in? It's cold out here. . . ."

"You're right."

"Mom's name was Maruja."

Back in the trailer, Laura learned that the soldier had wanted to be a pitcher on a Havana baseball team so he could travel and see the world, because he had a killer fastball that made the best batters in the Cienfuegos league dizzy.

"Once in an exhibition game I struck out Agustín Marquetti himself. But you don't know who don Agustín is. Number forty. Damn, I could have been a great pitcher. Like Manolo Hurtado, José Antonio Huelga, or Rigoberto Betancourt. Andrés Manuel Prieto was my coach, the best in the city. He had two pupils, that's all. My dream was to get into the Big Leagues and win a game at Yankee Stadium. And I'm telling you, I could have. My curve ball . . ."

"It's not too late."

"Don't fuck with me."

"Why not? There are other leagues. Tom knows a lot about sports. He can help you."

"You don't know anything about ball. Who's Tom?"

"One of the boys who's coming to kill you."

"No. No way. I have a broken elbow."

"Are you sure?"

"And besides, I'm crazy. Does it show?"

"Well, yes, but there's a cure for that too."

"You talk a lot. Are you a student?"

"Psychology. I want to be a psychologist."

"Would you take me as a patient?"

"When I graduate. I just won a scholarship to study in Los Angeles. We were celebrating the news when a tiger on ice showed up."

"You'll be very successful. I can read it in the stars."

"If you don't kill me first."

"What are you worrying about? You don't have to be afraid. You'll see. Your friends will save you. His name is Tom?"

"Tom's the big one, and Martin's the one with glasses."

"The thing is, I'm crazy. Crazier than a coffeepot. That's what my mother says, Caterina the Great. She knows a lot of funny old sayings. And she likes to sing: 'Zun zun zun, zun zundambayé. . . .'"

"Caterina the Great?"

"They call her the Great because she was born in Sagua la Grande but now we live in Cienfuegos. Well, she lives in Cienfuegos. I live here. In this garbage dump. Besides, Caterina the Great was an important whore who slept with half of Russia."

"Can I ask you something?"

"You can ask."

"Do you love her?"

"Mama? The man who doesn't respect his mother is a son of a bitch. I adore her. There are days when I miss her more than I should. If you tasted her guava preserves. . . . I'd like to hear from her."

"Talk to her on the phone. I'll pay for the call."

"She doesn't have a phone."

"Do you write to each other?"

"We did, when I was working at the Haitians' restaurant, but when I moved here I didn't send her my new address. I think she went to Havana. I have some postcards from her. And some photographs. Want to see them?"

"OK."

The soldier began to look through drawers. Laura, always at his side, helped with her cuffed hand. She used the opportunity to observe him with the eyes of a future psychologist. It wasn't only the trailer that reminded her of a young boy's room: the soldier, too, seemed like a child. A spoiled child. As he pulled papers from the drawers and found to his annoyance that they weren't pictures of Caterina, he threw them on the floor, like a kid who urgently needs to find his water pistol at the bottom of a huge toy box, because if he doesn't how will he fight his duel?

"You live in a circus," said Laura.

"Five Star Show. Traveling Rodeo. Performers and Gypsy Fortunetellers. Trained Animals. Private Dressing-rooms."

"I wonder what it was like?"

"What?"

"The circus."

"Nothing much. I can't find the pictures, damn it. I kept them in this drawer. A Manila envelope. Yellow. A photo where mama looks like the Queen of Clubs. Here it is!"

The Cuban showed the photograph of his mother as if he were displaying a lottery ticket. In front of the camera was a round-shouldered woman. The Queen of Clubs had her hair rolled up in toilet paper. She held her right arm in front of her, trying to shield herself from a photograph that apparently caught her off guard. "She doesn't like having her picture taken. She's always doing her *torniquete*," said the soldier. "You just have to know Caterina." The subject was barefoot, sitting on a rock at the edge of an untended garden, her back to a bay that filled most of the space.

"Torni what?" Laura asked, and the soldier explained that a *torniquete* is "the roller women use after their bath to smooth their hair when they want to look nice." Caterina the Great's feet were enormous and wide, with compact toes like a duck's. "Cien-fuegos has turned into an industrialized city. It's really something. It has cement factories, fertilizer factories, flour mills, even a nuclear plant that the Russians are building. A place with a real future," he said.

"I can see that," the girl replied, though there wasn't much to see. In the background some columns of smoke seemed to verify his information. The paper had pointed, serrated edges, just like Laura's black-and-white photograph of her mother. That insignificant detail made Laura remember she was only a few minutes away from dying.

"Can I ask you something else?" the girl said.

"You're interviewing me on TV! I like that. You're a reporter and I'm a famous ballplayer. I can talk about a lot of things. About Agustín Marquetti's average, Silvio's songs, constellations, or the customs of the white Haitians in Caracol Beach."

"I'm serious, soldier."

"I'm a lieutenant—that's much higher than soldier. Lieutenant Lázaro Samás, and don't forget it."

"Why do you destroy what you love?" said Laura.

"I don't know what you're talking about," he said coldly, and took back the picture.

"You claim you love your mother, and I don't doubt it, and you say Caterina was a whore, but you forced my friends to hit that girl on the street."

"Shut up."

"I'm still interviewing you."

"No."

"I can see you love animals, so why did you order them to kill that little dog?"

"Because."

"'Because' is no answer."

"Nothing to it."

"'Nothing to it' isn't an answer either."

"Do you want to know why? Do you really want to know why?" said the soldier hysterically, and Laura was afraid of another attack.

"You need help."

"Of course I need help! If I don't get help how the fuck am I going to kill that son of a bitch?" The soldier banged his fist on the table. "Today it sat under this table eating a rat. And it had wings. Two huge wings."

Laura pointed to the noose.

"And what about that, lieutenant?"

"What?"

"The rope."

"It's a rope."

"It's a noose."

"All right, it's a noose."

"Tell me about it."

"Tell you about it? OK, you asked for it. Today I tried to kill myself. I couldn't," he said, and he kicked the stool.

"Kill yourself?"

"Before the tiger did."

"The one that has wings?"

"Damn it! It was eating a rat under the table. The rat was squealing. It made a terrible sound. Its bones were breaking. Crunching. You have no idea. You have no idea what a tiger's like."

"Give me a weapon or give me my hand: I swear I'll help you kill that animal."

"You'd do that?"

"For you and for me."

"You're a tough kid. A real hellcat."

"Untie the knot."

"What knot?"

"The one in the noose."

"A hellcat," said the soldier. He tugged on the rope. The knot came loose. Laura gradually rooted out his secrets until she reached the source of his bitterness: the tattooed cemetery of dead men that blanketed his arm all the way to his wrist. At his shoulder he had a tattoo of a bow and three arrows. Coiled around the bow was a *majá* snake. A bird sat on one of the arrows. The handcuffs prevented her from seeing the end of the list. Laura turned the metal ring until she could she read the name of the last dead man, etched next to a cross of blood: Lázaro Samá.

"God almighty. Don't play with fire, girl. All right. Don't say I didn't warn you. Better watch out, " said the soldier. The pressure cooker of his madness had begun to build up steam again.

"A lie. It's all a lie," said Laura.

"What's wrong with you?"

"You're not Lázaro."

"What do you mean? What the hell do you mean? Oh my God!"

"Lázaro Samá is dead."

"What the hell. . . ."

"I can read his name here. Tattooed on your arm."

"You're crazy. Out of your mind."

"He's dead. Lázaro Samá is dead."

"Fuck you!"

"You killed him."

"I didn't kill anybody, damn it! I didn't kill anybody!" said the soldier, and he pressed the barrel of the pistol against the roof of his mouth.

34

THE CATS were witnesses, but the testimony of a cat has no legal standing. The scene can be reconstructed. From the sea a traitorous breeze was blowing. The silence of the night thickened with dampness and salt air. We know that a car drove down the street. Its occupants were listening to "Like a Rolling Stone" played at full volume. The Belgian soprano saw it from her bedroom some fifteen minutes after the alarm went off in the store. She did not want to go back to bed. She had a great deal to do. She was leaving that morning for London on a business trip. The car was moving slowly, she said, because she could hear a long section of the song. Martin and Tom hid behind some hedges. The harpoons caught in the underbrush. A cat was in their hiding place. The cat left unwillingly.

A truck came by. "Now!" said Tom, and he hit the driver on the back of the head. In their assault on the store they had gained two harpoons but lost the Oldsmobile. They needed a vehicle to get to their appointment and the milk truck did not seem a difficult target. "This resort community is so conservative a place that milkmen still deliver quarts of the precious liquid door to door, a tradition that has been lost in times like these when the ancient custom of providing service is rejected by some people." The sentence is don Claudio Fontanet's. He said it to Captain Sanders in the course of the investigation. The attack turned out to be simple: by now Tom and Martin were a couple of madmen. They understood one another. They did not have to plan it. Fear made them of one mind.

"Don't do it, Tom."

"It's late. Almost dawn."

"Let's go home."

"Shit. Don't you understand that we're thieves and they must be looking for us all over town?"

"I'm calling the police. That's what I'll do. I'll do it."

"Then you better report that I cracked open a milkman's skull."

"Don't do it, Tom."

"Now!" said Tom.

The driver lost consciousness immediately: he didn't even have time to feel pain. Tom took the wheel and they drove away at top speed, leaving behind on the asphalt a trail of broken bottles awash in a sea of milk. "I was on my daily route. I've worked nine years for this company. I never had any problems. I saw them when I got out of the truck and they didn't look suspicious to me," the milkman would tell Captain Sanders. "I just assumed they were a couple of students leaving an all-night party. I have eight kids. I know how young people are. I was wrong. Now that I've read what happened that night in the papers, I think if they had asked I would have gone with them to the auto salvage yard. I heard somebody say 'Don't do it, Tom.' It must have been the one named Martin. They hit me hard. I lost consciousness immediately. I didn't even have time to feel pain."

Gregory Papa Gory was walking along, telling himself it was time to make a will and leave everything to his half-witted godchildren, when dozens of stray dogs and cats emerged from their nighttime lairs, "and I was afraid I would begin the Great Journey without having put my affairs in order," he told Constable Ramos at the bar in the Bastille when he came back from the boys' funeral. The black albino had never seen so many street animals in Punta La Galia, and though he had been away for a while, if he didn't know about the existence of those creatures you can be sure nobody did, because Papa Gory was an exceptional chronicler who prided himself on his mastery of the behind-the-scenes workings of the perfect stage setting that now appeared on tourist maps with the insipid name of Caracol Beach. As if that weren't enough, from some balcony worthy of an operetta came the sound of a Verdi aria accompanied by a sudden chorus of sirens. Dogs and cats all ran in one direction. They jumped from the roofs of houses, used their claws to scale fences, and knocked over the plastic cans in which residents had deposited the previous day's trash. Gregory followed the trail of an emaciated, lame greyhound, and so he arrived in time to witness an unforgettable scene: the pack of vagabonds splashing in an ocean of milk, like schoolchildren paddling in the backwater of a river. At the head of the troops, a Doberman with hoodlum's eyes led the action: his diversion consisted of spreading his legs in a perfect gymnast's split, dropping to his belly, and letting his companions jump the hurdle of his body like racehorses in a steeplechase. If a dog has ever laughed on planet Earth, it was this acrobat presiding over the canine festivities. The cats preferred to fill the canteens of their bellies before participating fully in the celebration; they drank with concentration and good sense, taking care not to ruin their digestive tracts with shards of glass. Meanwhile, a Pekingese who had recently given birth and still had a silk ribbon tied around her neck bayed at the moon with more enthusiasm than skill, irritating the felines who, as everyone knows, tend to be very aristocratic animals. The Pekingese's puppies stayed at the edge of the pond, prudent in the face of the unknown, while the adults took advantage of the opportunity to frolic as they pleased, submitting to the power of an instinct that humans lost centuries ago: the wild, primitive instinct for freedom. Gregory Papa Gory found the driver of the truck still unconscious at the bottom of the steps of a nearby building, because the lame greyhound, who took no part in the noisy revels, was licking the man's hand, looking for a bone with some meat on it that he could sink his teeth into. The dogs were left biting at thin air.

35

WHEN LAURA told him to his face that he was an impostor and a fraud, the soldier pressed the barrel of the pistol against the roof of his mouth and forced her to place her index finger on the trigger, only to discover that the pistol wasn't loaded. Three times he squeezed the trigger. Three times he spun the chamber. Three times he pulled back the hammer. And nothing. Nothing was true. Lázaro Samá wasn't Lázaro Samá and none of his weapons were real. The arsenal was part of a stage set: the rifle with the telescopic sight was a useless artifact, the machine gun an ingenious but inoffensive object, the bow a simple toy. Only the map of Cuba was Cuba. And the flag, the island's flag. Though the star was reversed and badly drawn, and the blue of the stripes wasn't sky blue but metallic and as dark as the sea at night, and the red of the triangle looked like a leper's scabs: he had drawn it with his own blood, after all, poor Cuban. The madman collapsed at Laura's feet. The dog threw himself at the madman's feet. Laura fell next to the dog.

"Ah, damn it, just my luck!" the soldier groaned. "You don't know anything. Shut up, Strike!"

"Tell me."

"I remember the tiger."

"You told me. A Bengal tiger."

"I don't know if it's from Bengal but there was one of those animals. An African leopard, maybe. . . ."

"And what else?"

"What else? You don't think that's enough? Shit, I couldn't talk. My jaw clamped shut when I saw the soldiers. . . ."

"That happens."

"Like in nightmares. Haven't you ever dreamed that you want to scream and you can't, no matter how hard you try?"

"It's horrible."

"Horrible. Being scared is horrible. I'm scared."

"Trust me," said Laura.

"Shit!" shouted the soldier and he bit his left arm, as if he wanted to tear away his flesh. The epitaphs tattooed on his skin weren't those of his victims. One by one he had etched on his own body the names of his comrades-in-arms who had died in the jungle. They were documented there before the court of conscience, Ernesto, Poundcake, Fernandito, Tomás, Elías, the Fly, and Samá himself, leader of the squad. Sunday night was the eighteenth anniversary of that ambush, and to the soldier it seemed fair that someone should pay for the lives of his seven friends: he was the someone.

"Don't blame yourself."

"Go to hell."

"Then give me a piece of bread," said Laura, and she stood up. "Take care of your guests."

"Bread?"

"I want something to eat, lieutenant. I'm starving. My stomach's growling. Even my jeans are loose. The chocolate made me hungry. A piece of bread would be nice."

"Where would I find bread?"

"You must know."

Laura pulled at the soldier with the handcuffs. She held the reins.

"Bread. I had a piece of bread."

"Or some crackers."

"Crackers. In Cuba they had crackers that were really good. You ate them with butter."

Laura understood that the soldier had pretended to be Lieutenant Lázaro Samá in order to pay for the lives he owed, but in eighteen years of anguish he had never been able to take his own life by his own hand. That night, pursued by the phantoms of madness, he had decided to set a trap for an innocent bystander and force that person to shoot him through the heart. He wanted to die. That's what he wanted. He wanted somebody to kill him. That's all. He wanted another grave for Lieutenant Samá. Laura learned this because the madman had been able to confide in a person who felt no rancor. Someone had believed in him, had allowed him to tell what he knew about the Big Dipper and the constellation of Virgo and the record of Agustín Marquetti, the great Industriales ballplayer. The tiger could be hunted down. In the middle of his raving, the madman would suddenly remember some humorous event and go from grief to joy with absolute naturalness: then he talked of his dreams as a ballplayer and that wonderful Sunday in May when he attended a concert by Silvio and Pablo at the Bosque amphitheater in Havana. Yolanda, eternally Yolanda. Laura also found out that only she could prevent the killing of a poor lunatic who may have needed a room in a psychiatric hospital but not a nameless grave in potter's field; only she could stop Tom and Martin from becoming murderers overnight.

"Now tell me about Cuba," said Laura. "Don't forget I'm half Cuban."

"How do you see Cuba?"

"You ask a lot of questions," said Laura.

"All right, all right, how do you imagine it?"

"I don't know."

"Do you see it or not?" the soldier insisted. His chin quivered when he spoke of his country. "Cuba the Beautiful."

"I don't see it. I hear it. In my head. Cuba is a piano that someone is playing behind the horizon," said Laura.

"God almighty!"

"What about you?"

"A piano: you're worse off than me!" he exclaimed and, looking up at the ceiling, he said: "For me Cuba is Caterina the Great."

Laura finally found out about El Rincón, her mother's home, the place she had dreamed about since she was a child, a town with nice people and houses painted white with sloping roofs where the neighbors raise chickens in the courtyards and nobody has a dog that isn't a mongrel, like Strike Two. The soldier told Laura that on the outskirts of El Rincón there is a leper hospital not many people know about, where the dead who are about to die embroider dresses for the wooden Virgins, and a simply built basilica has a red dome that you can see from a distance: Babalú Ayé is worshiped there, blessed St. Lazarus, the patron saint of the helpless, the sick, and animals. Every December 17th thousands of Cubans carry stones on their backs for miles, burning their hands in candle flames. The keepers of vows tie their ankles together, flagellate themselves with tree branches or belt buckles, never making a sound; some crawl in the gutters, over stones and sewage; others, barefoot and repentant, carry enormous crosses, while their companions recite the rosary, one set of ten after another, Ave Maria, and give them rags soaked in vinegar to drink: "Each person knows his own sin," he said. "Zun zun zun, zun zundambayé, pretty bird at the break of day."

The soldier told her a dream. His dream. He was on the

shore at Caracol Beach, shirtless, on his knees, dragging a piece of firewood by a chain made of seven steel links. On his knees he entered the sea that separated him from his island, and on his knees he traveled the ocean bottom past coral reefs, anchors, tortoises, shipwrecks, and if the wood caught in the rigging of a sunken ship he put it on his shoulders, still on his knees, until he reached the north shore of Havana, and on his knees he continued on his way, gathering offerings for the saint, branches of *cundiamor*, cissus vine, leaves of purple basil, reeds of wild cane, stalks of sisal, sesame seed. That was his dream in the dream. He dreamed about going to El Rincón, to the basilica, to the foot of the altar, and keeping the promise to St. Lazarus that he made in the war: he would drag a piece of wood as heavy as a Bengal tiger if he could return to Cuba some day to give Caterina the Great the embrace he had always owed her. Babalú Ayé, the revered ancient of crutches, also called St. Lazarus, brother of Magdalene, Babalú Ayé, the old man of twanging speech and tightly bound hands, Babalú Ayé, the Bishop of Marseilles, Babalú Ayé, father of the world, the god of smallpox, Babalú Ayé, the saint who is not agreed to but received, Babalú Ayé, worshiped in dry jungles, Babalú Ayé, king of the lands of Arará, founder of a sanitarium in Dahomey, Babalú Ayé the feverish, Babalú Ayé the twisted, Babalú Ayé son of Obatalá, Babalú Ayé, he who works with the dead, Babalú Ayé would surely understand him and pardon him, because for the sake of something much greater than hope or fanaticism, something much, much deeper than disillusion, a reason as mysterious as faith and as intimate as love, Babalú Ayé is followed by mangy dogs, rachitic horses, hoarse roosters, feeble cows, tailless *hutías*, dethroned bees, gangrenous ducks, worldly parrots, depressed peacocks, emaciated cats, amputated flies, ill-tempered pigs, wingless butterflies, swamp-ridden earthworms, suicidal swans, outlaw snakes, wild ants, featherless turkeys, lost doves, sterile rabbits, famished

wolves, and, at a certain distance, silent, respectful, loyal, patriotic, thousands of Cubans in solemn procession, men and
women, young and old, sinners and penitents, vagabonds, lepers,
the maimed, the Mongoloid, the lame, the blind, the mute,
the half-witted, the diabetic, the desperate, the disabled, the
one-eyed, the tubercular, the deaf, the moronic, the paralytic,
the handless, the tongue-tied, the weak-hearted, the hopeless, the
asthmatic, the AIDS-infected, the paranoid, the solitary, the
melancholic, the neurotic, the mad, mad, mad, hundreds and
hundreds of poor madmen, some incurable, like him, Beto
Milanés.

"Beto?"

"Beto. My name is Beto Milanés."

The Cuban took an axe from the wall and placed the handcuffs on the table and hacked through the chain.

Dawn

He was almost dead when he began to sing.

— MARÍA LUISA ELIO

36

"DON'T CRITICIZE God for creating the tiger: thank Him instead for not giving it wings," said the *santero* Lázaro Samá, and he hoisted the sack of cement on his shoulders, not knowing a seam was torn: twenty-five pounds of dust turned him into a living statue. "Applaud, OK?" he said. Beto Milanés was climbing down the ship's ladder and was startled by the ovation that suddenly resounded under the metal dome. He was an inch away from slipping and falling onto the shovel of the freight lift. Down below, in the bottom of the boiling pot, an Abominable Limeman was dancing clumsily. "Yemayá Awoyó. Yemayá Asesú. Yemayá," sang the chorus. Those who didn't know the words kept time with their hands. What funhouse did they pull this clown from? Beto thought as he did acrobatics to keep his balance. That afternoon Beto would shake Lázaro's hand in the hold of the merchant ship *Playa Girón*, though another twelve hours would go by before he could identify him among the workers in the port, drinking a *malta* in the cafeteria of the Mambisa Terminals, because after the accident with the torn sack the black man was floured from head to toe, and through the thick dust Beto could barely make out his gleaming eyes and the half-moon of teeth as yellow as a golden plantain. He would recognize his voice. Hoarse. Centuries old. "Do you want a *malta*, boy?" he said. It's him, Beto thought, and he accepted the drink. Lázaro Samá was in charge of the crew whose mission was to unload the ship, and to raise the morale of his workers he would tell them that the famous battle at Playa Girón had been a picnic, a game, compared to the war they were waging sixty feet below sea level, against 50,200 paper sacks. "I took my shots at the Bay of Pigs with an antiaircraft gun and I know what I'm talking about: we don't give out medals here, comrades, but we do have bread and a creamy cheese that will make your mouth water." When they had completed the pharaonic task, at noon on Saturday, all the stevedores had the same death mask of cement imprinted on their faces, and since Beto had just joined the crew he wasn't sure into which magician's hat he had disappeared, that guy who ran off at the mouth and talked for three uninterrupted shifts. He was gone. Later he found out who he was: the man in charge of the union's militias. Lázaro stood out among the workers in the port because of his inexhaustible repertoire of jokes. A Santiagan chanter and enchanter who was always ready to help any compatriot in financial difficulties regardless of ideology, race, or religion. Beto liked him. The party began on Saturday in the cafeteria of the Mambisa Terminals, continued on the small launch that crosses the bay from Havana to the town of Regla, and ended in the house of the Samá family at five in the morning, with Beto and Lázaro each sitting in a chair in the doorway, drinking *aguardiente* and talking about the baseball championship, pollution problems in the port, and the mysteries of human beings.

"I'm going to tell you what it's really about, boy. Listen. Heads up. Open your ears. Pay attention," said Lázaro as he opened the second bottle of *aguardiente*.

"Shoot, Samá."

"It's serious. I've thought a lot about what I'm going to tell you. And I don't have any doubts about it."

"Pitch that ball."

"Here goes, champ. Men are divided into two groups: those who are near and those who are far away."

"What did you say?"

"Nothing to it. Men are divided into two groups," Lázaro repeated. "Those who are near and those who are far away."

"It went right past me, maestro."

"I'll explain it to you. It's the first alternative. The basic alternative. After that the mambo really gets complicated. Loyal men and traitors. Noble men and pigs. Rightists and leftists. Brave men and cowards. Stupid men and brains. Good men and bad. Capitalists and communists."

"The living and the dead."

"The living and the dead. Right. But before that, before loyalty and being a son of a bitch, you're either near or far away, which isn't the same as being close or distant. It isn't a question of geography but of history. Look. There are people who are as close as your shoes and you don't even see them. And somebody can be in the next world and you feel that person in your heart. Do you want lemon in your drink?"

"Just a squeeze. I don't understand anything."

"You will. You're a child of Yemayá."

"Yemayá? What are you talking about, I'm the son of Caterina."

"A saintly woman."

"Do you know her?"

"All mothers are saintly," said Lázaro.

In January 1976, Beto and Lázaro presented themselves voluntarily at a military recruiting office. Elite troops of the Armed Forces were fighting 1,150 nautical miles away, and hundreds of young men on the island signed up to do what they thought of as their duty. "They're very far away, Beto; we ought to get closer if we want to help them." Private Milanés and Lieutenant Samá were sent to the fourth company, second battalion, sixth infantry regiment, in action in the south of Ibondá de Akú. When they reached the theater of operations, the squad went on a reconnaissance mission in enemy territory. Through an error that Beto always considered the result of unpardonable cowardice, even when he could no longer remember it, they were ambushed during a dangerous operation. The men fought as hard as they could, isolated in a rat trap in the jungle, out of communication with the rear. The earth swallowed them up. The rival army's version acknowledges that the advance party of soldiers fought with suicidal valor under unfavorable circumstances, but the numerical superiority of the attackers and their control of the terrain's most advantageous positions eventually won the day. The only ones who managed to escape the inferno were Lázaro Samá, his right lung punctured by mortar shrapnel, and Beto Milanés, unharmed, perhaps, but with his mind ruined forever. He was or thought he was a traitor. Lázaro Samá forgave him because he was not the kind to blame a sick man. For several days he traveled on Beto's shoulders, like a sack of cement, refusing to die in order to save him, until he let himself be devoured by ants. The regimental commanders lost all hope and reported to headquarters in Havana that the reconnaissance unit had been wiped out, with no chance of survivors.

The night before the officials of the Military Committee of Cienfuegos reported the news to her, Caterina the Great dreamed that Beto fell down a well. At the moment of the accident she was washing a towel in the backyard. She began to run between the lines hung with sheets, agitating a flock of orange-colored chickens, and threw herself in after her son. The sun tinted the white cloth red. The stream of water overflowed the washtubs, and detergent suds invaded the abandoned garden. She had the same dream three times in a row, each time with great realism. She awoke convinced she had jumped in not because she hoped to save Beto but because she wanted to die with him. She cleaned the house from top to bottom, scoured the bottoms of the pots with steel wool, rolled up her hair with toilet paper, sewed the hem of a skirt she never wore, went to the corner market for the month's rations, used the broom to brush away the cobwebs on the ceiling, and prepared an enormous jar of guava preserves. What didn't she do to take away the bad taste of that nightmare! By late afternoon, dead with exhaustion, she realized there was no use in trying to erase what destiny had written in the palm of her hand. Then she began to soak the laundry, and she hung the sheets exactly as she had seen them in her dreams. Out of the corner of her eye she tried to identify the heralds of death, though all she detected were signs of life: the beat of a song by Los Brincos, a pigeon returning to the nests of her comadre Rafaela, a line of crazy ants on the wall. With the scene reconstructed, Caterina took up the challenge of the dream, certain that sooner or later someone would come to tell her what had happened to her son in Ibondá de Akú. The officials, in fact, arrived shortly before nightfall. She heard the motor of their car. The headlights shone on her in the backyard. She was soaping a towel in the washtub. Two doors slammed in unison. The wind held its breath. The Great turned the tap so the water would gush out.

"Fuck it," she said to herself as she shook off the suds. She began to walk, escorted by five of her chickens. In the spaces between the sheets she could see the sunset. She dried her hands on her dress: her fingers were wrinkled with water. As she faced her visitors she said calmly: "Come in, comrades, I've been expecting you."

37

THE CHICKENS had organized themselves into a Napoleonic wedge formation and cackled on their way to the coops without anyone driving them in. Pure routine. When the Great learned that her son had disappeared in Ibondá de Akú she went to sit on a dry tree trunk, at the far end of the yard, looking out on Cienfuegos Bay. She was dressed for the house, and her hair was rolled up with toilet paper. In spite of her appearance, no one disputed the majesty of her grief. "Beto," she said, and paused: "Beto, Beto, my Beto." None of her neighbors dared to interrupt her or comfort her. They had gathered around the house in groups of three or four; from the confessional of the tree trunk Caterina saw the ends of their cigarettes glowing in the darkness, and she felt protected, watched over by the gods of the neighborhood. "Let her cry," said comadre Rafaela, who had made some coffee to offer to the officials of the Military Committee. "It'll do her good: it's what she needs. To cry. This iron woman hasn't cried for a thousand years." Night had fallen, and along the shore road distant cars passed with their streamers of blue and yellow lights: only occasionally were the purr of a tractor, the cough of a horn, or the ring of a bicycle bell heard between deep spaces of silence. Someone turned on a radio and an announcer's voice crossed the yard, sports commentary mixing with the chirp of cicadas. "Quiet," shouted Rafaela from the doorway, and the crickets and the radio fell silent at her command. Caterina took a deep breath and began to toss pebbles into the bay. One after the other. It was a robotic action, repetitive and inexplicable. Some reached the edge of the water, some fell on the shore or into puddles on the rocks. As she purified her lungs with mouthfuls of salt air, Caterina began to feel more relief than sorrow, for when all was said and done, if that poor devil Beto couldn't have the life he wanted the kindest thing was for him to die in whatever way he chose. She didn't shed a single tear: the Great really was made of iron.

"What can you do?" she said, and threw the last stone with a good amount of force. The stone skipped three times before sinking into the waters of the port. None of the others had traveled as far, even when they skipped. Caterina smiled: she had tried the throw hundreds of times, trying to conquer the tedium of boring afternoons, and this had to be the first and only damn time she tasted the honey of victory. She walked back with a firm, almost military step, to an open rhythm, her feet crushing the wildflowers that by some miracle had come up between the rocks in her abandoned garden.

"We're very sorry," said the officials.

"I hope God knows why the hell He does what He does," said the Great, and she locked herself in the kitchen. After a while, when the neighbors had gone, Rafaela persuaded her comadre to open the door. There was an odor of gas.

"Girl!" shouted Rafaela as she ran to turn off the knobs on the stove. "Let's get out of here!"

"What I want is to die, Felita, I want to die," she said, not knowing that she was repeating her son's words. She pulled the rollers violently from her hair. The two friends embraced.

"Hush up! Don't say things like that, woman, Satan's listening behind the walls. Hope is the last thing you lose. I believe in miracles. Maybe he'll turn up."

"Maybe. . . . Do you really think so, comadre?"

"Me, I lost a pigeon about two weeks ago and today, just this afternoon, when you were washing sheets in the yard, I saw it coming back to the coop. Go on, honey, drink some linden tea and come sleep at my house, there's a terrible stink of gas in here."

"Know what I'm thinking about, Rafaela?"

"That's enough, woman: don't think about anything."

"Where the hell is that damn well?"

The next morning a Komsomol from Uzbekistan knocked on Caterina the Great's door with an implacable desire to exchange ten cans of Russian meat for two hours of sex, Cuban-style. He had not heard about events in Ibondá de Akú and had drunk half a liter of vodka at breakfast, and so he arrived ready for an experience he knew about only through his comrades' stories. The Komsomol knew barely enough Spanish to say hello. Caterina tried to explain that he had come at a very bad time, but when she saw his smile of a clown in the Great Russian Circus, she knew it would be a dialogue of the deaf. Besides, in a way she was grateful: ten minutes later and he would have found her in the kitchen with her head in the oven, asphyxiated in a cloud of butane. She accepted the cans and made love to him for three and a half hours, twice the usual time. The young Uzbeki was her last lover. She left the trade. Withdrew from the world. Lived on air, feeding on crumbs, like comadre Rafaela's pigeons. She needed little to let herself die: just patience. And she had plenty of fortitude.

"You're going to hell in a handbasket, Caterina," Rafaela would say when she brought her chicken soup for supper.

"The saints will help me get there," the Great would reply, weakened every day by grief.

What Caterina the Great did not know was that a month before she was notified of her son's disappearance, a group of military advisers and war correspondents found a soldier in the jungle several miles from Ibondá de Akú, desiccated by hunger, more dead than alive, almost a resurrected corpse, delirious with fever on an anthill. His rescuers, or perhaps it would be better to call them his pursuers, had been watching him for some time from the trees: he kept walking around the remains of a man covered by a blanket of ants and saying phrases in an incomprehensible dialect. Suddenly he would pick up an ordinary-size stone, toss it in the air, and hit it at chest height with a branch. When he missed, he would beat the anthill with the stick; if the stone traveled some distance, he would jump for joy. He offered no resistance when he was captured. He was the soldier Alberto "Beto" Milanés. Or what was left of him. They could never get a word out of him regarding what had happened during the ambush. He did not know. Madmen are innocents. Madmen are always somewhere else. He said there was a tiger. A yellow tiger. An impossible Bengal tiger. He spent three days sleeping in the camp infirmary, curled up in a ball on a cot, not getting up even to use the bathroom. Every two or three hours he would suffer a nervous attack and arch his body, from his head to his heels, with so much despair that his caretakers were obliged to confine him with leather straps. He awoke in a lake of excrement and urine, shouting and trying to drive away a nonexistent swarm of blowflies. He confused his companions-in-arms with famous ballplayers and said his name was Lázaro Samá, except he could not be Lázaro Samá because the corpse of the real Lázaro Samá, a lieutenant in the Cuban Armed Forces, was also discovered on the afternoon of the rescue, eaten like a piece of bread by an octopus of ants. One of the advisers who had saved his life, for better or worse, was a Puerto Rican named Sam Ramos, a soldier in the rear guard.

38

SAM RAMOS read this declaration of principles before the court that had to pass judgment on the events of that Saturday in June:

Let him who is not afraid to cast the first stone cast it! Fear is not an emotion that should embarrass anyone, and the man telling you this is a soldier who has fought in five wars, and if he is still alive it is because he was scared to death in all of them. Blaise Pascal's legs would cramp when he had to cross a public square, and the only thing his disciples could do was hold him up by the elbows, with a certain degree of furtiveness: from a distance, his biographers say, the French philosopher seemed to be flying two inches off the ground. Queen Elizabeth I of England could not bear the presence of a rose, not because of the thorns but because of the texture of the petals, which, for Her Majesty, was identical to the skin of a cockroach. Sigmund Freud, usually so composed, almost burst into tears when he had to board an airplane. The fair-minded, strong-willed, and demanding Captain Paul Sanders cannot deny that he is terrified of spiders. Several times in enemy air raids I have seen him stop in the middle of the stairway that leads down to a bomb shelter because on a lower step there was, is, used to be a spider; his subordinates would go down first, in rapid single file, and he would give each of us a little pat on the shoulder, which earned him a reputation for courtesy and the prestige of being a brave man. But let there be no misunderstandings: as far as spiders are concerned, Paul is a coward. Since the events in question took place, Wellington Perales has not gone spearfishing again due to a phobia regarding harpoons. Tigran Androsian is afraid of chickens. In his restaurant, the Mensheviks, he has forbidden all recipes that use chicken meat. When my son Mandy wants to upset Tigran, he shows him a wind-up rooster that he bought in a toy store. The Armenian defends himself with a rubber snake: Mandy becomes paralyzed when he sees a snake. Theo Uzcanga, in my presence, told the pregnant Agnes MacLarty that on the day she gave birth he would not be with her in the delivery room even if he were drunk because the surgical instruments of gynecologists, forceps in particular, cause him intolerable physical panic: he says that as a boy he was bitten by a scorpion and has never gotten over his fright. Agnes understood immediately: she is afraid of mirrors. It is not a trivial matter. My commander Owen Gilligan Jr., a five-star general and the hero of a thousand battles, lost his composure when it was time to have his passport photo taken; he would, however, agree to a group portrait, with members of the General Staff or his aides, and then have his face cut out of the picture to complete the document. This is how he explained his terror: head on, with the camera sights ten feet away, he saw himself in front of a firing squad; in profile, believe it or not, in profile he simply felt betrayed. In one of the many photographs he had taken, and which I keep as a memento, my face appears six heads to the left of the empty rectangle where his head had been. Zack, the white Haitian, is capable of throwing himself off a cliff if Madame Duhamel threatens him with a meat grinder. Gregory Papa Gory is afraid of bats. Don Claudio Fontanet, of dogs. Gigi Col, of thunder. And, to keep matters close to home, I myself become agitated, break into a sweat, lose my voice, and am very distressed if I discover that someone (whoever and wherever he may be) is wearing a hairpiece instead of a nice hat. If the valiant Captain Paul Sanders is willing to have a bomb blow his ass off to avoid a spider; if a hero like General Owen Gilligan Jr. feels stabbed in the back when his picture is taken, why not acknowledge that a poor madman would try to hang himself from a rope at the sudden appearance of a tiger, a yellow tiger, a tiger with swan wings, an impossible tiger from Bengal? Why? Professor Theo Uzcanga already said why: because not even God can understand this miserable life. Who will cast the first stone? Who? Who is not afraid to be the first? I, Sam Ramos, will not.

In the same document, as a kind of appendix, he attached a copy of his letter of resignation.

The only thing that Sam Ramos has not been able to understand is why he felt so much affection for Beto Milanés if the Cuban represented the enemy and Ramos was a soldier, a hard man not easily moved: just ask his son. He also has not found a good reason that would explain why the opposite also happened: in a few months Ramos had erased Milanés completely from his mind, like a telephone number you memorize, convinced you'll be able to remember it, and when you finally dial it you learn the number doesn't exist, has never existed in the city, or that you've called the wrong person, and then one day, you don't know how, why, or when, the number flashes, clear, exact, dazzling, on the screen of your eyelids, but by now it's too late and the man or woman, your friend, has left the country or gotten married or died, and you hear someone say I'm sorry, sir, I don't know that party, I don't know what you're talking about, if you like I'll put you on hold and maybe they can transfer you. Transfer what?

In the camp near Ibondá de Akú, General Owen Gilligan Jr. called Ramos to his office to give him two orders: the first, that Ramos be in a photograph with him and other command officers because he needed a visa to travel to Moscow, where the outcome of the war would be decided; the other, that he stay with the Cuban, morning, noon, and night, two missions that could be thought of as indicating high esteem, especially the second, because the Puerto Rican had always been a behind-the-lines soldier and this case seemed more appropriate to the brainy types in the intelligence section. Ramos thought about a possible promotion. He assumed that his appointment, in quotation marks, was due to his Caribbean origins and not to his unimpressive record as a perpetual sergeant with no medals. And so he became interpreter, nurse, confidant, godfather, biographer, bodyguard, and frightener of tigers for a prisoner of war named Alberto Milanés who claimed to be Lázaro Samá, a lieutenant in a duly constituted army, that is, an officer of higher rank to whom Ramos owed a certain deference, which was the height of absurdity. Sometimes, not always, Beto demanded that Sam Ramos salute him, and to his surprise Ramos found himself standing at attention before his own prisoner, who took a century to inspect his uniform until he found a speck of dust on his epaulettes. "Comrade Ramos, your demeanor and appearance are lamentable. I'm canceling your weekend pass. This court-martial orders you to clean the latrines." And Ramos would end up cleaning toilets at the speed of lightning so as not to be caught by General Gilligan, who had an extremely limited sense of humor. He did not ask to be relieved of guard duty because the Cuban amused him: he was a likable madman. Beto did a terrific imitation of the character played by Toshiro Mifune in the *The Seven Samurai*, one of his favorite films. Ramos cannot pinpoint exactly when he began to feel affection for Beto. It might have been very simple. He had not seen his little Nelson for ten months. Perhaps that explains the fatherly feelings elicited by the drama of this Cuban. That, and a notebook.

In Ibondá de Akú Beto Milanés had kept a diary that took up some twenty pages, written in a tiny hand with rounded capitals and no spelling mistakes. The rest of the pages were filled with telephone numbers, ciphers, drawings of felines (heads of cats, perhaps leopards), and an occasional odd phrase in the margins. Ramos read the notebook from cover to cover. One entry awakened his curiosity. Between two ridiculous, badly drawn hearts, the Cuban had written this sentence: "Not loving anyone is an immoral act." He would never forget it. From a military point of view, there was nothing of interest to discuss with the specialists from the intelligence section, and so Ramos decided to keep the notebook and return it to Beto as soon as the situation was clarified.

Sam Ramos devoted himself full-time to the care of the frightened boy whose lost-dog expression was not easy to contemplate. The two of them were admitted to the regimental hospital: Beto as a patient and Ramos as his attendant. The doctors who studied his case reached a somber conclusion: Alberto Milanés was incurably mad. Regimental doctors tend to be very fatalistic, and Ramos suggested to General Gilligan that the patient be transferred to Portugal, as organizations for international amnesty were requesting, with all the rights and privileges granted to a prisoner of war by the statutes of the United Nations. The general agreed. The prisoner was of little value to them. The Red Cross psychologist who treated him in a Lisbon asylum made a more hopeful but equally erroneous judgment: "The medication has begun to have the desired effect. We cannot cure his madness but at least we can erase fear from his mind. We can discharge him." It was not true, the tiger was alive and Ramos knew it, but he wanted to get back to Los Angeles as soon as he could to see Raquel and the boy, and so he discussed the matter with his "superior," the false Lieutenant Lázaro Samá. It was a difficult conversation. Beto had decided not to return to Cuba for fear of reprisals. He was afraid. He was convinced they would consider him a traitor. The case had already achieved a certain degree of notoriety because the war correspondents who found him in the jungle had published reports, stories, and false interviews everywhere, even in cookbooks. The intervention of Cuban exile organizations brought Beto to New York, and Ramos went with him, acting now as his private secretary. From New York they flew to Miami, from Miami to Santa Fe, and from Santa Fe, on the recommendation of a veterans' group, to the resort community of Caracol Beach. After some negotiation Ramos arranged for the white Haitians to give him a job and room and board in the restaurant on the beach. On the day the Cuban carried his first red snapper in garlic to his table, Ramos tried to return the notebook. He thought he would be happy to have it back. Beto threw the tray with the remains of Ramos's lunch (the plates hit a nearby table) and let out a terrifying scream, as if he had seen a Bengal tiger:

"Burn that."

"It's your notebook. Your memories."

"I want to forget, not remember."

"Don't be so hard on yourself."

"I'll be however I want."

"It's a part of your life."

"A part of my life!"

"All right. You know best. I'll keep it. Maybe you'll change your mind."

When they said goodbye in the cubicle at the back of the storeroom, Ramos had the impression that Beto was about to suffer another attack. He was trembling from head to toe as he stood at the door, blocking his way. It was midnight and a cold front had just hit Caracol Beach. The sea roared in the distance. Its fury swelled with each wave. A blast of wind hissed through a broken blind in the room. Beto covered the hole with a piece of cardboard.

"Don't go."

"Raquel and my son are waiting for me in Los Angeles."

"Can't you see I'm scared?"

"Rest now," said Ramos. "Tomorrow's another day."

"Stay and live here."

"I've thought about it."

"I'll make a place for you in this room. The place looks like Cuba . . . probably like Puerto Rico too."

"I'll talk it over with Raquel."

"Promise?"

"I promise. Maybe I'll move here one day."

"You'll come see me?" He did not wait for an answer. "The problem is you probably won't find me."

"Leave word for me with the Haitians."

"Know what? I want to die."

"There's time for everything in this world."

"Did you see the tiger? It's a lie that it doesn't exist. Of course it exists if I saw it. Out there."

"There are no tigers in Caracol Beach, lieutenant. I can assure you of that."

"It's coming for me. I've decided to kill myself."

"Rest now."

"God, what a wind!"

Two blasts of frantic air attacked the blind. The cardboard could not resist the sudden assault. Sam and Beto were at the mercy of the weather.

"Want some advice, lieutenant? Never make decisions at night. Things look different when the sun comes up."

"But I'm scared."

"Fear is a straitjacket."

"Fear may be a straitjacket, but what should I do?"

"Write your mother a letter. She must think you're dead."

"She's better off."

"Don't say that. You're absolutely wrong. She would love to hear from you."

"How do you know?"

"Because I'm a father," said Sam, and he turned his back on the boy and went out into the storm. The wind spat grains of sand in his face. He walked faster. He heard Beto yelling from the storeroom: "Don't go, you bastard! You miserable son of a bitch!" It was the voice of an outcast. Ramos sank as he walked. The sand was too soft, like half-cooked rice. He stumbled. He was fleeing, but his legs did not respond to the commands of his nerves. Stick legs. The waves crashed into the reefs and reached his feet in a confused swirl. Seashells. A final shout carried the name of Caterina the Great. Ramos was already far away. He was fleeing. He always fled. He slipped and fell on the sand. He did nothing to get up. A gull flew into the night, into the storm, and did not move an inch in the wind. Crabs, hundreds of crabs along the beach. Ramos thought about Raquel and his son Nelson waiting for him at home. A home he barely knew. He recalled the few pleasant moments in his life. He felt like a traitor but at the same time liberated by his betrayal. He had just freed himself of the deadweight of a madman. He swore he would forget him. And he did, at least for seventeen years. Ramos cut through the palm groves and reached the shore road. He stopped a taxi. He went back to Santa Fe. And from there to Los Angeles, on a regularly scheduled American Airlines flight.

39

SAM RAMOS did not see Beto for seventeen years, but he never lost the notebook. Some objects are stubborn. Raquel cannot get rid of an autograph album she filled when she was a mathematics student. It shows up in the most unlikely places. If she throws it in the trash, the album gets out of the basket and arranges for Ramos to kick it under a piece of furniture. It spends a few months there; then one day the Salvadoran woman who cleans for them finds it, assumes it is important, and puts it in a kitchen drawer that it will jump out of like a toy mouse. Sometimes Raquel asks: "I wonder where my album is?" And Ramos answers: "Don't worry. It'll turn up." Beto's notebook spent thirteen years in the pocket of an army jacket that Ramos had tossed into a trunk of souvenirs. He was going to give the jacket to Nelson, and the notebook fell out.

In the summer of 1990, Ramos received a letter from Beto. He still has it.

Sam: I hope this finds you and yours in good health. Caracol Beach is a nice place to live. You and I are men of the

Caribbean. Do you remember? Cuba and Puerto Rico are the two wings of a single bird. The sea is in our blood. Don't ever doubt it. Pack up your things and come out here, with your wife and your son, who must be a grown man by now. A quiet beach. In summer the days are brilliant; the winter is mild. There's a bowling alley. Zack and his family have opened a bar. What else. Come and I'll tell you: I became a saint. It was written. In Santa Fe there are a lot of Cuban *santeros*. I've taken the vow. I'm a child of Yemayá. Now she is in my head. I'm her chosen one, her *elegún*. She possesses me. She mounts me. Yemayá, messenger of Olokun, receives offerings in the company of the dead: she is very slow to respond to her worshipers. I'm writing to persuade you and to tell you that you're to blame for what's happened to me. Why didn't you let me die in the jungle? I'm sure you're thought of as a hero. Your son must be happy to have a father like you. I can imagine him telling the story about how you saved a Cuban who was wandering in the jungle. What a nice story. What a nice daddy. Does what I'm saying bother you? I didn't have a father, good or bad. Who asked you to stick your nose in my business? It's your fault my life is such shit. The tiger is looking for me. Only I know it's true. My being paranoid doesn't mean they're not after me. I'm surrounded. It's crazy. Crazy. Just my luck. God almighty. I need help. You say you like me, you said it, so why don't you come to Caracol Beach and give back what you once took from me: my death. Come. Nothing to it. I'll leave a trail of shit for you to follow. You'll find me at the Haitians' bar. Watch for any carelessness on my part and shoot me. Cowards die quickly. Cowards flee. When we flee we turn our backs. The tiger will carry me off. He's coming for me. He'll bite the back of my neck and drag me down to hell. Nothing to it. Child's play. Speaking of children. Bring your son. Great idea. I hit a home run. Bring your son. The boy will witness a wonderful scene.

Like in the movies. I'll fall on the sand. In slow motion. Background music. A harmonica. The sand will gradually turn red with blood. Don't turn my body over. Leave me like that. With my arms outstretched. A fistful of sand in my right hand. The fingers of my left hand spread open in a fan. Fabulous. Bring your son. I'll try to die with my eyes closed. Applaud, OK? Let the boy take a photograph beside my corpse, like hunters in the jungle who have their pictures taken with one foot on the side of the beast, in a triumphant pose. This world makes me sick. I spit on this letter. I spit in your face. My gums are still bleeding. They're rotting. Rotting. God almighty. The tiger will find me through the smell of my blood. Kill me. It's only fair. You pride yourself on being fair. I'm sure you are. What the hell. I remember you took care of me with affection. I was your prisoner of war. I still am. And will continue to be. I challenge you. Accept the challenge. Don't abandon me. I dream about being your final battle. Here I am. On my knees. For God's sake, am I asking very much? Don't fuck around. I'm worth a fortune. I've tattooed the names of my seven dead on my left arm. Zack did the work. Good work. If you kill me Zack could etch my name on your skin so you won't forget me. It would look nice. God almighty. Best regards, L.S.

In the envelope was a photograph of Beto standing on a hill of wrecked cars. Ramos burned the photograph. But he kept the letter.

Shortly before submitting his resignation to Captain Paul Sanders, Sam Ramos decided to write the memoirs of his six wars, starting with the last one, the battle in the auto salvage yard. He went to see Theo Uzcanga for advice. He visited him in his top-floor studio. As he climbed the stairs he wondered how he would be received but his fears floated away like soap bubbles in the face of Agnes's cordiality when she invited him to have some buttered toast. Her pregnancy had given rise to a series of whims that Theo went out of his way to satisfy: he stopped smoking because the smell of the ashtrays bothered her, he painted the house blue though he preferred white walls, and he became a specialist in the preparation of buttered toast. Agnes looked wonderful with her new, round-as-a-tambourine face. She sat in a comfortable chair, adjusted the globe of her belly over her thighs, and asked for more and more toast.

Theo advised that in order to thoroughly understand the tragedy of Beto Milanés and the students from the Emerson Institute, Ramos should talk to the witnesses, though he warned him about the difficulty of obtaining accurate testimony, for the simple reason that two of the protagonists were no longer of this world, and the only image that remains of the dead is the one kept by the living, "which is not always a guarantee." Ramos followed Theo's advice to the letter. He talked with everyone involved except Gigi Col, who returned to Mexico and sent her statement by fax. Laura Fontanet saw him in Los Angeles. At first the girl refused to confide in Ramos. She had her reasons. She did not trust him. "The police are not very likable," the constable would acknowledge. Laura told him something about the party at Martin's house and Tom's somersaults off the diving board, but the sergeant could not clarify much about the hours she spent with Beto in the trailer except for a few circumstantial facts regarding Strike Two. They met again in March 1995, during Wellington Perales's trial. Laura was present on the day Ramos had to make his statement in court. Two hours later, as he was walking down the courthouse steps, don Claudio Fontanet came up to him and said his daughter wanted to speak with him again. "She needs to get it off her chest," he said. Sam Ramos had supper with the Fontanets. When it was almost midnight, Emily and Claudio left Laura and Ramos alone in the study to talk.

"Do you believe in ghosts?" said Laura.

"Of course," said Ramos.

"Last night I saw the tiger. I mean, I dreamed about it."

"Interesting."

"Interesting? You think it's interesting? What a ridiculous word!"

"I dreamed about the tiger too. Many years ago."

"Is it true you found Beto in the jungle?" Without waiting for an answer she declared: "Applaud, OK?"

Laura offered him a drink. He accepted.

"What was Beto like?"

"A madman. A poor madman."

"Do you think you're very sane? Martin and Tom appear to me all the time. Martin comes for his glasses. Tom never talks."

"It makes me sad. . . ."

"I can't stand pity."

"Being sad isn't a synonym for feeling pity."

"Why wasn't I killed?" Laura asked.

Ramos swallowed an ice cube. "Paul Sanders has an explanation. He thinks that none of his men dared to fire at a girl. I think that attitude also saved my son."

"Your son? Oh, right. The transvestite."

"He was wearing a skirt. A leather skirt."

"I remember. Your son is an angel, constable."

"You're very kind. I'm not a constable anymore. I resigned."

"I escaped because your son intervened. What was he doing there? They almost killed him. Thanks to him I'm here talking to you. More rum?"

"All right. More rum."

"Why did you resign, if you don't mind my asking?"

"Because I'm tired."

"So am I."

"You're very young."

"Captain Sanders's theory doesn't convince me."

"It convinces me."

"Maybe. Nobody knows anything. Another question. Why do you think Martin smiled when he died?"

"I assume it was involuntary. He was nearsighted. He had lost his glasses at the liquor store, and he had just turned eighteen. Like you, Laura."

"No, not me: I'm a hundred years old," Laura said.

40

SAM RAMOS does not blame himself for the death of Caterina the
Great. God must know why the hell He does what He does. In
the spring of 1995 he sent a letter by certified messenger telling
her what had happened in the auto salvage yard, omitting the
most gruesome details, and in the envelope he included the notebook Beto had written in Ibondá de Akú in order to tell his
mother he finally had forgiven her. Sam thought it was the right
thing to do. He talked it over with Raquel and she agreed. Caterina was the one for whom all those pages were intended. Among
the documents found by the constable when he inspected the
Five Star Circus trailer was a pocket diary with the address of
Rafaela Sánchez in Cienfuegos. Caterina's comadre says that on
the day the package arrived she almost went crazy. Rafaela had
received only a couple of postcards in the past fifteen years, and
so when she heard the mailman's whistle she supposed it was a
mistake—fairly frequent because of the inadequacies of the mail
service—and left the pea soup she had promised Caterina cooking on the stove. For them the world consisted of two houses at
the top of a hill. Rafaela's first reaction when she read Ramos's

letter may show how deeply she was disturbed: she went up to the roof and opened the doors of the cages, telling the pigeons to fly away. She sat down on a wooden crate under the television antenna. A snow of bird feathers fell on her shoulders. She crumpled the letter in her hand and thought the best thing would be to hide the bad news from Caterina, who had gradually grown accustomed to solitude. But then Rafaela looked toward the courtyard next door and saw her dressed in the flowered housecoat that was covered with countless perspiration stains. Caterina was repairing the mesh of the chicken coop. She looked skinnier than her own skeleton, as if she were made of wire. Each time she swung the hammer she lost her balance and leaned against the stakes in the fence to keep her bones from falling apart. The attempt at carpentry was too much for her. Only someone who knew Caterina well would know that the task of hitting nails into the fence was a desperate effort to use her time in something less painful than spending the whole day cursing her fate. The flock of chickens had decreased, soup by soup, until it was reduced to its minimal expression: a scruffy old hen to which Caterina liked to compare herself during the rare moments of humor she occasionally permitted herself: "You're even uglier than me," she would say. The wind was blowing from the ocean, and the odor of goat droppings diluted the stink of the pea soup that Rafaela had forgotten to take off the burner. "Oh, dear God, tell me what to do, give me a sign," she said.

In Cuba time is measured by the rain. "A lot of rain had fallen," people say when they want to move any story into the past. Since the false report of Beto's disappearance in Ibondá de Akú, many rainstorms ago, Caterina had been balancing on the edge of the fragile barrier that separates sanity from dementia. Hardly any visitors came to her house, which she kept as tightly closed as a box of presents, and she never went down to the city because, she said, she hadn't lost anything in Cienfuegos. This explanation hit the nail on the head: the only thing she had accumulated in life was the memory of everything she had lost. Rafaela had concluded that Caterina's almost otherworldly suspension over reality had the advantage of keeping her afloat and, by the same token, might permit her to reach the end of the wall without having to walk, old and alone, the tightrope of madness. Rafaela knew that if she kept the news from Caterina that afternoon, she would never be able to look her in the eye without feeling shame. They both depended on loyalty in order to live.

"Hey, listen, you crazy old fool, hey, you're burning the beans," Caterina shouted at her from the courtyard.

At eight-thirty they sat down to supper, as Rafaela recalls. After dessert, Rafaela swallowed hard and began to read the letter. When she reached the paragraph in which Sam Ramos refers to the death of Beto in Caracol Beach, her throat closed up.

"Something didn't agree with me," said Rafaela, and she went out to smoke a cigarette. Under the night sky. With the crickets.

Caterina read Beto's notebook without stopping or displaying any emotion. Rafaela spied on her through the living-room window, her cigarette hidden in her cupped hand so as not to attract attention. The Great finished reading in silence. She made no comment. She sat on the living room sofa, in front of the television set, and watched a late movie for a while. An Italian film. A love story. A love story with a happy ending. "Volare, oh, oh. . . . Cantare, oh, oh, oh, oh . . . ," she hummed. That's all she did. Shit, am I hearing right?, Rafaela said to herself. She left her hiding place, went into the living room, and confronted her friend: "What the hell's wrong with you? Are you crazy or what?"

"I'm sleepy."

"Go to sleep. If you're sleepy, go to sleep."

Caterina fell asleep on the throne of the sofa. Rafaela moved the fan closer to her. It was unbearably hot. She kept watch for a few hours. At five in the morning, Caterina woke to the sound of static. She turned off the television. Rafaela was in a chair, exhausted.

"Don't be angry, Fela, but I'm going," said Caterina.

"Where, comadre?"

"Home."

"How are you feeling? If you want to talk, we'll talk. . . ."

"Later."

"Later never comes."

"This Beto of mine is a tough customer."

A tough customer. The old hen grew tired of waiting, pecked open the mesh of the chicken coop, and came in the window, shitting on the sill and the furniture. It found nothing to eat on the dining-room table, where Caterina had left Rafaela an affectionate note ("You old fool, I'm going out for a little fresh air. Don't worry if I come back late. The movie last night was nice."), or in the bed of her Soviet lovemaking, which was neatly made with a patchwork cover. Hours later, Rafaela found the chicken in the bathroom, lying on the flowered housedress, deader than a stone on a stony road. This was the sign that God had sent her: the sign of farewell.

"God almighty!" she exclaimed.

Caterina had found the well in her recurring nightmare, the one, many rainstorms ago, that had announced the end of her life: the void. Rafaela searched the neighborhood from one end to the other. She asked in the corner market, livelier than usual that morning because the keg of beer had arrived. A neighbor had passed Caterina on the highway: "I was surprised she didn't return my greeting. I said hello and she kept walking. She's not all there, I thought, and with good reason, right?" Rafaela spent the entire day asking questions, without losing hope. At Coppelia's they told her that a woman answering Caterina's description had been there that morning, how could they forget. Witnesses to the scene say she occupied a table on the terrace, right next to the street. She asked for a glass of water. She talked to herself. Suddenly she raised her dress in an extremely vulgar gesture and showed the other patrons a pubis that was gray, dry, and shriveled, like the sex of a mummy, while she brazenly shouted a string of filthy words and curses; after a few minutes she left, still yelling, walking through the curious crowd that had gathered at the ice cream shop to watch the show. The porter at the baseball stadium saw Caterina in the stands, attentively watching the practice of a children's team. "I was glad to hear about Beto after so many years," the porter admitted. "But I tell you, Felita: they ought to put your comadre in a straitjacket and lock her away in Mazorra for a while." They were talking about the boy when out of the blue Caterina began to hit herself on the forehead with her fists, as if she wanted to drive the devil out of her head. The porter went for help. When he came back, she had disappeared. "Poor woman," he declared. To make matters worse, the witnesses' accounts were contradictory. Caterina had been in many different places at the same time. We know that at noon she was walking around the outside of the cement factory, crying, they say, but at twelve o'clock she made a stop at the bus terminal and asked an acquaintance of Rafaela's for the coins she needed to buy a ticket to Havana. Three hours later she was sleeping on a bench in the Prado, according to some, "taking up the whole bench, her legs spread open like guava branches," and at exactly three in the afternoon, others testified, she was making a scene in the lobby of the Hotel Jagua, where the police detained her on the complaint of two tourists from Madrid who could not endure the sight of that grotesque woman who said she was the hottest whore in Cienfuegos and insisted on selling them her services for ten cans of potted meat. These were the stations of her cross: the backdrops for a dead son. Rafaela refused to believe so much nonsense. She was not prepared to accept the fact that her friend had lost her way in the labyrinth of insanity. Each new piece of information weakened her joints until her hands became swollen: the fluid running through the veins of her body now was so cold it burned—pure liquefied fear. Rafaela decided to go back before nightfall. She had forgotten to lock her pigeons in their cages. Had she left the radio on? She would lose her ration of beer. The keg came to the neighborhood market every three or four months. She traded beer for cigarettes with a neighbor. She wanted to smoke. The heel of her shoe had broken. Her stomach was so empty it pressed against her spine. Hunger hurts. With so many things on her mind, the walk home seemed endless. Poor woman.

"What a mess," she said.

Rafaela saw Caterina in the last place she expected to find her: at the edge of the bay, at the bottom of her barren garden. She almost didn't recognize her. Her comadre had walked about thirty feet into the sea. The water came to the middle of her chest. When a wave passed, she disappeared for a few seconds. Rafaela persuaded her to return to land and walked with her to her house. She wanted to ask about the events of that chaotic day, but Caterina's mind was blank. She didn't remember visiting the ice cream shop, let alone the baseball stadium or the bus terminal. "What would I do in Havana, comadre?" After she gave up whoring she had stopped walking past the cement factory to avoid running into her Russian lovers. The Hotel Jagua? She had gone there only once to celebrate Beto's success when he defeated the great Agustín Marquetti. She had spent the whole blessed day fixing the mesh in the chicken coop.

"And what about that pea soup? Didn't you invite me to supper?" said the Great in order to get out of a difficult situation.

"Dry your head."

"I'm cold. Is it cold, comadre?"

"Yes, comadre, it's freezing."

"It rained, didn't it?"

"Just look at you. Damn, you're a sorry sight."

"No, yes, sure, that's why I'm soaked. Oh, Felita! This boy is a tough customer."

A tough customer. Rafaela heated the pea soup. After supper she invited her friend to spend the night with her. In reply, Caterina confided in Rafaela for the last time: she told her who Beto's father was, but revealing his name now makes no sense, not even in this novel. The Great was calm. Serene. She had managed to climb out of the well. Out of the corner of her eye, Rafaela saw Beto's notebook on the table, surrounded by a circle of burning candles. Felita's feet hurt. And her knees. Elbows. Chest. Skeleton. Life. She closed her eyes. A song assailed her from the back of her mind: "Volare, oh, oh. Cantare, oh, oh, oh, oh." And she heard these words again: "What the hell's wrong with you? Are you crazy or what? I'm sleepy. Go to sleep. If you're sleepy, go to sleep." And she fell asleep.

When she was alone, Caterina the Great, the grand lady of the port of Cienfuegos, and a native of Sagua la Grande, began to cry and did not stop for twelve hours. We know she spent the entire night locked in her room, drinking mint liqueur from the bottle and not letting anyone in this time except the devil, who knows how to pass through walls like music. "Zun zun zun, zun zundambayé, pretty bird at the break of day," the neighbors heard her singing. The notebook floated in a bog of wax. She was still shedding dead tears when her comadre Rafaela kicked down the door and found her dangling from a rope, like a rag on a clothesline, four hours after she had hung herself.

41

SOLDIER'S NOTEBOOK. The wood in this pencil smells just like the kitchen in my house. Tomorrow I burn this book. The war cut out our tongues. God almighty. What happened, happened. You can't turn back the pages. Strike one, strike two, strike three. I have to think about something else. Imagine I'm in Cienfuegos watching the ships go by. Merchant ships from Russia. Oilers. Greek freighters. Sailboats. Barges. A lot of barges. I can't. I have to make plans. Lots of plans. I won't go back to Havana. What the hell. I need a corner. A nice little corner to hide in. Nobody cares what happens to me. Nobody. What happens to me! A pain in the balls. I feel like I'm at the bottom of a well. I'd better go home. That's it. Home. Nothing to it. Mama's waiting for me. Mama loves me. Mama suckles me. Mama. Forgive me, mama. Forgive me. Know what? I want to get out of the well. Climb the walls. Up there I see a circle of light. It attracts me the way it attracts flies. Flies, flies, blowflies. I move toward that light. I climb. One foot after the other. I dig my nails into the earth. Awful things are slithering along the shaft of the well. I'm falling. I'm falling. I fell. My friends toss my body back and forth in the dark. They live in the hole too. They move around in the dark. Like worms in the dirt. What am I doing here? Virgin of Regla have mercy on me! I'm a failure. Poundcake claims the human race is full of failures because you can count the winners on the fingers of a centipede. My mind is wandering. I have to concentrate. Focus. I light a match. My friends look at me. Look in my eyes. They don't say anything. My friends are scared. The match goes out. It burns me. So much fear in one place makes you brave. My friends are really good people. Do they know I'm thinking about running away, escaping? I'd love to escape. Flee. But how? The well's too deep. Blind. Run away, but where? To the end of the earth. To the devil. To hell. Think, you moron: I'm thinking. Let them accuse me of being a traitor. Let them say whatever they want. That I'm a coward. A deserter. A traitor, a turncoat. If I go not even the *san-teros* will find me, but if I escape I'll never be able to go back to Cuba; if they catch me on the run, I'll spend the rest of my youth in jail. Why do we have to be brave? I'll dig a grave and fall in. I'll disappear. That'll be the end of it. When the dog dies the rabies is cured. I'm not even brave enough to run away. Worst of all, I heard the leopard. Fernandito spitting from his hammock. Fernandito says it's a tiger. From Bengal. Out there. I'm going to die in Ibondá de Akú! Oh, mama. My sweet mama. Virgin of Regla! I don't even know how to pray. The animal was circling the camp. I didn't see it but I heard the twigs snapping out there. Holy God! Light and Progress for you. Light and Progress for you. Light and Progress for you. The tiger? The one in the movies? The one in the zoo on 26th? My scar's itching. It's nerves. It has to be nerves. Maybe a bomb will blow me up like Lázaro's son, may he rest in peace. The hand never turned up. Dead and missing a hand. My gums are a mess. A mess. I keep dribbling blood. Ibondá de Akú is covered with blowflies. Like a garbage dump. I'm the garbage. Ships. I have to think about the ships. I close my eyes. All I get is rain on my head. Shit, Fernandito, stop the damn spitting. You spit too, Fernandito tells me. Spitting helps. I fill my mouth with spit. Ready, aim, fire. The two of us start spitting, each from his own hammock. Knocking down blowflies with our spit. I spit. I spit. I spit until I'm dried out. Ready, aim, fire! One of Fernandito's mortar shells hits me right on the forehead.

42

THE BOYS scaled the heights of the car cemetery half an hour before sunrise. Martin saw the light of dawn over the rows of cars, and faced with the imminent battle told Tom he was going home because he couldn't stand it another minute. He had reached the limit of his resistance. Reality was erased like a blackboard in school. That garbage dump filled with metal fossils became a nonexistent place to him. He could feel in his own flesh the cold of an alien daybreak and he let himself be defeated: he was only eighteen, Sunday was dawning, second by second, and his parents were expecting him for a family dinner of leg of lamb. Everything else was hell. Tom, on the other hand, found Martin's presence indispensable to his being brave. His terror was identical to his friend's, but he could not permit himself the luxury of being a coward that night. Every good basketball star needs to feel the company of other offensive players on the court. Every winner needs a loser.

"Don't go."

"I'm sorry."

"Think about Laura. You asked us to go with you to get beer. Remember?"

"There was no beer, Tom."

"We were leaving your house."

"The party was nice, wasn't it? We only needed something to drink. How could I know what would happen?"

"You heard your father's message on the answering machine. . . ."

"Go to hell."

"Laura and I could be making love now."

"I can't see. I can't see anything without my glasses."

"Shit."

"I'm really scared, Tom."

"It's almost sunrise. Time's up."

"You broke my glasses. I was going to get out of the car. You stepped on the gas. You think you're so great? My parents are expecting me for dinner."

"The madman's there."

"Where?"

"There."

"I don't know. I can't see."

"I hear him laughing."

"The family gets together on Sunday. It's Sunday, isn't it . . . ?"

"He's laughing. . . ."

"I'm a coward."

"He's laughing at us."

"What do I care, Tom? You can think whatever you want."

"Don't go."

"I'm going."

"The sun's almost up."

"It's late. Very late. I'm going. I'm going. I'm gone."

When Martin turned and began his retreat, Tom suddenly tackled him and they both rolled down the slope of wrecked metal in the auto salvage yard. They fought hard and senselessly and with love. How can that terrible moment be described if neither of them lived to tell about it? With what right is the scene recreated if the boys were alone, absolutely alone under a moon that had dimmed in a few hours and barely illuminated the cars except for a faint gleam as eerie as it was inadequate? Would it be better to use this page to reflect on the indecency of wars, which do not end when the politicians sign their peace treaties but live on in the survivors, the victims of an arduous campaign that still goes on inside each one of them, between their guts and their hearts? And as Tom and Martin struggle among the cars, and embrace, push, weaken and go mad, would it be better to say at the top of one's voice that those truly responsible for the massacre do not appear in this novel because they first arranged to send others to the front lines, to the mindless battle of politics, so that others would be blown to pieces and they could say in public forums that the people fulfilled their glorious obligation to history? But does that make sense? What good would it do? Tom and Martin won't read this book: if the document exists, this fiction about facts, it is because they could not rely on the shield of letters, sentences, paragraphs, parapets of words. The only way to change destiny would be to lie, and not even a lie would save them: death, too, is a tyrant. How patiently she weaves the cloth and sews the winding sheet! Life is a totality of coincidences. And accidents. If Laura had not proposed dancing at Machu Picchu, where would her two friends be now? Anywhere at all except in their graves. If Martin had not smoked the joint, would he have had the courage to offer the house in Caracol Beach for the party? And if Wellington Perales had not asked Gigi Col and Langston Fischer to ride with him, would he have listened to the boys' story on the highway? Why did he fire into the air? And there is more: if the *santero* Lázaro Samá had not carried a torn bag of cement, would Beto have gone with him to the town of Regla? And if they had not emptied two bottles of *aguardiente*, would he have gone with him to Ibondá de Akú? Who knows. If Mrs. Dickinson had not called so often for so many absurd reasons, would Constable Ramos have responded in a timely way to her warning of danger? If Agnes had not spent time counting her wrinkles in the bathroom (just think how much she hates mirrors!), would she have gone with them to the store to buy beer? Why didn't Martin get in touch with his parents? A telephone call would have saved him. If Tom had not been offended by his friends' joke, would he have seen Beto's Oldsmobile at the crossroads? Why didn't Martin dare to use the wine and liquor in the cellar? It would have been so simple. If the cowboy with the Halloween pumpkin face had not parked his Ford in the only free space at the Bastille, would the Bengal tiger have continued the hunt? How patiently death weaves our winding sheet. Tom and Martin were certainly two innocents, a pair of desperate friends who fought hand-to-hand with the legitimate illusion that someone would come to separate them, to save them. What did they say to each other? Is any reader audacious enough to imagine it? In those anguished, eternal minutes, who will deny that Martin and Tom did not think of how imprudent it had been not to inform the police: they could be in a holding cell now, a miserable, damp little cell, wonderfully damp, and why not suppose that they also questioned the immaturity of confronting the madman under such inequitable circumstances when the possibilities of their survival were minimal. Perhaps the blows they exchanged alleviated their fear because they both needed to beat the terror out of their bodies. They insulted each other, they pummeled each other, they ripped each other's clothes in the fight, until, at the most unfair moment of the night and of this novel, when Martin was about to surrender, I give up, I give up, Tom lost his balance in a stupid maneuver and from a height of six feet fell onto a heap of scrap metal where a thin steel bar split his heart like a mandarin orange. He did not even have the consolation of a death scene, which, knowing Tom's temperament, would have allowed him to attempt a play and win applause, as in the many athletic contests he had resolved in his team's favor just as the referee was blowing the final whistle. End of story. He was nailed to the ground. Blood filled his mouth and choked his final words. He might have said something, even something stupid about real buzzards, but he was not authorized to say goodbye. He died in fifteen seconds of death rattles, not understanding what had happened: Martin was growing smaller; could Tom have thought that the person leaving was his classmate and not himself, the great champion of the Emerson Institute? The lights certainly faded without any switches, the world grew still in a silence so profound it deafened him, and the flame of life went out between God's fingers. OK was gone.

"What happened, Tom? Tell me, I can't see a thing!"

Tom was dead. Martin screamed at God that he had passed the wrong sentence. It couldn't be true. How. Tom. When. Why. Tom. The river of blood flowing out of his mouth left no room for doubt. Martin began to kick the flat tires of the cars, searching for an opening in the walls of the night that eventually wrapped him in the cloak of madness. He fractured the big toe on his right foot, according to the autopsy, and the pain in his broken bone made him fall down next to his friend. Tom's eyes were open. He was always curious. Seeing is believing, he used to say. The first sign that Martin had begun to lose his mind was the act of buttoning Tom's shirt to the neck; the second was lowering his left eyelid, automatically creating an expression of childish complicity that replaced the look of horror stamped on Tom's face by absurdity. "Nobody dies with one eye open and the other shut," reads the most frivolous sentence in the forensics report. Martin put the revolver in his waistband, picked up the spearfishing harpoons, and limped toward the only source of light in the auto salvage yard: a tin-plated trailer, outlined in blue, red, and yellow bulbs shining in the midst of cars as ragged as the tent of a traveling circus on a gala night. The soldier had said he would teach them to kill a man. Martin already knew how. It wasn't so difficult. The question now, now that cowardice had just given him a name to engrave in the pantheon of his arm, was who would pin a final decoration on his shirt: the medal of a bullet.

"Samá, Lieutenant Samá, you fucking son of a bitch!" Martin shouted from the hill of metal and he fired the first shot. "My glasses! Oh, no, my glasses!" Again he heard the bell in Mrs. Dickinson's store, and until he squeezed the trigger a second time and the small round window in the trailer shattered, his mind would not turn off the alarm that was calling for help—first and foremost, for himself. Then he heard a dog barking. Growling. He found him in the underbrush. A pup carrying a knife in his mouth. The dog dropped the knife. His tongue protruded. Panting. The dog. The silhouette of a dog. Martin kicked him in the ribs. The stabbing pain in his broken toe traveled all the way to his spine: "Tom, Bingo came back, Tom, Tom, what happened to my glasses!" Strike Two went back the way he had come.

43

IT DID NOT bother Ramos that Wellington Perales followed Captain Sanders around like his shadow, since that slight disloyalty left him just where he wanted to be, off the field, watching the game from the bench, an ideal place for devoting himself to the salutary project of doing absolutely nothing. Deep in his heart he was enjoying Mrs. Dickinson's distress. The idea of breaking into the store, he acknowledged, was much more daring than shitting on her porch. Between sobs, the unbearable Mrs. Dickinson was blaming the robbery on the young people who had turned the Lowells' house into a den of iniquity. Ramos walked away and sat down for a while in his patrol car, where Tigran the Terrible was about to die of boredom.

"Are you tired?" asked Tigran. "Tell Mandy, OK? That son of yours likes action movies. What did you find out?"

"I'm just paint on the wall."

"That makes two of us."

The constable did not want to know about the case. Paul could handle matters—really very simple for a strategist of his caliber. Wellington would learn that facing danger can be tedious, inglorious, even fairly contemptible, and he would be free to reestablish communications with his son, for whom the night was beginning to hold great appeal, just as the Terrible had foreseen.

"It's time to get out of here," said Ramos.

"What!" Mandy exclaimed. "I was starting to enjoy police work." Tigran the Terrible made a resigned face. "You have something up your sleeve, dad. I know you."

"It's a very strange night, son."

"I agree."

"You must be getting old, father-in-law," said Tigran.

For Captain Sanders, the burglars at the fishing-gear store had to be the same ones who had assaulted the liquor store on the highway. The clerk's description of the car was a perfect match to the red-painted Oldsmobile that had crashed into Mrs. Dickinson's store window, and in both cases the perpetrators' conduct had been identical: in the first, they threw the fruits of their crime all over the parking lot; in the second, with so many valuable items to choose from, they had taken only two spearfishing harpoons. The lion isn't as fierce as they say, Ramos thought, and he kept his conclusions to himself. One of the maxims that Captain Paul Sanders liked to repeat in the field was: "My subordinates talk when chickens piss." And there were no chickens urinating there, if you discount the fine-feathered Mrs. Dickinson who went on hatching insults until the last page of this novel.

"Two ordinary spearfishing harpoons. . . . I don't understand, captain. With all the expensive things to choose from in this store," said Wellington, who was well-versed in the subject.

"You think so?"

"I'm a diver."

"Search the vehicle," ordered Sanders.

On the visor of the Oldsmobile, Wellington Perales found an owner's registration indicating that the vehicle belonged to a citizen of Cuban origin, one Alberto Milanés. When Sam Ramos heard the name an alarm sounded in his head. "I'm going to die in Ibondá de Akú." The phrase lit up with the insistence of a neon sign. The jungle. The Bengal tiger. The madman. The anthill. The notebook. He checked the documents in the hope it was a coincidence, a fluke. Beto's eyes in the photograph erased any chance of error. He was no longer a young soldier, skinny and defenseless, but an adult with a bull's neck, though the scar was still badly sewn on his right cheek and his eyes still had the lost-dog expression that had disarmed Ramos with the leveling force of tenderness. He heard a voice: "I want to die." Resonances. Mandy went up to his father and put his hand on his shoulder, squeezing the joint hard. He knew who the Cuban was. Mandy took his father by the arm and walked him to the patrol car. The Terrible was still sitting in the backseat.

"I need some water," said Ramos.

"It's him, isn't it?"

"Who?"

"Alberto."

"Alberto! What are you two cooking up?" said Tigran.

"You told me a lot about him. The boy you rescued in the jungle. The madman with the tiger—it's him, isn't it?"

"I guess so, son," said Ramos. "They have the same name."

"What tiger? You want to adopt a tiger?" said the Armenian.

"What are you going to do, dad?'

"I don't know."

"Too easy."

"I swear I don't know."

"Let's go!"

"Where, son?"

"Home at last," said Tigran.

"Butt out, Tigran."

"Wait," said Ramos.

"I'll drive."

"Thanks, son," said Ramos.

Mandy pulled off the headband, hitched up his miniskirt, and got in behind the wheel. Ramos sat beside him. He was taking deep breaths. His lungs were full of fear. In an instant he relived his wars. Defeats. Pure defeats. Raquel. He needed Raquel Gould. As they were leaving, Captain Paul Sanders was calling Operations Center in Santa Fe to request background information on an individual named Alberto Milanés y Milanés. About a hundred yards past the store, Mandy pressed the gas pedal all the way to the floor. The acceleration pinned Tigran to the back of the seat.

"Men are divided into two groups: those who are near and those who are far away," said Mandy.

"How do you know that?" Ramos asked in anguish.

"I read Alberto's notebook too, years ago. Where are you, dad? Near or far away?"

Ramos clenched his fist with so much force that his nails pierced the palm of his hand like needles in a pincushion.

"We have a head start," he said.

"But where the hell are we going, damn it!" Mandy exclaimed. "These fucking tits are a pain in my ass!"

"To the auto salvage yard," said Ramos.

Mandy pulled off the false eyelashes.

"How do you know?"

"Ah, son, don't ask so many questions."

"If you only knew, dad. . . ."

The transvestite was transported mentally some ten years back, to the afternoon during Lent when he hid from his parents, read the notebook of that Cuban they were always talking about in his house, and experienced a paralyzing jealousy. He had just realized he would never be the good soldier planned for since the day of his birth: he liked men too much and had no doubt that his preference, viewed in those days as a defect, would earn him the contempt of the two people he loved most on earth, and who adored him in return—his parents. Ramos could sympathize with the delusions of a lunatic who found tigers on every street in New York, but he would not tolerate his heir's being homosexual, for that acceptance would oblige him to acknowledge his own defeat. "Nelson, you can learn from Beto," he would say. "Why aren't you more like him?" Beto. Always Beto. Beto Milanés. Beto the Perfect. Beto the Brave. Beto the Cuban. Mandy was tempted to burn the diary but he thought it would be better to set fire to himself in a blaze of manhood. If he did not commit suicide that afternoon it was because Raquel came up to the roof to hang out an entire army of military uniforms, and Mandy hid behind the fireplace vents. When his mother went back downstairs, the alcohol had evaporated in the winds of Lent blowing north to south with the strength of a storm. After that episode, Mandy began a game that fed his appetites. The hero of the notebook would be his secret lover, his imaginary man. Night after night he took him to bed and seduced him with slow caresses, violated him, possessed him and let himself be possessed under the sheets. No one can deny that in this way, man to man, he could share Beto with his clueless father. That Saturday, when he had proposed adopting a child, he had mentioned the name Alberto, and the Terrible suffered a fit of jealousy that he resolved with a handful of Armenian vilifications; before the pitched battle in the living room of their apartment, Mandy had lied and said his first homosexual relationship had been with an ardent Cuban whom his father had taken prisoner in the jungle of Ibondá de Akú, not knowing that just a few hours later he would have the opportunity to meet him. That was where he was heading, speeding over the asphalt road at ninety miles an hour. "Don't drive so fast, you'll get us all killed," said Ramos.

44

AT THE BOYS' WAKE don Claudio Fontanet would tell about a bad dream he'd had that night. On Sunday he woke earlier than usual and his shoes were where he never left them, at the foot of the bed, ready to start running, and the shirt he planned to wear to Mass hung on the door of the closet with its buttons undone (Emily had a mania for buttoning his shirts to the neck and covering them in plastic). Claudio could not bear to sleep wearing his watch, but when he washed his face that morning the watch was on his right wrist (he usually wore it on the left one) and the strap was not all the way through the buckle. He decided to check the house. On the dining-room shelves he found the photograph of Maruja on the beach, which Laura kept in her room; in the kitchen, the telephone book was open to the page that listed emergency numbers in Caracol Beach.

"There are a lot of crazy people out there."

"Don't worry if I don't come home to sleep."

"What I'm worried about is your driving too fast on the highway."

"Yes, daddy."

Don Claudio was recalling the conversation with his daughter when he found the pistol he always kept in the night table, unloaded, on the desk: it was loaded. He remembered the nightmare. He had dreamed about Maruja, which was unusual because his first wife had disappeared from his fantasies on the night he married Emily. Although the lawyer could not recollect all the details of the dream, he could not get the suspicion out of his mind that these alterations had to mean something. What?

"What?"

"That's what I say. What are you doing up so early?" Emily asked from the top of the stairs.

"What?"

"Why are you holding the pistol?"

"Throw on some clothes, Emily: we're going to Caracol Beach."

"But the sun isn't up yet, Catalán," said Emily.

A train whistled behind the baseball stadium. The sound of the locomotive arriving, or perhaps departing, mixed with the bells of an invisible church calling the faithful to six o'clock Mass. Agnes and Theo experienced that dawn ten miles from the auto salvage yard, and though the moon was the same one shining on Tom and Martin and Beto and Laura, for the teachers it had a different meaning. The city smelled like a village, the business street like a tilled garden, the air like water, the water like earth, the asphalt like cedar, Sunday like Thursday, the ocean like the countryside, the old like the new, and so much perfection took them by surprise.

At noon, the woman in the flowered apron who had hung the birdcage on her terrace rang the bell of her neighbor Agnes's apartment to tell her the news she had just heard on television: a half-crazed Cuban refugee and some students from the Emerson Institute of Santa Fe, after burglarizing liquor stores, smashing tourists' cars, attacking prostitutes, destroying local businesses, and killing pets, had been surrounded by members of the local police in the auto salvage yard at mile ten on the highway to Caracol Beach, according to a statement by officer Wellington Perales, who assured the press that the criminals had resisted the forces of law and order with firearms and harpoons for hunting sperm whales, and as a consequence they had found themselves obliged to open fire, although the officer in charge of the investigation, Constable Sam Ramos, refused to draw any premature conclusions.

"I said to myself I better tell Agnes, she probably doesn't know anything about it because she worked so late last night."

"No, no, no, no, no," said Agnes, slowly, with no variation in the timbre of her voice.

"Look. I wrote down the names of the victims for you."

When she saw the names of Tom and Martin, her knees buckled. No, no, no, no no. The walls, the furniture, her neighbor standing in the doorway, even the door itself began to melt, tilt, twist, violate the axis of verticality. The lady of the canaries turned as if she were spinning on a casino table, and Agnes fell in a puddle of urine. No. Yes: when her neighbor had begun her extremely detailed account of the news, Agnes tried to imagine how so many calamities could occur in so short a time, hoping to find some error in a report so suspiciously precise, exact, unappealable, and when the tragedy was confirmed the floodgates of her kidneys opened and the contents poured down her legs. Agnes went out and began to run. Run. Run. No, no, no, no, no. She ran through the parks where children were flying kites and as she passed she knocked over a food vendor's stand, and she ran along the gutters of avenues with no regard for the traffic on that first Sunday of vacation, she ran along the wide commercial streets filled with merchandise on display. And she kept telling herself she was having a nightmare, of course, a nightmare, because who would ever think of Martin, Tom, and Laura breaking into stores, killing pets, abusing defenseless old men. No. No. There was a mistake. Several mistakes. She kept running, with more enthusiasm now. She ran and ran and ran in circles around the rotunda that the mayor of Santa Fe had constructed in memory of the unknown soldiers killed in the nation's last five wars, and no matter how much she ran she did not get tired, no, she did not get tired no matter how fast she ran. In her flight to nowhere she ran past the Emerson Institute, where messengers from a prestigious florist were unloading dozens and dozens of wreaths of white roses, suitable for young people who were deceased. Why was she running? Why did she refuse to accept the facts? Why? Because if she had gone with them to the party at Martin's house, perhaps they would still be alive. She runs. Because she, Agnes, would have liked another chance to make love to Tom. Because she considers herself guilty. She opens her eyes. Because she was fond of them. Because she loved them. That's why.

Agnes did not stop. She ran through the middle of a school parade. A policeman tried to stop her but she wriggled out of his grasp like a fish in a fisherman's hands. She ran and ran, with no destination in mind. A crazy Cuban? she thought. A political refugee? Harpoons? An auto salvage yard? And those two red-headed girls eating ice cream on the corner. No. The buses were carrying legions of Japanese tourists. Yes. A father teaching his son to ride a bike. A bike with training wheels. Yes. That boy playing a saxophone in the park. The score on a music stand. The hat for contributions. No. A man reading the newspaper. No. An old woman consulting the lists of lottery numbers. The faces of models, successful men and women, smiling from billboards. Yes: it was Sunday. It is Sunday. The third Sunday in June. A transparent morning. They must be alive. Yes. Martin and Tom. Laura. What happened to Laura? Her name was not mentioned among the dead. Laura. Suddenly she found herself a hundred yards from the cemetery: the gate was opening slowly. A procession, then another procession, went through with their burdens of grief. A band. Another band. The march. The funeral march. Agnes ran faster, her spleen hurt, and then her legs began to fail and her knees weakened. As she ran up the stairs to Theo's top-floor studio, she thought she would never make it. Never. Up there. She knocked her forehead three times against the door.

"Theo, open up! Theo, Theo . . ."

When Theo opened the door, she was still banging her head. The teacher held an asthma inhaler: he dropped it to the floor in order to hold her.

"I know," he said in a strangled voice. The headmaster of the Emerson Institute had just called to tell him. Agnes clutched at the life raft of a friend.

"Give me a drink, Theo, a drink, a bottle of vodka, a pistol, anything to finish me off."

Theo would never forget what she said. That God must be out of His mind. That nothing was true, not even poetry. That Reinaldo Arenas had done the right thing when he blew his brains out. That politicians ought to stop putting up monuments in the park and decide once and for all to ban by decree the right to happiness, because that's what they want after all, because this life, Theo, this miserable life, it's not only that no one can understand it, that would be too easy:

"But nobody loves it either."

"Laura's alive," said Theo, and slammed the door shut.

The force of it knocked plaster off the wall.

45

BETO MILANÉS cut the chain of the handcuffs with the axe. And the first shot rang out. In an instinctive reaction, the soldier pushed Laura down and both of them rolled under the table. The memory of the war in Ibondá de Akú choked off his mind. The trailer filled with blowflies. Beto began to tremble like the boys in the backseat of the Chevrolet. Laura pulled the veteran up from the floor and began a desperate flight with him. She heard Martin's voice: he was coming through the auto salvage yard, shouting insults. The second shot shattered the glass in the round window.

"Lieutenant Samá!" Beto implored. "Lieutenant Lázaro Samá, don't leave me! Lieutenant Samá!"

"Let's go, Beto."

"The tiger . . . The tiger's out there."

"There is no tiger."

They left the trailer. Beto seemed terrified. The ghosts of his friends came out from among the cars. They rose from the ruined chassis, shadows behind the shadows of vans, and they glinted in the rearview mirrors of buses. They hid in the cabs of trucks, and they never stopped calling to him, reminding him it was time he let himself be eaten by the tiger. Quite a few of them laughed. Poundcake sat in the air, a fakir, and two domesticated rats ran along his body.

"Run!" Laura ordered.

Martin, hunter of men, saw them come out and fired three times in quick succession. By this time Captain Paul Sanders's men were advancing along the highway in a column of patrol cars, and they heard the gunshots in the silence of the night. Wellington turned on the spiraling howl of the siren.

"Nobody opens fire until I give the order," said Captain Sanders, and Perales transmitted the directive to the other cars. Perales would be the first to disobey it.

Ramos, Mandy, and Tigran ran along the narrow alleys of the auto salvage yard. The constable gradually fell back and his son took the lead, with the Terrible about three feet behind. Gasping for breath, afraid he would arrive too late, cursing himself for having devoured an enormous pizza with pepperoni and black olives, Ramos was thinking about his last meeting with the Cuban, in the room at the white Haitians', and with each step the room rocked like a cabin on a ship sailing the waters of the past, and he reproached himself for his bad, his terrible memory, that consolation of cowardice: now, when he was old and fat, he knew he had forgotten Beto because seventeen years ago he was terrified, panic-stricken at complicating his life with the existence of a luckless madman who had invaded his heart. He was fond of him. He would have liked to have a son like him. He loved him, but in the end he betrayed him. If fear is a straitjacket, forgetting is a cell in a lunatic asylum. He preferred to keep him in his memory and invent episodes that had not happened in order to construct a pious excuse: Beto Milanés has been cured, Raquel. Beto Milanés is living happily. Son, do you remember Alberto? Alberto Milanés. He's just returned to Cienfuegos. Beto Milanés is safe.

How ungrateful human beings are, Raquel: Beto doesn't even remember us. Over the years Ramos confused what had really happened with his inventions. When he came to Caracol Beach, he asked about the Cuban and learned he worked in the auto salvage yard. "He never comes round. He doesn't go out, at least not at night, when I'm up," Zack told him. "He's my best friend." Ramos did not go to see him. He did not want to face the challenge Beto had thrown down in his letter: "You say you like me, you said it, so why don't you give back what you once took from me: my death. Come. I'll leave a trail of shit for you to follow." Not loving anyone is an immoral act. Not loving anyone is an immoral act. Not loving anyone is an immoral act. It was an unlucky day when he read that sentence. Many people are terrified of love. After five wars, a transvestite son, and sixty-two years, he was one of them.

"I'm going ahead, dad," Mandy shouted.

"Be careful, son."

Laura, meanwhile, had managed to bring Beto to a side alley in the auto salvage yard. At that moment, the background was illuminated by the spotlights of the police, who had begun to cordon off the site, and they heard the voice of Captain Paul Sanders warning them to surrender. Laura thought she had been rescued. Strike Two was running along the passageways in the yard, holding the rubber knife in his mouth. Suddenly he stopped. He dropped the weapon. Like a hunting dog, he was trying to orient his senses. He bit at the toy. He continued the search. Just as Laura and Beto were approaching the exit of the cemetery, Martin jumped out from somewhere in the night and barred their way. Laura did not recognize him at first. In only a few hours the peaceable Martin had been transformed into a wild animal: he carried the fire of rancor in his eyes and a gaff for hunting sharks in his hand. The girl tried to give him a reasonable explanation but Martin pushed her aside with his hand and confronted the

Cuban. Beto leaned against a wall of scrap metal and offered no resistance. Flies. Flies. Blowflies.

"Kill me," he pleaded. "Kill me. Kill me. That's what you came for, to kill me."

"That's right, you bastard."

"Let me talk to you, Martin," said Laura.

"Butt out, Laura."

"No."

"Damn it!" said Martin.

Damn it, Martin wanted to die too. He heard a dog barking and found him in the underbrush. It was the puppy carrying a knife in its mouth. Another bat swooped close. Another car blew its horn on the highway: in simple chords the sound reproduced a popular tune. Against the backdrop of the night garlands of fireflies winked again. The reordering of reality brought no consolation because by this time the top student at the Emerson Institute had lost his mind forever. He was not in this world: madness is a kind of wandering. He pointed the gun at the soldier's face. That's what Tom would have done. Sure. Of course. Tom was a hero. He scored thirty points. Some bad isn't bad for you: it does you some good. Tom whispered in his ear to kill him now. Kill him. Tom hit the nail on the head. He had to start looking at things in a different way. Kill him. Tom was almost never right but almost always on target, which isn't exactly the same thing. Tom was at his side. Kill him. He could hear him. Kill him. He could touch him. Kill him. "You let me know when the smoke hits your gut, OK?" He always said OK. The tiger sprang out of the tree. The blowflies became agitated. Kill him. Kill him. Kill him. Kill him. Kill him. Kill him. Boy.

"Kill me. Poundcake, kill me. Leo . . . Aspirin! Here they come. . . . Damn it! Fuck! Caterina . . . Caterina!"

"Butt out, Laura," shouted Martin.

"You're wrong. . . . Let me explain."

"Don't explain anything, girl. Let him kill me, damn it. Bang bang. I've taken the vow. A clean slate. Walk. Walk. Yemayá, Babalú Ayé. Light and Progress. Here, Poundcake, aim for the chest, Poundcake. . . ."

"We're crazy, we're all crazy!" said Laura.

Mandy arrived with the pads of his breasts outside his blouse, his miniskirt pulled up to his buttocks, barefoot because he had lost his high-heeled boots along the way. He stopped a few yards from the confrontation. Behind him you could hear the footsteps of the Terrible and of Sam Ramos, still some distance away. Mandy wanted to speak but the words knotted in his parched throat. Beto was the Lone Ranger, the crocodile hunter who had been drinking his rat poison in the Haitians' bar.

"Enough," Mandy said. "For God's sake."

Laura thought she had been rescued. That transvestite had to be an angel. Beto mistook him for the tiger.

"Watch out," said Beto. "The tiger . . . Lázaro: the tiger, damn it!"

"I know your name is Beto," said Mandy.

"The tiger. . . ."

"What tiger?" said Mandy.

"Don't move, he's to your right. Poundcake!"

"It's Tom," said Martin and he took a few steps forward.

"Martin, listen to me," Laura pleaded.

"It's the tiger. From Bengal. It's following me. Kill me. Don't let it eat me. The ants. Kill me, for God's sake. Whoever you are, kill me."

"It's Tom," Martin repeated.

"Where's Tom?" Laura screamed. "I'll explain it to him."

"Tom's all right. I can't see a thing."

"Where's Tom?"

"Tom's dead. Tom. Don't you have my glasses? What happened to my glasses? Dead. Where are they?"

"For God's sake, what the hell is going on?" said Mandy, and he dropped to his knees. "Dad, dad, run!"

Martin raised the pistol to his temple.

"Don't do it," said Mandy. "This world is shit, that's right, shit, but there isn't any other. Don't do it, damn it. Enough. Don't kill yourself. I've tried suicide plenty of times. Plenty. If I told you all the afternoons I stood on the edge of a building or doused myself in alcohol and held a lighter in my hand. Until one day I understood that as long as there's one person, at least one, who loves you, nobody has the right to take his own life. Not loving anyone is an immoral act, you faggot."

"Go to hell. What did you say?"

"Faggot! Here comes Sam Ramos. . . . Remember? Sam, the fat man. . . . Your friend Sam Ramos, from Puerto Rico. . . . He loves you. He's coming to save you again. . . . He's almost here."

"Tiger . . . Tiger . . . Tiger . . ."

Beto began to claw at the ground until he found a stone. He threw it at Mandy. He hit him in the chest. It wasn't a stone but a metal nut. A threaded nut. Beto crawled along the ground on all fours: "What the hell. You'll see, damn it. You'll see who Lázaro Samá is. Beat it, tiger. . . ." He made a mudball and threw it at Mandy. The ball fell apart in midflight.

"You said it yourself. Remember, Beto? In the notebook. Not loving anyone is an immoral act, God damn it, an immoral act," said Mandy.

"I'm going to die in Ibondá de Akú!" shouted Beto. That was all he said. Yemayá mounted him. When Ifá gives the sign, doves are sacrificed to Yemayá. Ifá, son of Obatalá, is the great *orisha* of divination. Beto tensed like a violin string and began to spin on his axis, following the contours of energetic whirlwinds. No human being can resist so many storms. His body was shaken by invisible gusts of wind. Bolts of lightning. Yemayá, you of the seven paths, Yemayá Awoyó, you who are far away, Beto was praying. Laura was beside him, paralyzed with astonishment. Suddenly the Cuban was moving his arms as if swimming in a sea of air; suddenly he seemed to be rowing toward a hypothetical shore. He was drowning. Beto's movements gained in intensity, following the rhythm of a secret melody, ranging from soft undulations of his extremities to uncontrollable fury. Yemayá, you of the seven paths, Yemayá Awoyó, you who are far away, in the sea, mistress of the water, you who devour the innocent lamb, Mother with hair of silvery metal who gives birth to the lagoon, don't let me die, don't let me die. Mandy fell back, stunned. Before him was the crazy soldier his father had rescued in the jungle, the man he had fantasized in his adolescent hallucinations, possessed now by a devastating power that shook him like a puppet in a choreography he could not understand but that must mean, because of the beauty in what was terrible and the grace in what was fatal, a dance to life. Yemayá Awoyó, you who are far away, in the sea, mistress of the water, you who devour the innocent lamb, Mother with hair of silvery metal who gives birth to the lagoon, our protective Mother, perfect woman, unique woman who widens the sea, Mother who thinks, save me from death, help me. Beto was trembling from head to foot. "Lázaro Samá, don't leave me," he shouted. He had reached the limit of his endurance. His muscles stopped responding. His weary heart lost its strength. His mind went blank. He opened his mouth in a silent scream: his vocal cords could not produce the shout. His gums were bleeding. He had a golden insect on his tongue. He fell in a heap to the ground.

"Caterina Milanés," he said.

Caterina's name rose up and crossed the horizon. The tiger opened its wings and a gust of wind carried odors from the sea. Salt air. From its feathers hung dozens of amulets, dried and lengthened gourds, beads of Oyá, branches of *cundiamor*, stalks of bitter grass, copper medals in the shape of crutches, lockets, *lucumi* reed, scapulars of red *matipó*, seeds of *santajuana*, sacred hearts of Jesus made of tin, like promises on a cloth to Babalú Ayé. Zun zun zun, zun zundambayé, pretty bird at the break of day! When it closed its wings the wind stopped. And the moon went out.

"Kill me," said Beto.

"Kill me," pleaded Martin.

Flies. Flies. Blowflies. At that moment Laura heard the wings of the blowflies. She covered her ears. The tactic proved to be counterproductive because it locked the murmur inside her eardrums. She had been hearing that buzz ever since Beto attacked her in the liquor store parking lot; at the time she thought it was a problem in the dashboard of the Chevrolet; later, in the trailer of the Five Star Circus, while the soldier was looking for Caterina's photographs in the desk drawer, she supposed it came from some electrical equipment, the water pump, perhaps, but in the narrow alley of the auto salvage yard she finally solved the puzzle: death was approaching, furiously beating its tiny wings. Flies. Flies. Blowflies. Moving faster than a swallow she saw a flame in the air, no bigger than a wind-up doll. It darted through the mist and settled on the roof of a broken-down trailer-truck. It gathered new strength there. Laura recognized Maruja Vargas. Naked, diminutive, her mother held out her arms. A melody on the piano came from her fingers of smoke. A contradance. The music showed her the way to salvation. The blowflies stopped pursuing her and charged at Beto. The dog barked and barked under the shell of a truck. He came halfway out, barked, and went back to his hiding place. He stuck out his snout and growled suspiciously. He advanced a few steps, then one more, then retreated. He barked from the shadow behind the tires, not letting himself be seen. He barked. He barked. He barked. Strike Two was barking at Yemayá, at Maruja Vargas—in some way, at God.

46

THE BEST WAY Agnes and Theo could find to say goodbye to the boys was to receive them into their own bodies. They dried one another's tears with kisses. They began to make love as if they were inventing it. While he nibbled at her neck with his lips, she asked him to tell her about Laura. Laura had said something about their amorous encounter in the top-floor studio. Perhaps only a small part of what she remembered. But that afternoon Agnes wanted all of it. Everything: what they had felt and how it had felt. Laura has a golden ass, said Theo. How funny, she had a hard time taking off her jeans, peeling off her shell, she said, and ended up cutting them with scissors. "A drop of anise rolls along your thigh with the indifference of a ship sailing away," the professor recalled. Agnes smiled. Lie to me if you want. Theo would never lie. Laura's alive. I called the hospital. She's under observation, a crisis of nerves, but out of danger. Laura. Did you fuck her here, in this bed? Tell me. Yes, Agnes, said Theo, in this bed, and the cheerleader wanted me to open the windows in the room. Open the windows, said Agnes. Laura's beautiful. Yes, she's very beautiful. Theo confessed something that Agnes knew very well because she had seen her naked in the bathrooms in the gym: the girl's breasts were small, firm. Round and soft, how can I say it? And her nipples are pink. What Agnes did not know was that when his fingers touched them the tips of Laura's nipples hardened like kernels of corn—that's what Theo whispered in her ear. They harden like kernels of corn, touch me, and Agnes's nipples also hardened like kernels of corn. Call me Laura, said Agnes, and she closed her eyes so that Laura would reappear in the top-floor studio. Naked. Are you sure she's out of danger? That's what they said. The cheerleader is healthy. And strong. She'll recover. Time heals all wounds. Touch me. Touch her. Tom, she said. But Tom is dead. Tom. Agnes remembered the athlete's clumsiness: he seemed so frightened that she scaled him, muscle by muscle, until her breasts were on his eyelids, his cheek, in his mouth, that icy mouth that the coroners would be sewing now with silk thread in the Santa Fe morgue but that surrendered then with a murmur of pleasure, as if he were hungry, and Tom, Theo, bit her belly while she asked out loud that he go on kissing her, kiss me Tom, kiss me Theo, she said, come in, come on, do it, and Theo came in, he did it, repeating the sequence so that Agnes could relive the memory of that fiery athlete because Theo had understood and accepted that Agnes would love the way she had loved Tom in another body, his, and that she wanted the way she envied Laura in her own skin, that's why she touched herself, rubbed her pubis against his thighs, Theo's, Tom's, Laura's, and Theo thought it was all right this way, it ought to be this way, it would be this way. Agnes had a right to take her revenge, to defeat this son-of-a-bitch fate, and he said: teacher, Agnes, teacher, I'm Tom, Tom? yes, and I'm a little nervous, Agnes, here's Tom, Agnes, said Theo, you've never been with a woman, have you? said Agnes, never, said Theo, said Tom, said Theo, but Tom's here, and he's loving you, love me, I want you Tom, this is for you, it's yours, for you Agnes, and for Laura, the girl with the golden ass, look Agnes, Laura loves you, Laura, do you love me? Laura's alive, Agnes, Tom, and at the moment when the bodies of the two friends in coffins of precious woods were carried on the shoulders of grieving class-mates, Agnes and Theo made frenzied love in order to steal a few grams of life from the misfortune of death, and while Mrs. Liza Lowell was pounding her fists against the walls of her house in Caracol Beach, a shrunken, empty house, as absurd as a theater where the stage has been set for a work that will never be seen, while don Claudio Fontanet embraced Tom's parents and did not know what to say to them because he had forgotten the words or those words do not exist, should not exist, cannot exist, and Ramos threw his pistol in the ocean minutes before he mailed in his resignation, and while Tigran the Terrible was trying to con-vince the soldier's puppy that his new home could become a place even more hospitable than the Five Star Circus and Mandy kept calling him different names in the hope he would respond to one of them and Strike Two ran with his tail between his legs looking for a rubber knife under the furniture, while all this was happen-ing outside, Agnes and Theo were making love between warm sheets and knew that the afternoon of that Sunday was fantastic, bright, unrepeatable, and the days would return to nights, lights to shadows, shadows to bodies, and the dead you love to your heart.

"They've gone," said Theo.

Agnes's eyes glanced at Theo's, eyes that were black, black, black, glassy with tears but spirited enough to wink at him in a way that was charming, unexpected, frankly amorous, and she knew the worst was over, that Martin would always get the high-est grades and Tom would score more baskets than anyone else. She, Agnes MacLarty, gymnastics instructor at the Emerson Institute of Santa Fe, thirty-three years old, with a few wrinkles, would do all she could to stay with the asthmatic Theo Uzcanga for the rest of her life, both of them afraid, it's true, dependent and fearful, it's true, but breathing, if not happy, then with the hope of being happy because this miserable world, after all, is the only one we can count on and down here, you know, only love saves us, only love saves us, only love saves us, only love saves us. The constellations will line up again in the firmament. And the city will smell like a village and the business streets like tilled gardens and the air like water and the water like earth and the asphalt like cedar and the old like the new. It depends. It depends. The nights are dark before the dawn. And even butterflies will flutter around the street lights convinced they are tulips and dogs will cross at the corners when the traffic lights change. Agnes and Theo had begun to need one another. Later on they would find out how to forget the boys.

47

MARTIN RAISED the weapon and fired the last bullet at the sky. Because of that shot Captain Sanders's men closed in, lighting the scene with the beams of their powerful flashlights. As they raced into the auto salvage yard, Paul told Ramos in the station, Wellington almost broke a leg when he stumbled over a corpse. The body was run through by an iron bar. "Wellington fell next to Tom and got a shock he'll never forget. It wasn't pretty, Sam: this wasn't a dead dog or an insulted streetwalker—this was a dead body. A dead body on a skewer. Your officer took off his jacket and covered the dead man's face: his glazed, staring eye seemed to deny the importance of what had happened. That expression of his was unbearable. We moved forward. When we discovered the others in that narrow alleyway, none of them reacted. We have them, I said to myself. You think the stupidest things at times like that. The one holding the harpoons looked toward us. He squinted, getting his eyes used to the flashlights. I had the impression he was waking up."

Martin felt as if he were waking up.

"Where are we?"

"Let's go home, Martin. My good friend Martin. The best."

"Home?"

"Home, Martin."

"I'm scared," said Martin.

"Everything's all right now."

"And my glasses?"

"They'll turn up."

"I can't see."

"Martin, don't worry. Everything turns up."

"That would be nice."

"Right. It would."

Laura realized that her good friend was going to surrender, and she thought she ought to leave as soon as she could for Los Angeles and erase that night forever. Forget the soldier with the tattoos, for whom she had begun to feel an incomprehensible pity, forget the lepers in El Rincón, forget Caracol Beach, and Martin, and Tom. In the century that this instant of hope lasted she remembered herself as a little girl in Punta La Galia and saw herself sitting at a rustic table, drinking a fruit drink from a dry coconut shell. The Haitians were singing old Edith Piaf tunes at the back of the kitchen. She knew the drink was too sweet and the orange slices had bitter seeds. She was wearing a skirt with hand-embroidered flowers, her mother had on blue overalls, and her father wore a shirt and suspenders. At that moment she noticed that don Claudio looked like Sting.

"Tell him to kill me, Laura, I can't take any more," said Beto. He was far away. In the jungle. Watching his friends die one by one. They had been ambushed. He could have warned them, as he recalled, but fear is a straitjacket. A straitjacket. Somewhere in the world someone was singing Yolanda's song. It was probably the student, José Londoño, who never received any letters and spent the day humming songs by Silvio and Pablo. Yolanda. Yolanda. Forever Yolanda. He heard the laughter of Ernesto

Aspirin Gómez, the squad medic, and he knew that Tomás Ruedas and the telegraph operator Leo Rubí, alias the Fly, were playing checkers in the trench, among the worms, and did not imagine they were surrounded by the enemy. The earth pounded like a drum. A strong odor of rancid meat filled Ibondá de Akú. The blowflies settled at the back of his eyes. The tiger spread its wings and the medals jingled against one another, adding the tinkling sound of amulets to the chorus of crickets.

Ramos had lost his sapper's instinct: he could never atone for so many mistakes. He sat down on the bumper of a ruined ambulance, certain the worst was over. He had picked up the high-heeled boots that his son lost when he was running. He rested his forehead in his hand. His head weighed a ton. He could not feel his legs. His heart was pounding. Yes, old: you're old, he said to himself. He did not believe in God, but he thanked God: he had a feeling he had recovered his son. Mandy looked grotesque with his padded cotton breasts. I have to give him back his heels, he was thinking when Tigran placed a bear paw on his thigh.

"Oh, his heels! I hate those shoes," said the Terrible.

"Nelson's barefoot. He could step on a nail."

"Take it easy, father-in-law."

Strike Two came toward them. The Armenian patted his head. The dog wagged his tail. Tigran imitated the movement with his head.

"What a sweet puppy dog!"

"Damn, what world do you live in?" Ramos shouted.

"Isn't he sweet?"

"No, you moron, there's nothing sweet about him."

"Go talk that shit to your grandmother." Tigran lost control for the first time that night: "Nobody fucks with me. You hear? Nobody. I don't have to ask permission to be what I want to be. That's all I can count on: what I want. The world's what I can touch with my hand. This hand. I don't give a shit about the rest.

Who do you think you are? Who? You can shove your comments
up your ass. Everybody faces his fear the best he can. I don't like
shoes with such narrow heels, and I think this dog's sweet, very
sweet, and so what? There's a couple of madmen over there who
want to kill themselves, and what do I care? Let them kill themselves. Let them kill themselves and be done with it. They have a
right to die. As long as they don't touch my Mandy, to hell with
the rest. I don't know what I'm doing here. All right, I do: I know.
You brought me here. By force. You brought me by force. We're
your prisoners. Why did you come to the house tonight? Why?"

"Do you want to know why?"

"You never came before."

"I wanted to beg his pardon."

"Never. Not even when your son tried to kill himself.
Because it's true: yes, that fool tried to kill herself, set herself on
fire with alcohol. You never came. Never. Mandy was beginning
to adjust to the military indifference of her father. All his crap. As
if the great Sam Ramos had died in the war. It could have happened, right? Well, you died, you were dead and buried. Why did
you pay us a visit, that nice visit, that goddamn visit? What right
do you have to interfere with our lives? What about your life? Do
you think it's exemplary, irreproachable, heroic, decent, honor-
able, honored, dignified, significant? Ha, that makes me laugh. I
could die laughing. Why don't you look in the mirror, you filthy
pig? The Ramos family loves to compare men to pigs, right?
Nobody fucks with me."

"All right. All right now. No more," said Ramos, retreating
before the flood of Tigran's words.

"What's all right? Don't talk like a fool."

"I'm sorry."

"Fuck sorry. You can rot in hell. Where's Mandy? Where the
hell is Mandy?"

Tigran ran down the narrow alley.

"Mandy!" he shouted.

And Ramos smelled the aroma of white rice again. Tigran the Terrible! What a nickname, Ramos thought. Terrible because he had decided to live in his own way. Terrible because he loved Mandy with his balls, as he had said that night. Terrible because he confronted prejudices. Terrible because he showed himself just as he was. Terrible because he acted on impulse, by instinct. Terrible because he did not believe in false convention. And if he turned out to be a good partner for his son? And if he made him happy, why ask for another miracle? Ramos liked the Armenian, and even though that emotional closeness might be a flaw in a career soldier, feeling vulnerable turned out to be a comforting, almost cheering experience. He began to hit his thigh with the shoe until he tore his trousers. He was tired of pretending to be a physical and moral fortress; he would stop demanding of himself irreproachable conduct or integrity dictated by a rigid set of rules: from that Sunday on he would try to reconcile with his principal enemy, a bald Puerto Rican named Sam Ramos, and to make that reconciliation possible he had to ask his son for help. He would finally participate in the only war worth fighting: the one a man fights with himself to achieve the victory of being able to say "I love you." But he didn't know it then. There, in the auto salvage yard in Caracol Beach, sitting on the bumper of a wrecked ambulance, he didn't know it: he only kept hitting his leg with the red shoe until he broke the skin. "I love you, Mandy," he muttered, and scratched his head. His nails opened the scab that covered the cut he had gotten shaving. The trickle of blood rolled from his ear to his right nipple. He had never called him that: Mandy. Mandy. It didn't sound so bad. Mandy. "Dad, dad, run!" he heard his son shout. But it was Tigran who answered the call. Like a cossack.

48

SOLDIER'S NOTEBOOK. Will this be the last page I write? They're calling me They're calling me They're calling me Oh my God Caterina Caterina tell me something Caterina tell me that your son-of-a-bitch son is a brave man Babalú Ayé Blessed St. Lazarus if I get out of this I promise you I'll drag a log to your altar I swear old man I'll do it I don't know how but I'll do it On my knees Even if I die on the way I have to finish this letter Caterina you're far away save me from death help me Caterina the Great Caterina the Holy Caterina of the Orange-Colored Hens Caterina the Queen of Cienfuegos Caterina of the Warm Bed Caterina the Plump Caterina Patron Saint of My House Caterina Who Goes to Bed with Russians Caterina of Los Brincos Caterina the Comadre of Fela Caterina Who Throws Stones into the Sea Caterina the Whore Caterina of Guava Preserves Caterina Mother of Beto tell me something Caterina Milanés tell me I'm innocent The pencil broke God almighty What do I do now? What do I do? With the broken point I write I love you [The pencil mark fades until it is barely a dry furrow on the paper] I'm going to die in Ibondá de Akú! I'm going to die in Ibondá de Akú! I'm going to die in Ibondá de Akú!

49

YEMAYÁ PULLED his hair so he would raise his head and receive death with dignity. "Lázaro Samá, don't leave me!" Beto shouted and fell in a heap on the ground. To the best of Laura's recollection the Cuban made no effort at all to escape the siege but contrary to what one might expect he buried his hands in the mud, lowered his head, and acknowledged a defeat that in his case could be considered a victory. Everything started to happen again except life—which was ending. Martin began to cough. The nightmare had come to an end. It was Sunday on the planet. A Sunday Tom would not ever see because he was run through by a piece of metal in the auto salvage yard, but like it or not it was Sunday, a terrible, cruel Sunday, and dawn broke right on time behind the skeletons of the cars and in the distance a rooster crowed, another rooster, dozens of roosters, and Liza Lowell would be larding the leg of lamb with aromatic herbs and the bells of the church in Santa Fe would soon be calling the faithful to Mass and he could tell God what had happened. Maybe He would understand. God isn't God for nothing.

"Easy, boy, lower the harpoon," said Captain Paul Sanders. Later, in the police station, he would tell Ramos: "I saw you sitting on the bumper of an ambulance, Sam, and your attitude made me think the worst was over. That fox Sam has the situation under control. The girl started to move away until she was out of danger. Your son didn't move. He behaved like a brave man. His clothes saved him: no cop will fire at a woman. The one with the harpoons, Martin, he was defeated. Maybe I imagined it, I admit that, but in the beam of the flashlights I thought I saw tears streaming down his cheeks. He was crying. I told him to lower the harpoon, and I put away my weapon to make him feel safe."

"That's it, easy, lower the harpoon, nothing's happened here," said Paul, and he put his pistol in the holster.

As Martin turned toward the captain, the harpoon moved a few degrees. He was unprotected. A second would have been long enough for him to realize that to keep holding the weapon in his hand was imprudent, but his joints were fused into one piece and his body responded like a suit of armor to the commands of his nerves. He died smiling. Laura tried to warn him. Her jaws locked. Beto had said it: "Haven't you ever dreamed that you want to scream and you can't? It's horrible." It was horrible. It would be horrible for a long time. Understanding that smile became an obsession for the girl: she still hasn't forgotten it. Laura lost consciousness. She woke in the General Hospital of Santa Fe. She was mute for six weeks, battered by memories, until one day she stopped hearing the flight of the blowflies. Nothing would be the same until she could erase Martin Lowell's enigmatic look, an expression that could be explained by reasoning so simple it's frightening: he was nearsighted, he had lost his glasses, and he was only eighteen years old. Wellington Perales misread the boy's gesture. "I showed my own fear," he wrote in the report he presented to Captain Sanders, in which he acknowledged his errors with great civic courage. Ramos would defend him in the trial that concluded the investigation: "It had been too strange a night. Unbearably strange," Ramos stated before the court, which early in March of 1995 would acquit Perales because there was no premeditation: "Let him cast the first stone who is not afraid to cast the first stone. The man saying this is a soldier who has fought in five wars and is still alive because in all of them he was scared to death." Wellington Perales thought the harpoon was aimed at him and he remembered the young man run through by the piece of metal, and the Panamanian who had nailed a question mark to his father's forehead, and the gentleman with the dog, the streetwalker Gigi Col, and sharks, and he squeezed the trigger, emptying the pistol clip one bullet after the other. "I acknowledge my responsibility and accept whatever sentence is imposed on me: my conscience has already condemned me forever," he wrote in the report with a shaking hand. Immediately afterward the other police who were taking part in the operation used their weapons and unleashed a storm of bullets without order or plan and filled the night with blinding flashes. Tigran threw himself on Mandy and sheltered him in his arms. Sam Ramos jumped to his feet as if he were on a spring. The rain of bullets did not allow him to advance. His shout rebounded among the station wagons. Nobody heard him. Nobody. When the storm was over, Martin Lowell was lying in the narrow alley way in the car cemetery, torn to pieces in the middle of a pile of scrap metal. Beto Milanés held on for a little while longer, and as his veins were emptying he had enough life to see the tiger again, its swan wings spread now, as imperious as an evil angel. His soul mounted the tiger, straddled it, holding on somehow to the animal's neck, and undertook his final journey to the hell of Ibondá de Akú. Sam reached his son and the Terrible, whom the bullets had miraculously spared. The couple were joined together, leg to leg, cheek to cheek, heart to heart. Mandy leaped from Tigran's chest to his father's, where he found refuge. His right eyelid was twitching and he did not know what to do with his hands: he rubbed them together, he shook them, he ran them over his skirt until he broke his nails on the leather seams. His blouse and hair were spattered with blood. The Terrible moved a few steps away, observed the scene without understanding it, and went after Wellington Perales. He advanced with the clumsiness of a bear through the wreckage and the dead bodies, cursing in Armenian. Wellington squatted and hid his head between his knees. Ramos kissed Mandy on the forehead. His mouth was dry. His lips stuck to the skin. It tasted dusty. Then he looked into his son's eyes. He said something, he does not remember very clearly, and helped him put on the charming tricolor headband. It was a small, ridiculous, inadequate victory. Only then did the sun begin to rise over Caracol Beach.

Epilogue

That shadow that advances when my body stops is me.

— FRANCISCO HERNÁNDEZ

SOME TIME LATER, not very far from the auto salvage yard, in the small cemetery in Santa Fe, a drunken, dull-witted employee left his crossword puzzle unfinished. Annoyed because he could not recall any synonym for the word "mercy," he placed in the main oven of the crematory the dog that had belonged to his god-father Langston Fischer, the old pharmacist in Caracol Beach, unaware that the incineration process had not yet concluded for the corpse of a man whose entire body was riddled with bullets and whose left arm was covered with tattoos. If nobody had claimed the body, who would care about his remains?

"Clemency!" the employee exclaimed, and sent the ashes of the man and the dog flying. Clemency. That was the word he needed to fill in the last eight squares of the puzzle. He ran to write it down just in case, just in case he forgot it. Clemency. It isn't a word that is used very often. A gust of air carried the cloud of dust toward a cypress grove. The animal's ashes flew after the man's, and since the wind was whistling through the trees, it seemed as if the dog was barking at his killer.

Appendix

ABOUT THE CHARACTERS

AGNES MACLARTY (Santa Fe, 1961). Gymnastics instructor. Began to practice sports at a very early age. In 1972 she joined the women's team representing the United States in the world championship competition, held in Sofia, Bulgaria, and placed third on uneven bars. In March 1995, she gave birth to a daughter, named Grace, and left her position at the Emerson Institute to care for the child. She allowed her picture to be taken, naked and eight months pregnant, for the cover of the collection of poems, *A Drop of Anise*, written by Theo Uzcanga, her husband, and published by Ediciones del Equilibrista, with a prologue by the essayist Alejandro Rojas-Celorio. At present she works as a choreographer with the principal dance companies in Florida. Consulted by the author, Agnes MacLarty authorized the intimate pages fictionally recreated in Chapter 46 of this novel. Theo agreed: he was not about to contradict his wife, who was pregnant with their second child.

ALBERTO BETO MILANÉS (Cienfuegos, 1955–Caracol Beach, 1994). Son of Caterina the Great. Little has been said in this novel about his predilection for astronomy, but his family and closest friends assure us he became a specialist in the field. Aurelia Casas, a girlfriend of his youth, has a dozen letters in which Beto demonstrates this with exact observations. Igor Sergeyevich, a mechanical engineer, in a fax sent from St. Petersburg, indicates that one night, which he remembers very clearly, he went to the club at the Hotel Jagua with Caterina and Alberto, and vividly recalls the impression the boy made on him: "He knew the name of each star, and had precise information about it, its astral position, its distance from the earth, the influence of the moon on agriculture." Andrés Manuel Prieto, a Cuban baseball coach, testifies to Beto's athletic potential, "a fleeting but brilliant star in the firmament of our national game," according to statements he made by telephone to our editors. "It's true he struck out Agustín Marquetti, when the count was a difficult three balls, two strikes. Easier said than done." His life and death are recounted in this novel.

CATERINA MILANÉS (Sagua la Grande, 1937–Cienfuegos, 1995). Mother of Alberto, alias the Great. Rafaela Sánchez Morales states in a letter the reasons her comadre engaged in the practice of prostitution, but asked the editors not to include the information in this book, unless "in your opinion, it is absolutely necessary," and therefore we have thought it prudent not to explore the subject. In the above-mentioned correspondence, Rafaela reports that Caterina studied dressmaking in Cienfuegos, and also emphasizes her culinary skills, which won her fame as a pastry chef in the port city. In 1973, the Municipality of Cienfuegos awarded her the Clandestine Fighter's Medal for her contribution to the struggle against the dictatorship of Fulgencio Batista. Her body lies in the cemetery in Sagua, under the simple epitaph "La Grande."

CLAUDIO FONTANET (Barcelona, 1940). Criminal lawyer. In 1972, at a Carnival party, he met the Cuban immigrant Maruja Vargas y García, whom he married that same year. They were a handsome couple. After the birth of their daughter Laura, they took up residence in Santa Fe, where he opened an office in association with an important firm of litigators. He was widowed soon afterward, and a short while later he married Emily Auden, his present wife. They too were a handsome couple. Claudio had a clinical eye for spotting golden women. In the early eighties he won national fame defending the rights of a group of Cuban exiles known generically as "Marielitos." He won most of the cases and earned the affection of Little Havana, in Miami. Some call him Catalán. He had a thriving practice. After the events in the auto salvage yard he suffered a severe emotional crisis, which led him to enter a sanitarium under the care of Dr. Andrew Burton. Once cured, he retired and dedicated himself to drawing. He had his first show in the winter of 1997.

EMILY AUDEN (North Carolina, 1944). Anthropologist. Visiting Professor at the National Institute of Indigenous Studies, Mexico City (Summer Program, 1982–1984), her studies of Mayan culture have appeared in a variety of academic journals. A tenacious polemicist, she expounded and defended bold theories that attempted to re-create the daily life of the mysterious Mayans (inter-family relations, the role of women and children in the politics of the state, funeral rites, etc.). "Weary of plowing the desert," as she herself said in her last known essay (in the journal *México Oculto*, April 1986), she abandoned research to dedicate herself "to less controversial subjects, such as the presence of Cataluña in the Philippines or the history of the American labor movement under President Harry S Truman, 1949–1953." The wife of the attorney Claudio Fontanet, she resides in Santa Fe, "far from my Mayan princes and transformed into a broker of contemporary art."

GIGI COL (Tijuana, 1972). The data presented here were supplied by her friend Tigran Androsian, the Terrible. "A she-lion in bed. She practiced the noble profession of prostitution with an extraordinary knowledge of the subject. With just the tip of her index finger she eventually dominated several wealthy clients, some of them very good-looking, and made them suffer a dependence so incurable that quite a few offered the moon and the stars if she would accompany them to the altar. She refused to exchange freedom for matrimony. Often, and with some sadness, she would speak of her family in Tijuana, on the other side of the border, and we knew for a fact that she regularly sent a good part of her earnings to her relatives. Her only defects were obstinacy and sincerity. Because she called things by their real, unadorned names, she earned the hatred of certain hypocrites who need lies to do what they do. Today she lives in Ciudad Juárez, where she opened a second-hand clothing store. We write at Christmas. I adore her. They tell me she adopted a little girl. That's just like Gigi. She's one tough cookie. And stubborn."

GREGORY PAPA GORY (Port-au-Prince, 1929–Santa Fe, 1995). A primary and secondary school teacher, a lover of the Caribbean, "a region of powerful cultural roots," he contributed to the newspaper *The Macandal Journal* in order to publicize the virtues and correct the defects of the Haitian community abroad. A widower, childless except for dozens of godchildren who inherited his estate, a patrimony of great symbolic value though of limited economic significance. His sudden death in an automobile accident cut short his plan to write a book in homage to the pirates of America, especially those of African descent, who, in his judgment, were distinguished from their contemporaries by a desire for justice rarely recognized by the scholars who have dealt with the subject, almost always in a prejudicial manner.

LANGSTON FISCHER (New Orleans, 1930). A graduate of the University of California with a degree in chemistry, 1952–1953. Little is known about him. The proprietor of the Andalusia states that Dr. Fischer was a frequent visitor to the bowling alley, but never as a player. "He would sit on the sidelines and not move from the spot. It was a little unsettling. Sometimes he was accompanied by a gentleman in glasses. They would drink whiskey, and they liked the Galician meat pies. They always left late and never left a tip proportionate to their bill." In September of 1995 he left Caracol Beach, presumably for his native New Orleans, where, apparently, a younger brother lives, or lived. He suffers from migraine. His godson, a local cemetery-worker, states that his only dog was Bingo, the murdered Pekingese, and that he kept him in the pharmacy safe until he could have him secretly cremated at the cemetery in Santa Fe.

LAURA FONTANET (Santa Fe, 1976). As a child she studied piano with Eloísa Galarraga and took lessons in flamenco dancing at the Municipal Lycée. She traveled through Central America accompanied by her father, Claudio Fontanet, and her stepmother, Emily Auden. A distinguished student at the Emerson Institute, 1993–1994, and an outstanding athlete, she applied for a scholarship with her senior essay, "A Psychology against Despair," highly praised by the Awards Committee headed by the psychiatrist and neurosurgeon Dr. Andrew Burton. Professor Theo Uzcanga insists that Laura has a special sensitivity to literature, although she has never had the courage to acknowledge it; at the Institute she preferred to seem a frivolous, somewhat uninhibited young woman, an image that corresponded to her temporary leadership of the cheerleading squad. In December 1997, she traveled to Cuba accompanied by Emily Auden, and visited the Basilica of St. Lazarus. In the town of El Rincón she met a first cousin, the plumber Vlady Vargas, with whom she maintains a correspondence. She participates actively in campaigns for solidarity with the island. She is studying psychology at the University of California at Los Angeles.

LÁZARO SAMÁ (Santiago de Cuba, 1930–Ibondá de Akú, 1976). *Santero.* An active combatant in the clandestine struggle in the south of Oriente province by order of the national directorate of the 26 of July Movement, he joined the Rebel Army in February 1958. He fought under the leadership of the legendary commander Camilo Cienfuegos. After the triumph of the Revolution, he attended the militia school and took part, with the rank of lieutenant, in the battle of Playa Girón. In 1971, after the failure of the Harvest of Ten Million, he returned to civilian life and began to work in the port of Havana, where he assumed leadership of the workers' militia. Felipe, his only child, died in 1967 when he tried to cross the no-man's-land surrounding the American naval base at Guantánamo. In 1975, Lázaro Samá returned to military life as an internationalist fighter, and because he was an officer in the reserves, he was named head of the reconnaissance unit of the fourth company, second battalion, sixth infantry regiment on duty in the south of Ibondá de Akú. He died in an ambush. One of the meeting rooms at the Mambisa Terminals, in Havana, today bears his name.

MANDY (Los Angeles, 1974). For the publication of this book, Nelson Ramos forwarded the editors an autobiographical note: "Many people considered me a child prodigy. At thirteen I was a black belt in judo, at fourteen a recognized karate player, at eighteen a boxing champion, and at nineteen I went to bed with Rigo Restrepo, the Colombian masseur with the face of a quail who traveled with us to the District Finals in Marksmanship. When I reached my legal majority, and having enjoyed so much success, I decided to live alone, away from my parents, and use my own funds to open a beauty establishment where streetwalking transvestites could receive advice on the latest trends in gay fashions. Well, 'alone' is only a manner of speaking, because Tigran spent almost the entire week with me, protecting me tooth and nail from spiteful lovers, an attitude toward our relationship that earned him the nickname of the Terrible, a witty inspiration of the Mexican Gigi Col, our spiritual adviser." Mandy asked us, in a postscript, to publish the note without changing a comma because he was convinced the novel would be tinged with tragedy and he thought a few drops of humor would not be a bad idea in the midst of so many sad events and characters "buffeted by fate."

MARTIN LOWELL (New York, 1976–Caracol Beach, 1994). Top student at the Emerson Institute, 1993–1994. His senior project, "From the Frenchman Blaise Pascal to the Russian Mendeleyev: Toward a World without Boundaries Between Science and Humanistic Thought," received the highest grades and posthumous publication in the yearbook of that educational institution. Items found in his desk drawers after his death included a collection of toy lead soldiers, a stamp album, and a notebook of aphorisms that synthesized his youthful evaluation of the world: "Never doubt it: there is someone meant for you, ready to give everything on the sole condition that you believe in her." In the aforementioned notebook, he had also written two long poems in free verse, dedicated to an "impossible love"; today it is assumed they were composed for Laura Fontanet, a conclusion suggested by the titles: "Blue Jeans" and "Let's Go Listen to Sting Next to a Fountain." The brothers Bill and Chuck Mayer cannot speak of Martin without crying: "A great friend," they say. "The best. We'll never forget him." His life and his death are recounted in this novel.

MARUJA VARGAS (El Rincón, 1950–Santa Fe, 1981). Don Claudio Fontanet says he fell in love with her at first sight at a Carnival party, although he notes that he decided to propose when he heard her play contradances by Ignacio Cervantes on the piano, on February 24, 1972, "at 8:37 in the evening. I've never forgotten: it was a Thursday. Maruja wore yellow overalls. She loved overalls." In March of 1968, Maruja's parents decided to take her out of Cuba legally, and the young woman went to live in Santa Fe with her godparents, the Gaza de Galarragas. Eloísa Galarraga, who was Maruja's piano teacher, and then Laura's, acknowledges that she had a great aptitude for music, and therefore cannot explain why Maruja abandoned her concert career just when she was about to give her first public recital. "She missed the island. She seemed to be a sad girl. Don Claudio, who is an extraordinary Catalonian, brought joy to her life. More than a daughter, Laura was her friend. She told her about the island and taught her to read with *The Golden Age*. Then we learned that her health was as fragile as India paper." Maruja Vargas died in May 1981. She is buried in Santa Fe, under a royal palm that don Claudio planted at the head of her grave.

BILL AND CHUCK MAYER (Santa Fe, 1975 and 1976). Members of the Council of Pissers, a brotherhood that was dissolved barely twelve hours after its founding because of the sad passing of Martin Lowell and Tom Chávez, its other two members. Bill Mayer, a notable sketch artist, underwent medical treatment to cure him of his incipient addiction to marijuana. In May 1995, he matriculated at the University of Florida, where he is studying engineering. Chuck, the younger of the Mayer brothers, reacted more desperately to his friends' tragedy: he allowed himself to be caught up in a religious sect, the Children of Heaven, based in Utah, thereby confusing his emotional state even further with an absolutely groundless guilt complex. Depression brought him to the verge of suicide. In the winter of 1996, "shock troops" led by Sam Ramos and consisting of Bill Mayer, Professor Theo Uzcanga, Wellington Perales, don Claudio Fontanet, and the headmaster of the Emerson Institute (who planned the attack in detail), traveled secretly to the mountains of Utah, attacked the "monastery," and rescued Chuck by force in a pitched battle, thus preventing another misfortune in the chain of fatalities that began to be forged on that third Saturday in June in the auto salvage yard in Caracol Beach.

MISS CAMPBELL (Boston, 1936). In the winter of 1994, Miss Marina Campbell resigned her chair in mathematics at the Emerson Institute. Bill Mayer and Laura Fontanet have contradictory views regarding the teacher. One would think they are referring to two different people. For Bill, Miss Campbell is an angel come down from heaven; for Laura, she is a snake. The girl asserts that she has proof to support her theory; the young man believes that loneliness should not be confused with malice: "She's suffered," he said. "Suffered!" exclaimed the cheerleader: "I'll save my compassion for those who deserve it." To which Bill Mayer responded with a citation from Laura Fontanet's own senior project, "A Psychology against Despair": "Almost all adults are traitors, although they do not admit it, because most of them have forgotten the children they once were. Forgetting is an undemonstrable but real betrayal.

However, not only the chosen few have a right to forgiveness. Why else does the world have so many gods?"

MRS. DICKINSON (North Carolina, 1936?). We do not have precise information regarding this woman, whose name was Anna Margaret Ingrid, according to some, and simply Dorothy, according to others. With great difficulty it was established that she took a secretarial and bookkeeping course in one of the Western states but never practiced her profession because at the end of the 1950s she came into a small inheritance, large enough for her to settle in Caracol Beach and open a fishing-gear store. Neighbors interviewed for this publication state that she was a quiet woman who loved cats and solitude. She had no visitors. Every Sunday she attended six o'clock Mass. She never went to the beach. It is said she was allergic to the sun. On weekends she rented Westerns at a local video store. In the autumn of 1994 she left Caracol Beach. On the morning of November 15 of that year, her porch was found to contain a pile of human shit. She told no one where she was going. Occasional mail still addressed to her former residence is forwarded, as per her request, to a post office box in Massachusetts. The only somewhat intimate detail known about her is that she was skilled in throwing darts.

PAUL SANDERS (Hawaii, 1931). Son of General Abraham Sanders Munkacsy, a hero of the Second World War, Paul studied at the National Artillery School in Pennsylvania. A captain with command experience in the wars in Korea, Vietnam, Grenada, and Iraq, where he was an analyst for the Air Force General Staff. He lives in Caracol Beach, surrounded by his fourteen daughters, six of them twins in three births. "I never acknowledge defeat, but Betty has conquered me," he says. Betty is his wife, and mother of his daughters. The oldest served as a nurse in Desert Storm. Decorated by four presidents for services rendered to national security, Paul Sanders was director of training on the army base at the Panama Canal, Second Military Attaché at the American Embassy in Budapest (1971–1972), and an International Adviser to the United Nations in the conflict in Ibondá de Akú (1975–1979). He has just retired to civilian life. He has a house in Santa Fe, although he spends a good part of his time in Grand Cayman. He enjoys tennis.

PETER SHAPIRO (Texas, 1952). Rancher and businessman. Seventy-two hours after the events in the auto salvage yard, Shapiro's legal representatives filed a suit in a Florida court against Nelson Ramos and Zack Duhamel. The claim held them responsible for the destruction and burning of the Ford in the parking lot of the bar. Wellington Perales conducted the necessary investigations, thanks to which the attorney Claudio Fontanet presented conclusive evidence in favor of the defendants. The testimony of Tigran Androsian was crucial to the trial, his amorous version of events impressing the members of the jury. When he returned to Texas, Shapiro publicly criticized Armenian and Haitian immigrants in Santa Fe, an attack that could be read as a racist diatribe against homosexuals. Gay groups surrounded his ranch with endless demonstrations, rock concerts, and fashion shows in which the models, most of them lesbians, riotously paraded in nuns' habits. Shapiro had to leave Texas.

RAFAELA SÁNCHEZ (Cienfuegos, 1945). Neighbor and comadre of Caterina Milanés. She had no children, a lack that she filled with barnyard fowl. She had a pigeon coop with twenty pairs that bred constantly, although only a few were so-called messenger pigeons. In any case, she never used them for sport. And she never ate them, although the same could not be said of the ducks and turkeys, which she sold for a good price on the black market. Caterina spoke often about Rafaela: "My sister Felita," she would say with genuine affection. Her love of pigeons was born in her youth, when she lived with her uncle Idelfonso, a lighthouse keeper in the port of Cienfuegos "and the island was full of gulls." With the help of Rafaela Sánchez, certain passages in this novel were reconstructed fictionally, in particular those that take place in Cuban settings. When Caterina died, the People's Committee for her district authorized Rafaela to move into the Milanés family house. As far as the neighbors knew, Beto disappeared in the war in Ibondá de Akú. "That's fair," said Rafaela in a letter to Ramos: "After all, it's the truth."

RAQUEL GOULD (Los Angeles, 1940). Barely three sentences have been written in this book regarding this wonderful woman, always so discreetly in the shadows. The daughter of the economist Albert Gould, author of the classic *The Finances of Sorrow*, Raquel displayed an exceptional arithmetical gift even as a child. In 1955 she shared the gold medal at the International Olympics in Exact Sciences, held in Quito, Ecuador. She held a degree in mathematics but abandoned a promising teaching career to follow Ramos in his pilgrimage through military camps and academies; she filled the long periods of solitude, typical for a soldier's wife, with a love of reading that made her a celebrated literary critic. Her essays on the North American short story have been published in several anthologies. When she turned fifty-five, Tigran and Mandy surprised her with the best possible present: *The Secret Soul of Raquel Gould*, a beautiful edition of her reviews, with a prologue in which Sam Ramos dares to compare love to a naval battle.

SAM RAMOS (San Juan, Puerto Rico, 1932). Career soldier. He lived in Caracol Beach from 1993 to 1996. At present he resides in his native San Juan, Puerto Rico, and is writing his memoirs, where he recounts life-and-death experiences in the five wars in which he was involved, always as a soldier behind the lines. Professor Theo Uzcanga has said of him: "Having a close relationship with a gentleman like Mr. Ramos is a privilege, since men like him teach us that we humans are superior because of the strength we derive from knowing how to, and being able to, ask for forgiveness. Fighting under the command of this bold Puerto Rican has been, at least for me, a stroke of good fortune I do not deserve." In the winter of 1996, Sam Ramos led the rescue of Chuck Mayer in the frozen mountains of Utah, an episode that served as the central theme of his first literary project, *The Seventh Crusade: The Monastery of the Children of Heaven*, an adventure novel with a happy ending, which is dedicated to his "rescue team": Theo Uzcanga, Wellington Perales, Claudio Fontanet, Bill Mayer, and the "strategist" Harvey Weinberger, headmaster of the Emerson Institute, a man often mentioned but never named in this book.

THE TATTOOED NAMES (Various). Beto Milanés had the names of his seven companions in the squad, including Lieutenant Lázaro Samá, tattooed on his left arm. Only the sketchiest information is available concerning the other six soldiers. They are, or were: ELÍAS BENE-MELIS (Camagüey, 1956). Alias Camagüey. It is known that he worked in a printing shop as a linotypist, for his name appears on the masthead of a journal of the Academy of Sciences of Cuba. He died in the ambush at Ibondá de Akú. ERNESTO GÓMEZ (Havana, 1957). Alias Aspirin. A nurse in the National Red Cross. A basketball fan. He completed his obligatory military service in the Ceremonial Battalion of the General Staff. He died in the ambush at Ibondá de Akú. FERNANDO LÓPEZ (Havana, 1957). A railroad worker. Before leaving for Ibondá de Akú he married Zenaida Peña, with whom he had a son he never knew. He died in the ambush at Ibondá de Akú. JOSÉ LONDOÑO (Santiago de las Vegas, 1955). Alias Poundcake. A student at the Technological Institute in Rancho Boyeros. He died in the ambush at Ibondá de Akú. LEO RUBÍ (Bayamo, 1956). Alias the Fly. A telegraph operator. He won first prize in folkdancing at the XV National Festival of Amateur Dance, as documented in a Certificate of Honor. He died in the ambush at Ibondá de Akú. TÓMAS RUEDAS (Cárdenas, 1957). Alias the Brain. He did not complete his studies for the priesthood at the Seminary of San Carlos. A graduate of the Pedagogical Institute of Matanzas. An English translator. He lived in the port of Camarioca, near the world-famous Varadero beach. He died in the ambush at Ibondá de Akú.

THEO UZCANGA (Guatemala City, 1960). "The poetry of my friend Theo Uzcanga has the stunning simplicity of popular songs. As a consequence, it is wise. Theo might say, along with Maestro Eliseo Diego, that poetry is a conversation in the dark," the essayist Alejandro Rojas-Celorio states in the prologue to the first edition of the collection of poetry, *A Drop of Anise* (Ediciones del Equilibrista, 1997, 34 pp., 300 copies signed by the author, Octavio Smith Prize). As a child he moved with his parents to Orlando, Florida. He received his degree in Latin American literature with the thesis "Reinaldo Arenas: A Celestine from Pre-Dawn to Pre-Dusk." His essay on Alfonso Reyes, "Something Had to Be Done about the Unpresentable Minotaur," won the Gabino Palma Prize, 1997. He resides in Caracol Beach with his wife Agnes and daughter Grace. They expect a second child. He is preparing a new book, *A Ship Sailing Away: Coplas from Vera Cruz*, with which he hopes to conclude the creative cycle inspired by the poetry of the Mexican Francisco Hernández. He is asthmatic.

TIGRAN ANDROSIAN (Erivan, 1969). Chess champion, student competition in Moscow, 1980. In 1991 he worked as an electrician for the Classical Ballet of Armenia. He left the company during a tour of Spain, where he requested and was granted political asylum. After extensive travels through Europe, too many for an inexperienced young man like him, he met a North American impresario in London who brought him back to San Francisco as his lover. There he tried his hand as a clothes designer. His collection of gold-printed silk kimonos was selected by a well-known magazine as the worst of the season: "They are costumes for scarecrows," Mandy has said with his peculiar critical judgment. Then he attempted to be a chess instructor, a set designer, an animal trainer, but his successive failures were so great that he ran away. He reappeared in Santa Fe, in a gastronomic enterprise: his restaurant the Menscheviks has been gaining in popularity. In mid-1995 he traveled as a tourist to Erevan, accompanied by Mandy, never dreaming that he would arrive just in time to close the eyes of his stepfather, who was living in an old-age home where all the residents were veteran interrogators of the KGB. He lives with Mandy. He is happy with his dog, whom he calls Boris. He has been recognized as a tireless fighter in the battle against AIDS. He is called the Terrible, a joke he does not care to refute.

TOM CHÁVEZ (Santa Fe, 1976–Caracol Beach, 1994). Eleven days after the events in the auto salvage yard, notification was sent to the house of the Chávez family informing Tom Chávez that he had won a brand-new Nissan sports car, for of the nine thousand contestants only he had correctly answered all 150 questions about the NBA devised by a newspaper, and consequently he was invited to the All-Star Game, on which occasion Michael Jordan himself would hand him the keys to the car before two hundred million television viewers. He deserved it. Since childhood he had been passionate about sports, game forecasts, and the records of his idols. He was a wholesome boy. All his classmates agree in pointing out his spirit of fair play. He could not tolerate abuse. He made the cause of the defenseless his own. All his life, which was certainly brief, he had only one moment of bad luck: his last. Bill and Chuck Mayer cannot speak about Tom without crying: "A champion," they say. "The greatest athlete in the Santa Fe area, no doubt about it." His life and death are recounted in this novel.

WELLINGTON PERALES (Panama City, 1972). He was always told that his father had been murdered by a gunman in Panama City, but it was a lie. In the course of the investigation into the events in the auto salvage yard, information from secondary sources indicated that the naval commander had been killed in an internal dispute among drug traffickers. This discovery has not invalidated the admiration young Wellington feels for his father, for according to Captain Sanders, who knew him in Panama: "Luis Napoleón Perales was a generous man who distinguished himself for bravery under the most severe circumstances." Sanders did not accept the resignation submitted to him by Officer Perales following the events in the auto salvage yard, for he believed the young man deserved a second chance, but he did transfer him for a time to the legal department, where he is still employed. What no one could prevent, since it depended entirely on himself, was that he gave up spearfishing. In the spring of 1997, Sam Ramos received an invitation to attend the wedding of Wellington and Sofía Carrasco, a Dominican, but at the last minute Ramos decided to stay home.

ZACK DUHAMEL (Caracol Beach, 1930). He learned the art of tattooing and the darkest secrets of voodoo at the same time, but never made use of this knowledge except for the afternoon when he engraved the names of seven dead men on Beto's arm. A confirmed bachelor, he has been severely criticized by the elders of the Haitian community. A friend of Beto's, who for him is "a great lion-hunter," Zack Duhamel improves as a human being as he grows older. After the death of Gregory Papa Gory his name has been mentioned as the person to occupy the moral throne so wisely filled by the albino. He is not an ambitious man. He works at the Bastille. He swims in his pool three hours a day. And he has a lover named Artemisa de la O. He lives with his mother, Madame Brigitte Duhamel, an elderly woman who celebrated her hundredth birthday in December 1997—on the nineteenth, to be exact.

THE FACTS OF THE CASE: CHRONOLOGY PREPARED BY SAM RAMOS

SATURDAY, JUNE 19, 1994
(Times are approximate)

19:00   The headmaster of the Emerson Institute presides over the graduation ceremony for the 1993–1994 academic year.

20:00   Sam Ramos reports for duty at the police station in the Resort Community of Caracol Beach, assisted by the young and inexperienced Wellington Perales, his new aide.

20:30   The soldier with the tattoos leaves the auto salvage yard at mile ten on the highway between Santa Fe and Caracol Beach.

21:30   A group of students from the Emerson Institute decides to continue the graduation party at Martin Lowell's summer home in Caracol Beach.

22:00   Professor Theo Uzcanga invites his colleague Agnes MacLarty to the Two Blind Cats Bar in Santa Fe.

22:15   The students from the Emerson Institute occupy the Lowell house in Caracol Beach.

22:30   Nelson, alias Mandy, arrives at the Bastille Bar in Caracol Beach.

22:30   Friends of Reinaldo Arenas pay homage to the great Cuban novelist in the Two Blind Cats Bar.

23:00   The soldier arrives at the Bastille Bar at the same time as the Texan Peter Shapiro. Incident in the parking lot.

23:40   In the Two Blind Cats Bar, Theo Uzcanga and Agnes MacLarty listen to Albita Rodríguez, the Cuban singer.

23:50   Martin Lowell discovers there is not enough beer to last until the end of the party.

SUNDAY, JUNE 20, 1994

00:10   Mrs. Dickinson, a neighbor of the Lowells, calls the police station to complain about irregularities at the young people's party.

00:15   Martin Lowell, Tom Chávez, and Laura Fontanet go to a liquor store on the highway.

00:30   Nelson gives a severe beating to the Texan Peter Shapiro in the Bastille Bar.

00:35   The soldier leaves the Bastille Bar.

00:35   Gregory Papa Gory arrives at the Bastille and sees the soldier leave.

00:45   The students' car almost crashes into the soldier's at a crossroad.

00:50   Sam Ramos leaves Wellington Perales in charge of the police station and reluctantly responds to Mrs. Dickinson's call.

00:55   Martin and Tom enter the liquor store on the highway. Laura chooses to stay in the car, dozing.

01:00   Tom notices the presence of the soldier in the liquor store, but does not attribute much importance to it at the time.

01:05   The soldier takes Laura Fontanet prisoner.

01:10   Sam Ramos arrives at the Lowells' house. He finds significant drawings on the wall.

01:10   Martin and Tom discover the soldier in the car. They attempt a desperate defense, without success.

01:20   The soldier imposes the rules of his dangerous game on the boys.

01:30   The Mayer brothers leave the Lowells' house, on orders of Sam Ramos.

01:40   Sam Ramos decides to visit his son Nelson. He calls Wellington Perales.

01:50   Martin and Tom destroy Peter Shapiro's Ford in the parking lot of the Bastille Bar.

02:00   Sam Ramos arrives at the home of his son Nelson. Meets Tigran Androsian, called the Terrible.

02:10   Peter Shapiro reports what has happened to his car to the police station.

02:25   Sam Ramos and Tigran decide to look for Nelson at the Bastille Bar. They ride through the streets of Caracol Beach in the patrol car.

02:25   On orders of the soldier, Martin and Tom kill the dog Bingo, a pet belonging to the pharmacist Langston Fischer.

02:45   On orders of the soldier, Martin and Tom attack the prostitute Gigi Col in the middle of the street.

02:45   Sam Ramos and Tigran find Nelson in the Bastille. Sam Ramos arrests his son in response to Peter Shapiro's complaints.

03:00   Langston Fischer files a complaint before Wellington Perales regarding the two boys who killed his dog Bingo.

03:10   The soldier leads the assault on the liquor store on the highway.

03:10   Gigi Col comes to the police station to file a complaint regarding the two boys who attacked her.

03:15   Sam Ramos calls the police station from a public telephone.

03:25   A complaint regarding the assault is received at the police station from the liquor store on the highway.

03:30   The soldier issues his final order.

03:45   The patrol car driven by Wellington Perales passes the vehicle in which the soldier and Laura, his captive, are riding.

03:50   Martin attempts to inform the police. The encounter on the highway. Wellington Perales's first mistake.

03:50   Mrs. Dickinson leaves a message on the answering machine of Martin's parents.

03:55   Wellington Perales requests assistance from Captain Paul Sanders.

04:10   The soldier and Laura arrive at the auto salvage yard.

04:15   Martin and Tom arrive at the house. Their friends have left.

04:45   Martin and Tom break into Mrs. Dickinson's store.

05:00   Laura persuades the soldier to confide in her. The soldier reveals crucial secrets of his life.

05:10   Sam Ramos, Paul Sanders, and Wellington Perales meet at Mrs. Dickinson's store.

05:15   Martin and Tom attack a milk delivery truck.

05:15   Wellington Perales discovers the soldier's true identity.

05:30   Gregory Papa Gory saves the life of the milk truck's driver. Stray cats and dogs have a banquet.

05:30   Sam Ramos, Nelson, and Tigran speed to the auto salvage yard.

05:30   Theo and Agnes leave the Two Blind Cats Bar.

05:30   Martin and Tom arrive at the auto salvage yard in the milk truck.

05:35   The soldier reveals his true identity to Laura.

05:40   Tom's death.

05:40   Sam Ramos, Nelson, and Tigran arrive at the auto salvage yard.

05:55   Paul Sanders, Wellington Perales, and twelve police officers arrive at the auto salvage yard.

05:55   Theo accompanies Agnes to her apartment. They say goodnight.

06:00   Final confrontation between the soldier and Martin. Nelson's intervention.

06:15   Martin's death. The soldier's death.

06:17   Dawn.

THE RUINED MAP

by Kobo Abe

Nemuro Hiroshi, head of sales for Dainen Enterprises, has disappeared. In fact, he disappeared over six months ago, but only now has his young wife hired a private eye to find him. The only clues the nameless detective has to go on are a photograph, a matchbox, and the sparse facts offered by Nemuro's alluring, though alcoholic, wife and his slippery brother-in-law. In pursuit of Nemuro, the detective is gradually drawn into Tokyo's seedy and dangerous underworld, and, before long, begins to lose the boundaries of his own identity.

Fiction/Literature/0-375-72652-7

OTHER PEOPLE

by Martin Amis

She wakes in an emergency room in a London hospital, to a voice that tells her: "You're on your own now. Take care. Be good." She has no knowledge of her name, her past, or even her species. It takes her a while to realize that she is human—and that the beings who threaten, befriend, and violate her are other people. In this eerie, blackly funny, and sometimes disorienting novel, Martin Amis gives us a mystery that is as ambitious as it is intriguing, an investigation of a young woman's violent extinction that also traces her construction of a new and oddly innocent self.

Fiction/Literature/0-679-73589-5

THE BOOK OF EVIDENCE

by John Banville

Freddie Montgomery is a highly cultured man, a husband and father living the life of a dissolute exile on a Mediterranean island. When a debt comes due and his wife and child are held as collateral, he returns to Ireland to secure funds, a pursuit that leads to murder. Here is his attempt to present evidence, not of his innocence, but of his life, of the events that led to the murder he committed because he could. Like a hero out of Nabokov or Camus, Montgomery is a chillingly articulate, self-aware, and amoral being, whose humanity is painfully on display.

Fiction/Literature/0-375-72523-7

THE HOUSE OF SLEEP
by Jonathan Coe

Jonathan Coe's novel follows four students who knew each other in college in the eighties: Sarah is a narcoleptic who has dreams so vivid she mistakes them for real events; Robert has his life changed forever by the misunderstandings that arise from her condition; Terry spends his wakeful nights fueling his obsession with movies; and an increasingly unstable doctor, Gregory, sees sleep as a life-shortening disease which he must eradicate. But after ten years of fretful slumber and dreams gone bad, the four reunite in their college town to confront their disorders and discover that neither love, nor lunacy, nor obsession ever rests.

Fiction/Literature/0-375-70088-9

THE ELEMENTARY PARTICLES
by Michel Houellebecq

Bruno and Michel were born to a bohemian mother (but they had different fathers, of course) at the height of the sixties. Following her inevitable divorce, they endured separate childhoods and developed distinct identities. Bruno—a failure to his own family and literary calling—is pursued by sexual obsession and madness. Michel—a wholly asexual molecular biologist—expresses his disgust with society by engineering one that frees mankind from its uncontrollable, destructive urges. An international phenomenon, *The Elementary Particles* is a furiously important novel that has become a sensation throughout Europe and beyond.

Fiction/Literature/0-375-72701-9

ABYSSINIAN CHRONICLES
by Moses Isegawa

At age nine, Mugezi leaves behind his secure life in the village to join his parents and siblings in Kampala, where he is first exposed to the despotism and hardship with which he will contend all his life. The nightmare reign of Idi Amin and its chaotic aftermath are the backdrop to Mugezi's troubled coming-of-age. He goes to work as a high school teacher, becomes enmeshed in a tragic romance, finds himself drawn into a potentially dangerous alliance with the military after Amin's fall, and witnesses the widespread ravages of the AIDS virus. The details of Mugezi's life provide an illuminating portrait of the contemporary, postcolonial African experience.

Fiction/Literature/0-375-70577-5

WHEN WE WERE ORPHANS

by Kazuo Ishiguro

The maze of human memory—the ways in which we accommodate and alter it, deceive and deliver ourselves with it—is territory that Kazuo Ishiguro has made his own. Christopher Banks, an English boy born in early twentieth-century Shanghai, is orphaned at age nine when his mother and father both vanish under suspicious circumstances. Sent to live in England, he grows up to become a renowned detective and, over twenty years later, returns to Shanghai, where the Sino-Japanese War is raging, to solve the mystery of his parents' fates. A masterful combination of narrative control and soaring imagination, *When We Were Orphans* is Ishiguro at his best.

Fiction/Literature/0-375-72440-0

LOVE AND GARBAGE

by Ivan Klíma

From an internationally acclaimed Czech writer comes a shrewd and poignant novel set in Prague before the Velvet Revolution, a book whose perceptions about love, conscience, and betrayal cut to the bone of life in both totalitarian and democratic societies. The writer-hero of *Love and Garbage* has responded to state suppression by becoming a street-sweeper. From his vantage point in the gutters comes a piercing vision of a world in which everything—from uncomfortable ideas to a former mistress—may be reduced to garbage, and only love has the power to grant permanence.

Fiction/Literature/0-679-73755-3

GHOSTWRITTEN

by David Mitchell

A gallery attendant at the Hermitage. A young jazz buff in Tokyo. A crooked lawyer in Hong Kong. A disc jockey in Manhattan. A physicist in Ireland. An elderly woman running a tea shack in rural China. A cult-controlled terrorist in Okinawa. A musician in London. A transmigrating spirit in Mongolia. With pyrotechnic virtuosity, David Mitchell weaves genres, cultures, and ideas like gossamer threads around and through these linked stories of nine souls in nine far-flung countries, stretching across the globe from east to west. In the end, as lives converge with a fearful symmetry, *Ghostwritten* comes full circle, forcefully revealing the idea that whether the planet is vast or small is merely a matter of perspective.

Fiction/Literature/0-375-72450-8

THE NEW LIFE

by Orhan Pamuk

The protagonist of this fiendishly engaging novel is launched into a world of hypnotic texts and Byzantine conspiracies that whirl across the steppes and forlorn frontier towns of Turkey. Through the single act of reading a book, a young student is uprooted from his old life and identity. Within days he has fallen in love with the luminous and elusive Janan; witnessed the attempted assassination of a rival suitor; and forsaken his family to travel aimlessly through a nocturnal landscape of traveler's cafes and apocalyptic bus wrecks.

Fiction/Literature/0-375-70171-0

THE CLUB DUMAS

by Arturo Pérez-Reverte

Lucas Corso is a book detective, a mercenary hired to hunt down rare editions for wealthy and unscrupulous clients. When a well-known bibliophile is found hanged, leaving behind part of the original manuscript of Alexandre Dumas's *The Three Musketeers*, Corso is asked to authenticate the fragment. Soon he is drawn into a swirling plot involving occult practices and swashbuckling derring-do among a cast of characters bearing a resemblance to those of Dumas's masterpiece. Part mystery, part puzzle, part witty intertextual game, *The Club Dumas* is a wholly original intellectual thriller.

Fiction/Literature/0-679-77754-7

THE KEY

by Junichiro Tanizaki

Scintillating, elegant, and darkly comic, *The Key* is the story of a dying marriage, told in the form of parallel diaries. After nearly thirty years of marriage, a middle-aged professor frenziedly strives for new heights of pleasure with his repressed, dissatisfied wife. During the day, they record their adventures of the previous night. But when they begin to suspect each other of peeping into their respective diaries, it becomes unclear whether each spouse's confessions might not be intended for the other's eyes.

Fiction/Literature/0-679-73023-0